"Don't be angry with me," she said quietly

When she reached her hand out to touch his back he jerked and she curled her fingers inside her palm. "I'm sorry. I shouldn't have touched you."

He turned and his eyes burned with a dark fire she'd seen before. "You can touch me any damn time you want to, lady. Just know that when you do, it sets off a jolt of lightning inside me and I'm hard-pressed to keep my own hands where they belong."

"Lightning?" Was that akin perhaps to the tingling sensation his fingers imposed on her when he gathered her close? When his lips touched hers and a flame arced from that spot to the depths of her body?

"Yeah. That's what I said. I missed you for four days, Miss Augusta. I dreamed of you every time I crawled into bed. Spent some damn restless nights in fact. And you're such an innocent you don't even know what I'm talking about, do you?"

Acclaim for Carolyn Davidson's recent titles

Maggie's Beau
"A story of depth and understanding
that will touch your heart."
—*Rendezvous*

The Bachelor Tax
"From desperate situation to upbeat ending,
Carolyn Davidson reminds us why we read romance."
—*Romantic Times*

The Tender Stranger
"Davidson wonderfully captures gentleness
in the midst of heart-wrenching challenges,
portraying the extraordinary possibilities
that exist within ordinary marital love."
—*Publishers Weekly*

CAROLYN DAVIDSON

The Texan

TORONTO • NEW YORK • LONDON
AMSTERDAM • PARIS • SYDNEY • HAMBURG
STOCKHOLM • ATHENS • TOKYO • MILAN • MADRID
PRAGUE • WARSAW • BUDAPEST • AUCKLAND

ISBN 0-373-29215-5

THE TEXAN

Please address questions and book requests to:
Harlequin Reader Service
U.S.: 3010 Walden Ave., P.O. Box 1325, Buffalo, NY 14269
Canadian: P.O. Box 609, Fort Erie, Ont. L2A 5X3

Writing for Harlequin has been a privilege.
Finding friends among the ranks of their historical
authors has been a joy. To Cheryl St.John and Deb Hale,
I offer my gratitude, for sharing your strength and
wisdom over the past years. This book is for all y'all.

And to my manager, Mr. Ed.

Chapter One

If *innocence* bore a Christian name, it would be Augusta McBride. For there before him was, without a doubt, the most lily-white specimen of womanhood Jonathan Cleary had ever laid eyes on.

Wearing a wide-brimmed, feather-embellished hat over golden hair, and clad in a long-sleeved, up-to-the-neck, fully buttoned dress, she stood on his doorstep, hands folded and reticule drooping from one wrist. Her eyes were wide, blue and wary. Pink and inviting, her lips glistened, and as he watched, he noted the reason for the moisture evident on that lush, full mouth. Her tongue touched her lips briefly, not for the first time, as if the flesh were dry and taut. He watched with male appreciation as that pink, pointed member dampened the skin and then retreated within her mouth.

"As I said, my name is Augusta McBride," she repeated, as if she'd been reading the lines in a book and had somehow lost her place and must begin again. "I'm here to collect donations for a shelter for..." Her voice trailed off as if she had become aware of the smile he wore, a smile he was certain signaled his approval of her appearance.

The dress she was bundled in covered all her curves sufficiently and did not offer a tempting peek at one square inch of skin, save a part of her throat. And that lack only served to whet his interest in what lay beneath its fabric. Starched percale could not subdue the lift of her full bosom, nor could the dress's long sleeves hide the perfection of slender fingers and pink, oval nails.

"The shelter for…what?" he asked quietly, commanding his eyes to rest on her rosy cheeks, lest he frighten her away with the full survey he wanted to repeat. He'd only caught a glimpse of her slender form for a moment before his gaze was captured by the perfection of a straight nose and wide-set eyes.

She was lovely, and where she'd been hiding since his arrival in Collins Creek, Texas, was a mystery he wouldn't mind exploring. For sure, he hadn't laid eyes on her until three minutes ago.

"The ladies of the community church have purchased a house on the north side of town, sir," she began, her voice an earnest, soft contralto. "It is designed as a shelter for women who need a place to live until they can…rebuild their lives."

"Rebuild." He repeated the word slowly, already dead certain of the problems the women in question might have in doing such a thing. "What's wrong with their present circumstances?" he asked, frowning a bit, as if he were truly puzzled over her explanation.

"Most of our residents come from a lifestyle that makes them *unappealing* to most of the citizens of Collins Creek. We are offering them a shelter while they make the appropriate changes that will give them an opportunity to—"

"Unappealing? Are they crippled or disfigured in some way?" he asked, cutting off her faltering explanation. He furrowed his brow, sliding his hands into his trouser pockets as he leaned against the doorpost.

"Oh, no!" she said firmly. "Not in any way."

"Then I guess I don't understand their problem," Cleary said, puzzlement alive in his voice.

She just about had her fingers twisted off, he noted, stifling a grin. Her hands were clenched so tightly her knuckles were white, and her eyes sought some destination over his left shoulder as she began a halting explanation.

"These women come to us from various places, several from the Pink Palace just south of town," she said, allowing her glance to touch his face briefly, as if she sought his understanding.

"The Pink Palace." He narrowed his eyes and met her apologetic look head-on. "You mean to say you're in the business of rescuing a bunch of *soiled doves?*" he asked.

"Um...I believe they've been called that. Among other things," she said quietly.

"And you want me to donate to your cause?"

She nodded quickly, and he watched as the feathers on her hat blew in the breeze. "Well, yes. We're asking the good folks of Collins Creek to help us in our fight against the evils incarnate in such establishments. Our ladies are only seeking a chance for employment in another—" her hand waved ineffectively as she searched for a phrase "—line of work. Yes," she said abruptly. "Another line of work."

"What are they suited for?" he asked, and then stepped back, offering her the opportunity to enter his parlor. "Why don't you come in, and we can discuss this further?" Her eyes looked past him into the shadowed room and she swallowed, a convulsive movement that drew his attention to the line of her throat, the only spot of pale skin available to his view.

"I don't think it would be proper of me to step inside your home, sir," she said, her eyes round, her voice a prim reproof. "I only wanted to offer you an opportunity to aid us in the worthy project we've undertaken."

"Hmm…" His index finger scratched negligently at his jaw and he tilted his head to the side, as if he were seriously considering such a thing. "I suppose I'd need to hear a bit more about your plans, first," he said, after a moment's pause.

She glanced up and down the street, where not a soul had ventured on this hot afternoon. "Perhaps you could come out onto your porch," she offered, a trembling smile forming her pink lips into an invitation.

"Certainly," he conceded. "I'll just get us each a glass of refreshment first. Have a seat on the swing, why don't you?"

He watched as she stepped to where the swing dangled at the end of the porch and then carefully seated herself, allowing her feet to rise from the floor as the swing moved in a gentle rhythm. Her smile in his direction lent wings to his feet as he raced toward the kitchen, where a jar of lemonade stood in the icebox. Pouring two glasses, he placed them on a tray and headed for the front porch.

"Here we go," he said, allowing the screened door to slam behind him. The tray found a spot on a small wicker table, and Cleary planted himself on the opposite end of the swing. Bending, he fetched a glass for his visitor, then the second for himself.

She swallowed carefully, sipping in a ladylike manner from the glass, and her mouth glistened from the residue. "Thank you so much. I was terribly thirsty. I suppose I didn't realize what a long walk it was from the middle of town, and I wanted to call on each house, lest I not give everyone the opportunity to help in our worthwhile endeavor."

"Well, I certainly admire your devotion to the cause," he said judiciously. "But I suppose I'm having trouble trying to figure out just what line of work your *ladies* might be capable of training for."

"We'd like to be sure our ladies know the basics of homemaking," Augusta began. "And that they would know how to work on a farm or ranch, should we find men available to take them as wives."

Cleary almost sputtered as he swallowed a mouthful of lemonade. "If you try to pass them off as typical brides, you might have a problem," he said. "On the other hand, some of the men I've known, who are on their own, would welcome most any female creature into their homes. It gets pretty lonely out in the open country where the best a man can do is find a dog to talk to."

"Well," she said primly, "we know they aren't typical brides, but most of them will make wonderful wives, given the chance."

"I'd say you've bitten off quite a challenge," he told her. "Who all is involved in this business?"

"Why, the minister's wife and a couple of the ladies who are willing to teach classes to our pupils. And we've hired a widow lady to live in and be a chaperon."

A chaperon. If any group of women on earth were less in need of such a dragon guarding the doorway, he didn't know where you'd find them. And he'd be willing to bet that those self-same pupils could teach her churchgoing friends a thing or two that might put grins on their husbands' faces.

"What sort of contribution did you have in mind?" he asked her, and was pleased by the quick smile she shot in his direction.

"Money will do very well," she told him. "Foodstuffs would come in handy, but I doubt you have an assortment of canning jars filled with fruit or vegetables in your pantry. We need clothing for a few of them whose wardrobes are somewhat limited."

"I'll just bet they are," he murmured beneath his breath, and was delighted as she bent closer to better hear his remark. A line of perspiration touched her temple and a single drop of sweat trickled the length of her jaw. Her eyes were not only blue, he noted, but that color was emphasized by a darker circle rimming it.

"How many ladies do you have at your shelter?" he asked smoothly, admiring the clear, soft skin on her cheeks. Though her hair was light, her lashes were golden brown and he noted the sweep of them as her lids closed for a split second.

"Four right now," she said. "But there are two or three more arriving before too long, I believe, from a place on the outskirts of Dallas."

"How did they hear about the availability of such a place?"

She sipped again from her glass, and a slowly advancing blush rose from her throat to color her face as she avoided his gaze. "I went to Dallas and approached them. I let it be known that help was available, should any of their number be interested in a new start in life."

He choked on a mouthful of lemonade, and his cough brought consternation to her blue eyes. "Are you all right, sir?" she asked, reaching to pound ineffectually on his broad shoulder.

"Yes." He gasped, inhaling air, then coughed again. "I'm fine."

She settled back in her corner and eyed him over the rim of her glass. "I think you doubt my word that I went to see those women," she said accusingly.

"No, I just doubt your intelligence that you allowed yourself to enter such a place. Don't you know what might have happened to you? You're exactly what some of those madams are looking for, Miss McBride. You might have been imprisoned in a room and never seen the light of day again in your lifetime."

She shook her head. "I'm not the sort of female men

look at that way, sir. And I wouldn't have the least idea what to do in a place…like…that.'' Her words trailed off as his gaze swept her form. "What?" she asked, her voice sharp.

"I'd say you're exactly the sort of female men look at," he told her.

"*You* haven't looked at me…like that," she said primly.

"Haven't I?"

She glanced aside, and then, with a swift movement that left him grasping his glass, she rose from the swing. "I'm sorry I bothered you, sir. I'll be on my way now. Thank you for the lemonade." Bending, she deposited her empty glass on the wicker table and marched to the porch stairs.

"Miss McBride." He called her name firmly and her feet came to an abrupt halt, right on the edge of the first step. "I'd like to make a contribution."

"What sort of contribution did you have in mind?"

"If you'll turn around, I'll tell you. I've never been fond of speaking to a woman's back." Though there was a lot to be said for the shape of this particular woman's backside, he decided. What little he could make out through the fabric of her dress was rounded and pleasing to the eye.

She turned on her heel and her blue eyes were steely, in direct contrast to their earlier softness. "Yes?"

"I'll make it a cash contribution." He stood, towering over her, and reached into his trouser pocket, where his money clip held several bills together. Without looking at their value, he pulled them from the clip and, reaching for her hand, pressed them into her palm, then curled her fingers around the wad of bills.

"Thank you for allowing me to be a part of your plan," he said nicely.

Her blue eyes widened and her hand tightened around the considerable amount of cash she held. "I'll tell the ladies how kind you are," she said after a moment.

He lifted a hand to brush at his mustache. "If it's all right with you, I'd rather this be an anonymous contribution."

"Certainly, whatever you desire," she blurted out, her gaze focused on his mouth.

He touched the underside of the dark hair he kept trimmed neatly above his upper lip, watching closely as her tongue touched her mouth again. "Whatever I desire?" His words were whisper, but they apparently caught her ear, for she jerked and then retreated from him, almost tumbling backward down his porch steps, one heel trying to catch hold of thin air.

He reached for her, hauling her with a total lack of dignity against the long length of his body. His thoughts had been right on target, he found, as firm breasts made an impression on his chest. She was not lacking in any way so far as he could ascertain, his hands gripping her hips through the starched fabric of her dress.

In fact, he'd say that Miss Augusta McBride was exceedingly well formed.

Exceedingly.

How she could have made such a complete and utter fool of herself was a point she would ponder later, Augusta decided. Her gait was rapid, her high-buttoned shoes sending up small clouds of dust behind her as she made the return journey toward the north side of Collins Creek, where the tall, white house held the first contingent of her— what had he called them?—her *soiled doves*.

And little did the gentleman know how fittingly that name described the women she had a burning desire to help. She thought of her own mother, whose working name had been Little Dove, when she'd been a resident in a high-class establishment in New York, a fact Augusta had only discovered two years ago.

Claude McBride, an Irishman with a heart as big as all outdoors, had fallen in love with the woman who sold him her favors. Had fallen in love and rescued her from the place that was a dead end for most of its occupants. That Dove McBride became a wife and mother, and made Claude happy until his dying day, were facts that her diary had established in detail.

After the funeral, when Augusta was sorting out her parents' belongings, she'd come across the leather book filled with her mother's flowing handwriting, and over the next several weeks had come to know the woman from a whole new perspective. Apart from being a beloved mother and devoted wife, Dove McBride had been a woman who would have been deemed unacceptable in polite society during her early adulthood.

Augusta had dutifully divided the proceeds from the family home and its contents with her brother and cried bitter tears as he'd left to seek a new life in the western part of the country. Alone, yet financially able to support herself until she decided in which direction to turn, she'd followed her instincts.

"I'll make a place for myself, and then send for you, sis," Wilson had told her earnestly. "If you leave here, be sure to let me know where you're going." And she had, sending a letter in care of the postmaster in Cheyenne, Wyoming, before she left New York City.

If Wilson could seek a new life in the West, so could she. And Texas promised to be more cosmopolitan than Wyoming or Colorado, she decided. With cities like Dallas and Houston developing into social communities that commanded respect, she'd headed in that direction.

How she'd ended up in Collins Creek was another story, one she refused to think about today. Her head high, her steps swift, she passed the bank, then the general store, waved at the minister who stood before the hotel's double doors, and smiled nicely at the barber, who nodded his greetings.

"Good morning, Miss McBride," came a salutation from her right.

"Good to see you out and about, Mrs. Pemberton," she said properly. "I hope you're feeling better." And then she went on her way, aware that the white-haired widow would more than welcome a chance to describe the details of her latest illness. Not today, Augusta thought. Not now.

She marched past the schoolhouse, the church and the cemetery, crossed the street and headed toward the row of simple two-story houses that made up the second street of Collins Creek. Five of them, there were. Two turned into boardinghouses for men without families, two owned by families who scrabbled to keep body and soul together, and the fifth, set a little apart due to a fence and a row of trees with low-hanging branches, designated as the *shelter*.

Without a proper name, and with no desire to advertise it should they come up with one, the ladies who ran the establishment merely considered it their good deed. Not for a day, or year even, but a project into which they'd vowed to devote their time for the foreseeable future.

It stood now, its majesty faded by wind and rain, and as it came into sight Augusta viewed it anew, moving through the gap in the front picket fence, where a gate hung with but a single hinge, leaning against the ground, awaiting repair. As were several other items that caught her eye. A porch step lacked a board and she carefully maneuvered over it, mentally adding it to her list of things she would get to this very afternoon.

Inside, the parlor was almost empty of furniture, a sofa against one wall, and, before the window, a library table upon which a lamp, complete with fringed shade, stood in graceful splendor. Two chairs sat on either side of the fireplace, mismatched but sturdy. Augusta's footsteps clicked against the bare floor as she walked on down the hallway and into the kitchen at the back of the house.

"Miss McBride." Pearl offered a greeting as she looked up from the bread she was kneading. Flour decorated her cheek, almost concealing the remnants of a black eye, now faded to a dull yellow hue, and the presence of two stitches next to the bottom lid. "I'm almost done with this, and Bertha said I should make the loaves next."

"Don't forget to grease the pans," Augusta reminded her, aware that learning basic household chores was important to these women. "Who's cooking supper tonight?"

"I hope it's gonna be Bertha," Pearl said glumly. "It's Janine's turn, but she's not real handy with pots and pans, yet."

"She can sew well, though," Augusta reminded her. "And she'll learn to cook. We just have to be patient."

"Yeah, but in the meantime, we could get awful hungry."

A second glance at Pearl's voluptuous form made that prospect doubtful, Augusta thought, and then she walked past the big table toward the back door. "Is Honey working in the garden?" she asked, peering out the screened door to where a patch of vegetables struggled to survive beneath the hot Texas sun.

"Said she was gonna water stuff and pull weeds," Pearl told her. "She's probably daydreamin' about goin' home to Oklahoma, if I know Honey. She was cryin' in her tea at noontime."

"I'll find her," Augusta said, stepping out onto the small porch and searching in all directions for the golden-brown hair of the girl she'd brought here only three days since.

"Honey?" she called, stepping from the porch and walking around the corner to where a slender young woman sat, slumped against the side of the house in the shade.

"Ma'am?" Honey looked up, wiping at her eyes, attempting to smile as she got to her feet. The fullness around her waist was proof of her condition, and again Augusta was smitten with pity for the child. For Honey was, indeed, too young to be so far from home, with a baby on its way and no one to care whether she lived or died.

"I pulled the weeds and carried water from the pump, ma'am," she said quickly. "The lettuce is big enough to eat for supper, I figured, and the first of the peas are pretty near full in the pod."

"Well, why don't you go ahead and pick the peas and lettuce, then," Augusta told her. "Do you have a pan out here?"

Honey shook her head. "No, but I'll get one, right quick."

She rounded the corner and disappeared from sight, the sound of the screened door opening and closing giving away her location. Augusta sighed. If only she could find a farmer who would be willing to take on the girl, and more than that, be willing to accept her child. That particular item had been on her list for two days now, ever since she'd brought Honey here from the Pink Palace, once Lula Belle had confirmed the fact of her pregnancy and decreed her unfit for her trade.

Mentally she made a note of Honey's situation again, listing it just beneath the broken step before the front porch, and then sighed again as she considered the growing length of things to be concerned with. Beth Ann must be lying down upstairs. Slender to the point of skinny, she'd wandered down the road three weeks ago, the second day they'd occupied this house, and announced that if she never had anything to do with a man again, it would be too soon. Lula Belle had pronounced her not pretty enough for her crew of ladies, too skinny for a discriminating gentleman to pay for, and without the proper manners necessary for a resident of her establishment.

All true, Augusta agreed. But Beth Ann was willing, and once they had fed her properly and taught her some basic elegance, she'd make a fine wife for some *discriminating* man, whether Lula Belle agreed with their theory or not.

And then there was Janine, who was content to sit and sew a fine seam, a talent that had come in handy, but certainly wasn't enough to find her a husband. Although Janine had quietly and firmly denounced that idea anyway.

They weren't cooperating the way Augusta had foreseen. Certainly, women misused as they had been should be eternally grateful for the chance to remake their lives into productive channels. She bent to pull a stray weed, left behind during Honey's travels through the garden.

"I've got a pan," Honey announced, standing beyond the pea patch.

"Well, pick the stuff that's ready," Augusta told her, "and then I'll show you how to shell the peas for supper."

And that should give her just about enough time to fix the front step, she decided, turning toward the woodshed, where their pitiful collection of tools hung on one wall, and where she might find a board fit to be used. In a few minutes, she'd managed to come up with what she needed from the dimly lit interior of the building. A can filled with nails, screws and assorted bits of hardware in one hand, a hammer in the other, and a piece of two-by-ten board under her arm, she advanced toward the front of the house.

She'd barely had time to roll up her sleeves, place her hat on the floor of the porch and lay out her equipment when a tall figure walked through the opening in the fence, bypassing the hanging gate with a scornful look.

"When you going to give up on this foolishness and come on back to Dallas?" Roger Hampton's voice was harsh, his drawl hardly audible beneath the strident tones.

She offered him barely a glance. "You might as well get on the next train," she said, wiping her hands on the front of her skirt. "I'm not going back to Dallas, not with you or by myself. This is my home."

"Huh! This dump is what you want to call your home? A place where you've chosen to gather up the scum of the earth under one roof and then waste your time and talent *redeeming* them?" His taunt was familiar. She'd heard it almost daily for the past week, ever since he'd followed her here from Dallas.

"You forgot to list my inheritance in that rendering of my assets," she told him bluntly, picking up the hammer and hefting it in her right hand. She looked up at him then, focusing on the pale hair, close-set eyes and sharp, narrow nose that made up his face. His lips were thin and she almost shuddered, recalling her narrow escape from his pursuit as he'd attempted to press his cool mouth against hers.

"Your money doesn't enter into it, Augusta," he blustered.

"That's a crock of—" She stopped, her mouth almost set to say the dreadful, unspeakable word she'd found on the tip of her tongue.

"Well," Roger said slyly, "where's the lady I proposed to, less than a month ago in Dallas?"

"She's right here," Augusta said quietly. "But she's a lot smarter and busier than she was then." She lifted an eyebrow as she scanned his length with a scornful air. "I probably should thank you for making Dallas so unpalatable for me. Collins Creek is a much better choice for my work, I think."

Her chin tilted upward as she smiled cooly. "Go away, Roger. I don't have time for you." Turning her back, she pried the hammer beneath the broken step and applied her weight to levering up the board. Wood splintered, and a piece of it slid beneath her skin, piercing her hand just beside her smallest finger.

"Now look what you've done," Roger said, stepping forward swiftly, reaching to take the hammer.

But she would not allow it, instead swinging her arm back and the hammer into the air. "Don't touch me," she warned him, painfully aware of the splinter that even now dripped blood onto the board she was trying to pry up.

"I don't think you've retained many of your ladylike qualities here in Collins Creek," Roger said spitefully. "Threatening a gentleman with a hammer when he's only trying to help you—"

"Get out of here," Augusta said, raising her voice as she swung the hammer in a downward arc. It missed his hand by a good margin, but he moved quickly, apparently fearing she might step forward, weapon in hand.

"I'm going," he said, settling his hat at a jaunty level. "I'll drop by again, Augusta. I think another week or so will be sufficient to make you see things more clearly." And then as he left, he muttered words she made no effort to hear, aware only of the sounds of his buggy wheels rolling down the road and the jingling of his horse's harness.

Her back to the gate, she looked at the broken step, then eyed the splinter in her hand. "I doubt it, Mr. Hampton. I've seen you clearly for more than a month already, and you're running out of time here," she muttered beneath her breath, and then turned around to sit on the top step, the better to inspect her wound.

"I'll be glad to give you a hand, ma'am." The offer came without warning, and she turned her head abruptly. Beside the front gate, a horse and rider stood motionless, apparently having been privy to the discussion between Augusta and Roger.

"Sir?" He was nameless but certainly familiar, he of the lemonade, and the wad of cash money she even now had tucked in her reticule. And on top of that, his dark eyes and smiling lips seemed still more attractive this time around.

"I didn't introduce myself when we first met," he said. "My name is Cleary. I thought I might drop by and properly make your acquaintance, seeing as how I have a vested interest in your…" He looked up at a drooping shutter, then back at the broken step. "Your project," he finished nicely.

"I should have mentioned my name when you came calling earlier," he told her, dismounting easily and tying his mount to the gatepost. "And when I recognized that I'd been less than gentlemanly, I thought I'd best make amends and see if there was something I could do to set things right."

Augusta's mouth refused to stay closed. She inhaled deeply, concerned at the lack of air available for her needy lungs, and then began awkwardly to roll down her sleeves. It would not do to receive a caller so dreadfully unclad.

"Don't bother," he told her, reaching one hand to halt her endeavor. "I'll take a look at your splinter if you like," he offered. "I have a dandy knife that will probably set things right in less than a minute."

She could only nod as he settled on the top step beside her and took her hand in his. One long finger tilted his hat back on his head, and as she watched, he turned her hand over in his, her fair skin looking even more pale against the tanned flesh of his palm.

His fingers were gentle, his skin callused, and the scent arising from him was a blend of citrus and leather. Augusta held her breath against its lure, and he glanced up quickly. "Am I hurting you?"

She shook her head. "Oh, no. Not at all."

"I wondered. You caught your breath, and I thought perhaps—"

But what he thought was not revealed as the front door

opened and Bertha's firm voice interrupted his healing mission.

"I didn't know we had company," Bertha said firmly. "Did you want to bring the gentleman inside, ma'am?"

"Uh, no. As a matter of fact, he only stopped by to…" Augusta looked up into his dark eyes. "Why did you stop by?"

He smiled and bent closer. "I already told you, ma'am. I hadn't properly introduced myself, and when I found you were being verbally assaulted by the man who just left, I thought it prudent to keep an eye on things."

"Oh. Oh, I see," Augusta said. And then she looked over her shoulder at Bertha, whose arms were folded firmly across her ample bosom.

"Was that rascal here again?" she asked, her voice booming a challenge. "I told you. We need to send him off with a load of buckshot in his behind one of these days."

At that, Augusta felt a torrid blush climb her cheeks and she rose to her feet. "I'm sure Bertha can take care of my hand, Mr. Cleary. But I do appreciate you stopping by and offering your help."

"Most folks just call me Cleary," the visitor said politely, and smiled at Bertha. Whether it was the look he flashed in her direction or the easy, elegant way he carried himself, Bertha nodded and lowered her arms to her sides as Cleary stepped down to ground level.

He looked up at Augusta and offered his hand. "It was good to make your acquaintance, ma'am. I hope you won't have any problem with your wound." He settled his hat more firmly over his forehead and turned aside. "I'll stop by again."

And then he was gone.

Chapter Two

The sound of a hammer against wood woke her, and Augusta sat upright in bed, unaware, for just a moment, of where she was. The walls of the bedroom were covered with faded pink flowers against a nondescript wallpaper, and brighter patches signified the absence of pictures, apparently taken by the house's former owners. Not a room she would have chosen in days gone by. But, she decided, looking around at the shabby walls, it could only get better.

She slid from the bed, cocking her head to the side to consider the silence surrounding her. Perhaps the banging of a hammer had been part of a dream, she thought. Certainly she'd been plagued with a number of scenarios throughout the night, ranging from a woman with hatchet in hand chasing her down the streets of Dallas, to the sight of a man's large, tanned hand holding hers captive.

She'd preferred the latter, she admitted to herself, thinking of her visitor the other day. Cleary, he'd said she should call him, but she hadn't. Instead she had only touched her palm to his offered hand before he left. *I'll stop by again.* A promise of sorts, she supposed, and a smile curved her lips as she tied her petticoat and slid a clean dress over her head.

From the front of the house, another flurry of pounding met her ears, and she went to the window, bending to peer from the open frame. Dark hair, topping a pair of broad shoulders, met her gaze and she watched in awe as the hammer rose and fell. Only two blows required to set a nail in place. Another nail was held between long fingers, and the hammering resounded again. He lifted the hammer a third time, and then as he ran a thumb over the nail, he looked up to where she watched from the window.

"Good morning," Cleary said, a cheerful grin lighting his dark features. "Hope I didn't wake you." And from the look on his face, she was certain he knew he had.

"Oh, no," Augusta said quickly, aware that her voice still held early morning huskiness. "I was just getting up." She bent forward a little, viewing the three boards that lay beside him, noting the two he'd already nailed onto the uprights of her front steps. "Things have been piling up on me," she told him. "I was going to get back to that today."

"Well," he said, drawing out the single syllable, "now you won't have to. I'm sure there are other chores more suited to your hands."

"I'll be right down," she said quickly. "Has Bertha offered you coffee?"

"She came to the door and frowned at me," Cleary said. "I suspect she'll be back to make sure I haven't walked off with anything that isn't nailed down."

"She's not at her best in the morning," Augusta said in a loud whisper. She ducked back into the room to find her housekeeper standing in the bedroom doorway.

"I'm always at my best," Bertha said stoically. "I didn't think seven in the morning was a good time for the man to come calling. But if you want him to have a cup of coffee, I'll pour one for him."

"Well, he isn't really calling," Augusta told her, bending to find her shoes beneath the bed. Her slippers were there and she donned them quickly, deciding they'd do as well as the high-buttoned shoes she generally wore. "I think we should be thankful for his help, Bertha. The ladies in town have not been receptive to their husbands coming here to lend a hand."

"Huh!" Bertha was a woman of few words, but the sounds she made were generally easy to understand. "Breakfast is pret' near ready," she said, turning to go back to the first floor. Bertha's heavy shoes clumped on the uncarpeted stairs and Augusta snatched up her hairbrush, bringing quick order to her long hair.

It had hung over her shoulders as she'd leaned from the window, and she scolded herself silently for being so lax in her deportment. Cleary would surely think she was not much of a lady.

She looked like an angel, he decided, golden waves falling to either side of her head, her eyes as blue as the back of a jaybird. Bending from the window above him, she put him in mind of the heavenly beings his mother had read to him about from the Bible. Surely, the angels who sang to the shepherds bore some resemblance to Augusta McBride.

Augusta. Much too dignified a name for the delightful woman he'd been thinking about over the past two days. *Augusta.* He'd call her Gussie, he decided, although even that did not suit her. But it was less off-putting, and he'd warrant his speaking it as he addressed her would bring quick color to that creamy skin.

He tore loose the final cracked board and removed the old nails, adding them to the pile he'd accumulated during his task. One more board remained, and he lifted the length of yellow pine, eyeing the edge and decreeing it straight before he placed it on the upright stringer. With six nails and a dozen swings of his hammer, it was in place and he stood, stepping on it to test its firmness.

It was done, the job completed in fifteen minutes or so. A coat of paint would cover the newness of the wood and provide protection from moisture. He looked up as Augusta stepped out onto the porch and closed the screened door quietly behind her.

"Do you have any paint?" he asked.

"Paint?" Her gaze swept over the steps he'd replaced. "You mean for the stairs?" Her foot touched the first step and she bounced on it a bit, smiling as she met his gaze. "I didn't plan on replacing all of them, just the one that was missing."

"Several had cracked boards," he told her. "They were unsafe, and I hated the idea of you falling and getting worse than a splinter for your trouble." He reached for her hand and, without thinking, she placed her own in his palm. "Let me see," he said, bending over to inspect the spot where Bertha had removed the splinter. It was scabbed over nicely, and a bit swollen around the edges, but Augusta had decided to leave the bandage off for today, allowing it to heal.

His index finger traced the line of her injury, and she felt the warmth of that touch send a cascade of heat up her arm, bringing gooseflesh to the skin that was, thankfully, hidden by her long sleeve. The man presented a danger, she decided. Though not in an evil way, such as Roger Hampton did.

But a danger, nonetheless. She could not afford to have her reputation sullied in any way, shape or form. Not with the success of her shelter hanging in the balance.

"Looks pretty good," he said, releasing her hand and placing his palm on his hip. "You might want to soak it in Epsom salts. It'll draw any infection out, lickety-split."

"Thank you, *Dr.* Cleary," she said softly, slanting a grin in his direction, then cradling her left hand in her other palm as he returned it. He made it too easy to be free and friendly, and she must be wary of following the dictates of her impetuous streak.

"I've been called a number of things in my life, but not that," he told her, running his index finger the length of his mustache, lifting a brow as he spoke. "But I do have some experience with wounds and healing."

"Well, if you're done lollygaggin' out there," a voice said from the doorway, "come on in and have some breakfast." Bertha spoke from behind the screen and Augusta was thankful for the reprieve. That, and the chance to spend more time with the man in front of her.

"Coffee's poured," Bertha mumbled, making her way back down the hallway to the kitchen.

"That invitation included you, sir," Augusta said, reaching for the door handle, and holding it open for her impromptu handyman.

"Are you certain?" His hands swiped ineffectively against his trousers and he glanced down at them. "I'll need a good wash before I'm fit company at anyone's table. And I suspect you're not used to itinerant workmen in your kitchen for meals."

"Well, we just happen to have a basin and lots of warm water," Augusta told him. "You'd better come along before Bertha changes her mind and feeds the hogs instead."

He brushed himself off, then climbed the sturdy stairs and walked past her, careful not to allow his trousers to touch her dress. "You don't have hogs." The words trailed behind him as he entered the kitchen and Augusta heard Bertha's quick retort.

"Well, who said we did?"

"The lady of the house tried to feed me a line of guff, but I'm too bright to fall for her nonsense," she heard Cleary reply, and stifled a chuckle as Bertha murmured agreement. Breakfast was indeed ready, as was Bertha, a skillet full of sausage gravy in one hand, a large ladle in the other. As Augusta entered the room, she shot her a look of warning.

"The girls are up and around," she said nonchalantly. "Should I tell them to wait a while so y'all can eat in peace and quiet?"

"I think it's too late for that," Augusta told her as footsteps clattered on the front stairway.

"I can feed 'em in the dining room." A bowl of biscuits appeared on the table and the sausage gravy was poured into a deep bowl.

"Is there any chance you might know any of our ladies?" Augusta asked Cleary in an undertone. She would not have him embarrassed, should he have been a regular customer at Lula Belle's place. On the other hand, if he were of that ilk, she'd better know now and keep her distance, lest his evil shenanigans give her shelter a bad name.

"Doubtful. I can't imagine how," he said, his glance meeting hers with an honesty she found assuring.

"Well, lookie here. We got company," Pearl said, posing in the doorway as if readying herself for a photographer. Sauntering into the big kitchen, she peered into the warming oven where a pan of cinnamon rolls waited, then wandered to the round table. "Got room for a couple more?"

Cleary stood promptly and nodded. "I'm sure you're welcome to join us. Are you alone?" he asked, and then, as Beth Ann cleared the doorway, he paused, his gaze taking a quick survey of the fragile woman.

"I'm sorry," she said, backing into the hall. "I'll eat later on. I didn't know you had company, Miss Augusta."

Augusta shot around the table, her hand outstretched. "Come in, Beth Ann." Not for the world would she allow the girl to feel unwanted in this house, no matter who came to call. And Cleary didn't seem to have any qualms about the additional seats required around the table.

"Can we use that for seating?" he asked, motioning toward a backless bench sitting against the wall.

"I'll help you get it," Pearl offered, her sidelong glance taking in his masculine form. Augusta thought the woman's cleavage could have been less noticeable, and she watched as Bertha gave Pearl a push and nodded at the front of her wrapper. Reluctantly Pearl tugged the sides of her bodice closer and sat on the bench, patting the area beside her.

"Why don't you come over here, and we'll get acquainted?" Her invitation was directed at Cleary, but he patently ignored it, holding a chair for Beth Ann, instead, as she edged her way back into the kitchen. With barely a whisper of fabric or an audible sound from her lips, she nodded her thanks and slid onto the seat.

"Give me a hand here, Pearl," Bertha said gruffly. "Y'all spend half the day layin' in bed and then expect me to wait on you. You'll find out that ain't the way it's gonna work here."

Without protest, Pearl rose and did as she was asked, her hips swaying as she placed plates and silverware around the table. "Should we lay a spot for Janine and Honey?" she asked, looking to Augusta for instructions.

"Are they up?" she asked, and then nodded in reply to her own query when they could be heard coming down the stairs. "Go ahead. They'll be hungry, too."

And wasn't Mr. Cleary getting an eyeful this morning? she thought, lifting the bowl of biscuits from the middle of the table and passing them in his direction. He took two, and she noted Bertha's pleased expression. "The way to a man's heart," was an adage that could be reversed, her mama had said, more than once. The way to a woman's heart lay in compliments on her cooking, and Cleary was obviously adept at that type of behavior.

Janine settled in a chair, and Honey slid onto the bench beside Pearl. "Did we forget anything?" Bertha asked, and

Pearl shook her head, breaking a biscuit in half and waiting for the gravy to be passed in her direction.

None of the women seemed to recognize Cleary, and for that Augusta was grateful. It would have been embarrassing had they known the man by name. Instead, she performed introductions as they began to eat, and he was inundated by questions from the women surrounding him.

Not known for their reticence, Pearl and Janine were vocal in their curiosity, but Cleary was not forthcoming with information, merely turning their queries in another direction, until they exchanged glances and returned to eating breakfast.

"Today, we're going to hang curtains in the parlor and work at building a place to keep chickens," Augusta told her charges. "I'd like Honey to water the garden and paint the front steps. Mr. Cleary has kindly finished repairing them for us, and I'll purchase some paint at the general store."

"It's easier to buy eggs at the store," Janine said bluntly. "Keeping chickens is a messy job."

"Raising chickens is a profitable venture," Augusta told her firmly. "Not only can we eat the young roosters, but we can sell the eggs at a nice profit."

"Next you'll be talking about a cow," Janine said. "I'm not sure we're gonna be allowed to keep livestock in town."

"Lots of folks have chickens in the backyard," Augusta said. "I've checked, and there are no ordinances against animals for your own use."

"Did you hear from that lady at the store that wants me to do some sewing for her?" Janine asked. "That brings in good money."

"Yes, and so does laundry," Augusta told her. "Mrs. Stevens and her husband own the hotel, and she's about persuaded him to let us do all the linens twice a week.

Harriet Burns, our neighbor, wants us to keep her in clean sheets for her boarders, too.''

"I'm not real fond of using a scrub board," Pearl said darkly. "We had a laundry lady when I was at the Pink Palace."

"That wasn't all you had," Augusta reminded her with a pointed look at her eye, where the lid still wore two stitches. "It was your choice to leave there, Pearl. If you want to go back to the lap of luxury, be my guest. But once any of you leave here, it's for good. We've already talked about that."

"I'm not going back," Pearl said quickly. "I've done worse things than scrub sheets in my day."

"We need income," Augusta told them. "That's the whole reason for working. We can't run this place without money, and we have to do the things that are within our capabilities. Laundry and sewing, keeping a kitchen garden, raising chickens and selling eggs to our neighbors are all moneymakers for us."

"Well, if you'll get the paint, I'll do the front steps. I noticed Mr. Cleary working on them this morning," Honey said shyly. "And in the meantime, I'll tend the garden and help in the kitchen."

"Can I be of assistance?" Cleary asked Augusta. She thought he looked almost hopeful as he met her gaze.

"You already have been," she told him. "You probably don't want to be associated too closely with our endeavors. It might not look good for you in town, whatever your business might be." And if she waited long enough, he might tell her just what it was he did for a living, she thought.

"I've never been one to worry about what folks think," he said bluntly. "If you need my handyman skills, I'll be happy to pitch in and help. And in the meantime, I'd be glad to run you into town in my buggy to get your paint, ma'am.''

''Well, that beats walking, any day of the week,'' Bertha said flatly. ''You better snatch up that offer in a hurry, I'd say, Miss Augusta.''

''I don't want to put you out,'' Augusta told Cleary, then watched his eyes light with some emotion she couldn't decipher.

''I'd be glad to accommodate you, ma'am,'' he said politely, his words accompanied by Pearl's subdued snort of laughter. He glanced at the buxom blonde, and her hand flew to cover her mouth.

In the midst of a conversation that bore undertones she couldn't interpret, Augusta turned to Bertha. ''When is John Burgess bringing the hens?'' she asked.

''First of the week,'' Bertha said. ''Gives us four days to have a coop ready, and a fenced yard for them to scratch in.''

''It sounds to me like you're going to need a load of things delivered from the lumberyard,'' Cleary told Augusta. ''We can go by and place an order if you like.''

She hesitated. ''To tell you the truth, I'm not sure how to go about building a henhouse. Nor do I know how much lumber to order.''

''Let's ask Harriet Burns if she has any gentlemen living in her boardinghouse who might be looking for work for a couple of days,'' Cleary suggested. ''I don't think you ladies are up to building such a thing, unless you've got experience at swinging a hammer.''

Augusta rose from the table. ''I'll take you up on your offer, Mr. Cleary. If you really want to help, you can figure out what we need from the lumberyard, and I'll provide the cash to buy it.'' She glanced at him quickly, thinking of the wad of bills he'd pressed into her hand two days ago. It had been a generous contribution, and she hadn't properly thanked him for it. Her own account was satisfyingly healthy, but Cleary's contribution had provided enough to buy more than a load of lumber, if she was any judge of the price of wood.

"Let's take a walk out to the back," he suggested, placing his fork on the table and nodding politely at the watching women. With one hand on the small of her back, he opened the screened door and led her out onto the back porch.

It burned there, that wide palm and the four outstretched fingers. His thumb rode the line of her spine and she felt a shiver spin from that spot, vibrating down the length of her back. Whatever it was Mr. Cleary's touch did to her, she could not afford to allow it. With a quick double step, she moved ahead of him and heard his stifled laughter at her back. It served only to stiffen her spine and renew her determination, and she walked briskly toward the spot she'd chosen for the proposed building project.

"We've got two dozen chickens coming, all pullets hatched early this spring," she told him. "They're already laying. The eggs are small, but given a couple of months, we'll have plenty of them, good-sized, too, every day. And then, once they're old enough, we can let some of them hatch their eggs, and we'll have a steady supply."

Pleased with her plan, she turned her head to observe his reaction. It was not what she expected. A wide grin exposed white, even teeth, and his hands were deep in his trouser pockets as he rocked back on his heels.

"I think you've forgotten one small item, ma'am," he said. "In order to have eggs hatch, you'll need a rooster in your little flock."

"Well, yes, of course," she said hastily. "I'm sure Mr. Burgess will be happy to provide us with a rooster." She made a mental note to bring the subject up when the gentleman came to deliver his white leghorns on Monday, next.

"You'll need roosts and nesting boxes," Cleary told her. "A henhouse with a sloped roof, a door, a couple of windows and a small exit for the hens to get out into the yard."

She dug into her pocket and brought forth a tablet and a pencil stub, kept handy for just such a purpose. With a glance, she tore off the top sheet, folded it and placed it back in her pocket, then offered Cleary a speaking look. "List what we need, and I'll make note of it," she said.

He did, itemizing two-by-fours and wooden siding, nails and hinges, chicken-wire fencing and upright posts. And then he had her read it back to him. "They'll need to cut some of the two-by-fours in half and you'll need about twenty feet of dowel rod for the roosts."

"Dowel rod." She wrote it down, then glanced up. "What's dowel rod?"

"Same thing you're going to need to hang curtains on in the parlor," he said. "Have you already bought them?"

"I'm ordering from the catalogue," Augusta said. "Surely they must sell rods also."

"You'll do better to buy it from the lumberyard and paint it yourself. Costs a lot less than ordering it cut to size from Sears, Roebuck. And we'll need to have paint for the henhouse, too."

"You must think I'm awfully dumb," she said quietly. "I just assumed it would be so easy to put things together, and the further I go, the less I know what I'm doing."

"Well, aren't you just fortunate I came along?" he said slowly, his grin matching his droll manner of speech. "I happen to know a lot about such things. I think what you need, ma'am, is a man around the house."

"Oh, I can't have that," she said quickly, looking back at the kitchen door, where shadows moved within the room. "I think they're watching me." A flush climbed her cheeks, and she turned away from the women who were no doubt straining their hearing as they tried to listen in on the conversation their benefactress was having in the middle of the yard.

"Well, maybe a man who'd come and go on a regular basis. Not a fellow who'd expect to stay nights."

"Did you have anyone in particular in mind?" she asked, looking stalwartly toward the back of the lot.

"I think you're a fine lady, Miss McBride, who's bitten off quite a mouthful. If I can be of assistance without jeopardizing your reputation in this town, I'd like to help."

"And what of your own business?" she asked, shooting him a look of inquiry. It wasn't likely he'd divulge his method of livelihood to her, but curiosity bade her ask.

"I'm on hiatus right now," he said. "Sort of between assignments. Which means I have time on my hands, and enough to live on very comfortably, so you wouldn't have to pay me a wage."

"Assignments." She repeated the word that had caught her attention. "Who do you work for, sir?"

"I'm not at liberty to discuss that, Augusta," he said reluctantly, offering her no excuse, only the firm refusal that halted her questions before they could be given voice.

"All right," she said. "If you want to spend your time working at a thankless task, with no chance of monetary gain, I won't attempt to stop you. I can only tell you that God will surely bless you for your interest in the shelter."

His smile was quick, and his eyes lit with humor as she spoke. "Thank you, Augusta. I may be so bold as to call you that, I hope. After all, if we are to work together, I think we should consider ourselves good friends, don't you?"

He'd almost blown the whole thing. Almost burst out in laughter when she'd so sweetly told him he could be expecting the Almighty's blessing for his interest in her work.

What he was expecting was a chance to spend time with a woman who appealed to him in a mighty big way.

A female like Augusta McBride was not what he'd ever thought to consider as the most important woman in his life. He'd had in mind a more independent creature, a woman who knew her way around in the masculine world and was able to fend for herself. And then he'd taken one good look at the creature on his front porch and rearranged all of his opinions as they related to females.

He'd spent more years on top of a horse than he wanted to count, and the past eight months had taught him that he wasn't getting any younger. The shoulder wound he'd suffered in Wyoming ached at night, and various and sundry places on his thirty-four-year-old frame proclaimed that youth had passed him by and left him with scars and wrinkles galore.

If ever a man wanted to settle down and have a family, his name was Jon Cleary. And Augusta McBride was the likeliest candidate he'd met up with—at least the most available woman who'd ever appealed to his instincts.

"I don't mind if you call me Augusta," she said now, only a bit of reservation tingeing her words. "Not in front of my ladies, of course, but in private. And I'll call you…" She turned up an unblemished face, and his gaze swept the vision before him.

"Cleary will do just fine," he said. "Did anyone ever tell you that you have—"

"Yes, I know," she said abruptly, interrupting him mid-thought. "I have blue eyes and yellow hair and my features are nicely formed. But that's not the part of me that's important, Cleary. Don't give me compliments. They make me very distrustful."

"Wouldn't think of it," he said hastily. "Wouldn't even consider the idea. What I was about to say was that you have a fine mind, with a bent toward organization. Why, just the way you gave orders for the day was enough to let me know that you have things nicely under control here.''

And wasn't that a lie, if he'd ever told one. She was a female knocking herself out for the benefit of a string of ponies who'd come in last. He could only hope that those female creatures she'd taken under her wing were appreciative of the effort she made in their behalf.

''Thank you,'' she said, writing furiously on her pad of paper. Then she looked up at him again, and he lost track of his thoughts. ''What else do I need to list? For the henhouse, I mean?''

''I think we've got it about covered,'' he told her. ''Now let's head for the lumberyard and the general store and see how much money we can spend.''

Harriet Burns had two boarders looking for work, and they were pleased to find a job at which to show their talents. Their quick looks in Augusta's direction were squelched with one glance from Cleary's dark eyes, and he pointedly told them they were under his direct supervision, no matter that Miss McBride was paying their wages. They agreed to show up after dinner to lay out the chicken yard, and Cleary told them he would be there to set the four corners of the henhouse.

''Now for the lumberyard,'' he said, satisfied at the progress gained at their first stop. In half an hour, he'd ordered the wood and tar paper for the roof, then they'd gone on to the general store. Hardware was heavy stuff, he told Augusta, not allowing her to lift the box of nails and hinges.

''Can we stop at the post office?'' she asked. ''I think it's about time for my catalogue order to come in.''

He obliged her by lifting her from the buggy and waiting patiently outside the barbershop, where the postmaster shared space with haircutting equipment. She emerged with a large bundle in her arms, and he quickly lifted himself from the side of the buggy as she appeared in the doorway.

"Why didn't you call me? You shouldn't try to carry such a heavy load by yourself." His hands were careful lifting the bundle from her arms, aware of the soft curves of her breasts that tempted his touch. The backs of his knuckles brushed against her dress fabric, and he was nonchalant as he relieved her of the weight.

"I'm used to doing for myself," she said quietly. "There's another bundle inside, if you have room for it in the buggy."

"We'll make room," he told her, placing the paper-wrapped package on the edge of the seat. The second one was settled on the floor in less than a minute, and then his hands surrounded her waist as he lifted her into the buggy on his side of the vehicle. He watched as she scooted across the leather seat to wedge herself firmly against her package, making room for him as he climbed in beside her.

"Got room enough there?" he asked cheerfully, noting the pressure of her thigh against his, the warmth of her shoulder beneath his arm.

"Yes, of course," she said, a trifle breathlessly to be sure, but bright-eyed and bushy-tailed as a sleek squirrel as they rode slowly back toward the north side of town.

He had her right where he wanted her. Under his wing and unable to back off. He kept the mare to a walk, talking quietly about the places they passed, tipping his hat to ladies who watched from the sidewalk and grinning at men who eyed him with a trace of envy.

Augusta McBride was perched beside him and the whole town was taking note. He'd managed to do a good stroke of business this morning.

Chapter Three

The day held promise. Cleary grinned to himself as he entered the livery stable and greeted the sturdy gentleman who leaned on his pitchfork and tilted his hat back in a silent salute. "Good morning, Sam. I'm in need of my horse this morning."

The genial owner nodded and asked dutifully about Cleary's health, having apparently received the story through the local grapevine that Cleary had instigated upon arrival in town. "You back in shape yet?" And then he answered his own question, to Cleary's delight. "Must be, the way you've been workin' over at the old Harvey place the other side of town."

"Feeling better every day. I figure swinging a hammer is good for what ails me," Cleary said with a friendly smile. That he'd never stipulated what ailed him was a moot point.

"Here's your horse," Sam Ferguson said, leading the gelding from its stall. He located Cleary's saddle and blanket and, in moments, had the animal ready for its owner's use. Hands deep in his pockets, he watched as horse and rider rode off at a sedate pace, down the main street and then between buildings to the side road leading to the old house Augusta McBride had made her own.

Lifting his face to inhale the morning air, Cleary sensed the promise inherent in a new day, one in which he planned to move his friendship with Augusta McBride into a new arena. But first, his reasons for heading toward her shelter must be in place.

The gate repair was next, Cleary figured. Then the shutter, hanging by a single nail and due to land on the ground should a wayward wind catch it. He'd had a hiatus over the past week, and perhaps it was only the calm before the storm, but he'd best enjoy it while he could. Should a message arrive and he be forced to leave town for any length of time, explaining his absence to Augusta might be a problem.

Mounting his horse, he nudged its barrel with his heel, his heart lifting as he viewed the cloudless sky, his thoughts speeding ahead with the anticipation of seeing Augusta again. She was melting a bit, her natural defenses against a stranger giving way to the friendship he was working to develop between them. And more than a friendship was in the offing, he'd determined.

The henhouse was a finished project, the fence drawn taut and secured to upright posts surrounding it. It swarmed now with white leghorns, each of them willing to donate to the cause in exchange for a steady diet and a pan of water. He grinned as he recalled the look on Honey's face as she'd ventured within the gate to feed the hungry pullets. She'd backed up, holding the pan of feed over her head as the noisy birds clustered around her feet, awaiting their meal.

The pan had hit the ground, scattering seed in a wide circle, and Honey had flown through the gate, shrieking loudly, as if the hounds of hell were at her heels. Obviously, the girl was not a product of country living, and yet she could be appealing, should the right young man in need of a wife's assistance come along.

Augusta was a different sort. Used to city living, yet more than willing to blend in with the small town atmosphere she'd sought in which to open her haven. Even in the chicken coop, her character had emerged. Facing the hens head-on, she'd reached swiftly beneath them for their eggs, scolding a possessive creature who ventured to threaten her with a vicious beak. Not a word of scorn passed her lips as she'd showed Honey how to face down the squawking pullets, scattering the feed before her, then filling the water pan with a pitcher before she left the pen.

A remarkable woman, he'd decided. One he could easily take into his life. There was not a doubt of her innocence, but she was worldly wise in the ways of women and their needs. And he was a man in need of the solace only a woman could provide. Once he'd managed to locate and bring the gang of ruffians he sought to a courtroom, he was definitely planning on making a more prosaic life for himself.

And that life would include Augusta McBride, if he could manage to bring it about. His gaze raked the house before him, seeking a trace of the woman he'd set his sights on. She would not be happy with his evasive answers for much longer, he'd determined. Augusta was adept at prying, and his current occupation did not lend itself to a courtship. In fact, the thought of the man courting her being a hired gun, albeit the government having sought his services, might turn her totally away from any tender thoughts she might harbor toward him.

The pursuit of a gang of train robbers did not bode well for a man's health, and Cleary hoped to preserve what remained of his weary bones and scarred body. And when all was said and done, he was using Augusta as a shield, his courtship of her a cover-up for the game he played.

Yet, in his heart, he acknowledged a need that would not be denied. Use her he might, and a niggling shard of guilt accompanied that admission, but the woman herself was a prize he yearned to own. One day, should he survive this operation, she would know the truth about Jonathan Cleary. He only hoped she would forgive him his deception.

He rode the edge of the property line, close beside the hedge of bushes, and tied his mount to a tree, where the animal could graze and remain in the shade. Replacing the bridle with a halter, he loosened the saddle cinch and headed for the woodshed. His gaze was satisfied as he beheld the pile of lumber he'd ordered for various projects, and he set about seeking the hardware necessary to mend the gate.

"Mr. Cleary?" Augusta's voice spoke his name and he looked up to find her in the doorway. "Can I help you find something?" she asked, and then stepped into the confines of the small shed. "I didn't know you were coming here this morning. I'd thought you might be weary of working by this time."

"No, ma'am," he said, denying her concern. "I'm exercising my shoulder every time I swing a hammer."

She frowned. "What's wrong with your shoulder? Did you fall and injure it?"

He hesitated, ruing his words, and then aimed a smile in her direction. "You might say that. It's almost as good as new now, but it's given me some trouble getting it back in shape." Not to mention the neat hole where a bullet had gone in and the torn, scarred flesh where it had made its exit.

Augusta McBride was not the sort of woman who would receive that confidence with a smile. Rather, she would be full of questions, and her persistence would know no end.

"I thought I'd fix the gate this morning," Cleary said, lifting a bag of hinges from a shelf. "These will work for the gate and the shutters, too. You have several that need to be secured.''

"Hinges for shutters?" she asked, a brow lifting as she questioned his intent.

"When you get a good wind hereabouts, you might need to close them in order to keep the windows safe from flying debris," he told her.

"Will they fasten inside?" she asked, and he nodded a reply.

"To keep out intruders, perhaps?" Her words were slow, as if her mind worked a problem.

"I suppose they could be used in that way," he conceded. "Though I doubt you'll need them for that purpose."

She stepped backward through the doorway and her hand beckoned him to follow. "I'll be available if you need help, Mr. Cleary. Can I carry something for you?"

"No," he said, bending to collect a board. The shutter had a cracked slat, and he might as well make a decent job of it. "But you can keep me company if you like."

"No, I believe I have more than enough to do indoors this morning," she told him. "We're teaching the ladies how to do simple sewing tasks. Janine is quite a talented seamstress, and she's willing to share her knowledge." Her smile was quick, as if she'd allowed a bit of humor to intrude on her serious endeavors.

"Are they willing pupils?" he asked, needing to keep her company as long as he could without being too forward.

"Willing, perhaps, but not as capable as Janine. Buttons and seams and darning might be the limit of Beth Ann's talents, but Honey is eager to learn."

"And Pearl?"

She cast him a glance from beneath long eyelashes and her mouth was taut. "Pearl is another story, I fear. She's adept in the kitchen these days, but she's so used to being waited on and cosseted, it's sometimes a problem, trying to expand her education.''

''Waited on?'' His brows rose in pure skepticism as he tried to envision that woman as a lady of leisure.

''She was in demand at the Pink Palace, I understand, and had the nicest room and all the benefits of being Mrs. Simpson's pet, according to Honey.''

Apparently a most talented lady, he decided. Surely talent was her only attraction, for the woman was almost beyond the age of selling herself by seductively revealing her face and form to the gentlemen who sought out such an alliance. And next to Augusta, Pearl was blowsy and wore the look of a horse who'd been ridden hard and put away wet. No matter Pearl's tricks of the trade, he'd take Augusta McBride over any amount of experience any day of the week.

Even now, Augusta's cheeks bore a hint of embarrassment, their tone definitely rosy as she discussed the women she sheltered within the walls of her home. An almost overwhelming need to touch that fine skin arose within him, and Cleary blessed the fact that his hands were filled with the supplies he needed to complete his work this morning.

''Well, you go on ahead, ma'am,'' he told Augusta. ''I'll try not to make too much noise when I work on the shutters. But I'm going to be working on all of them, and you'd do well to stay in the back of the house for your sewing class.''

''Yes, we'd planned on that. The kitchen table will do well for our needs,'' she told him, lifting her skirt as she hastened toward the back door.

He watched, aware of the fine lines of her ankles, his gaze narrowing as he caught a glimpse of the lower curve of her calf as she climbed the three steps to the back porch. And then the sight of Bertha standing on the other side of the screened door drew his eyes. The look of warning she flashed in his direction made his mouth twitch with amusement. He'd be facing a veritable dragon in that one, he decided, should he lay one finger on her lone chick.

Let her do her worst. It would be more than a finger he placed on the delicate skin of Augusta McBride. Before many more days had passed, he planned on initiating a slow seduction.

Gussie. He tasted the single word on his tongue, and his smile became full-blown. Bertha be hanged. He'd faced worse adversaries in his day. And in this case, the prize was worthy of his finest efforts.

"I'm not ever going to be a seamstress," Beth Ann announced at the end of an hour of attempting to sew on missing buttons, suffering numerous tiny wounds from the needle that refused to cooperate.

"You don't need to be," Janine told her, preening as she held up her own work. A dress from the missionary barrel had been remade into a garment for Honey. It would tie in the back, making allowances for her increasing girth as time passed. "I think this will do," Janine pronounced, folding the dress and presenting it to the young woman.

"I can't thank you enough," Honey said, humbly accepting the gift. "My things are all but tearing out at the seams already."

"If you can learn to do mending and sewing on buttons, it will be sufficient for now," Janine told the two young women. "Not everyone can sew a fine seam, but with practice, you'll do better."

"Why didn't you become a dressmaker?" Augusta asked her bluntly. "Surely it would have been a more—" She halted, not knowing the words to describe her thoughts.

"More acceptable occupation?" Janine supplied with a quirk of her eyebrow. "Perhaps, but not nearly so lucrative."

"Nor so dangerous," Augusta reminded her.

"Well, there is that," Janine agreed. "And I have the marks to prove it." She shuddered involuntarily as she spoke, and Augusta felt a moment's curiosity as she wondered at the events that had driven Janine from the Pink Palace to this place. It was an unspoken rule that no one need divulge any more than they wanted to regarding their past or their reasons for being here.

And that included Augusta, thankfully.

"If you don't get your mess out of my way, we'll be eatin' dinner on top of your mending," Bertha said from her place before the stove. "You'd better ask that man if he wants to sit down with us," she told Augusta, grudgingly offering the hospitality of her kitchen to Cleary.

Even now, his hammer rang out sharply as he put shutters in place on the front of the house. Augusta nodded and hastened toward the hallway, her heart strangely affected by the prospect of speaking to the tall gentleman. She exited through the front screened door and turned to where he labored at the furthest window. A glance at the gate proved his ability. It hung straight and was fastened with a shiny new latch.

"Mr. Cleary?" She halted six feet from him, her eyes drawn by the muscles in his upper arms, straining the material of his shirt as he swung the hammer one last time, a final blow that set the nail firmly in place. His vest lay over the porch railing and his shirtsleeves were rolled up above his elbows, allowing him to work without the hindrance of fabric pulling and tugging as he used the hammer.

He was strong, not overly thick through the upper body, but muscular nonetheless. And she felt a slow flush climb her cheeks, reproving herself for noticing such a thing.

"Yes, Miss Augusta?" he answered, turning his head to meet her gaze. His eyes were warm, regarding her with a look of pleasure, as if he took delight in the sight of her there before him. His lips curved beneath his mustache, and she felt her heart beat a bit faster as his smile widened.

"We're about ready to eat dinner, if you'd like to join us." Her words were stilted, delivered in a breathless fashion, and his smile tweaked a corner of his wide mouth.

"I'd appreciate that, ma'am," he told her politely. "Would you like to hold this shutter in place while I finish up the last bit of securing it to the house?"

"Yes, of course," she said quickly, stepping to his side, wondering briefly how he'd accomplished hanging the others without help.

Cleary looked down at her as she awaited his instructions. "I need to make it readily available, should you want to close it," he said, explaining his method. "But it needs to be firmly attached when it's opened." Grasping her right hand, he placed it on the edge of the wide slats.

"Hold it right there," he instructed her, speaking past several nails he held between his lips, and she obeyed.

Aware of the faint scent of masculine flesh, she breathed carefully, drawing shallow gasps of air into her suddenly inadequate lungs. It was no use. He was male, a bit warm, sweaty even, she decided. Yet it was a pleasing smell, that of soap and perhaps hair tonic, along with an undefinable aroma that teased her into edging just a bit closer.

Her hair brushed against his chest as he leaned over her to ply his hammer to the latch he imposed on the wooden siding. And then his hand touched her shoulder as he fit the hook into the latch, holding the shutter immobile and in place.

"You can let go now," he told her, and her hand fell from the shutter as she stepped aside. His palm against her shoulder tightened its grip, and she halted in her retreat. She looked up at him, aware that, though he held her firmly, he exhibited no force, only a touch that warmed her to the tips of her fingers.

"Thank you, Miss Augusta," he said politely. His eyes were heavy lidded, she noted, their depths dark as he took her measure. "When will you learn to call me *Cleary,* without the formality of a title attached?" he asked quietly. "Once you do, I'll be able to use your name as I please." His mouth twitched and widened to a smile that lured her.

"Cleary," she said obediently, softly, with a whisper of anticipation, as if she waited for some momentous occasion to present itself.

"Augusta," he replied, his gaze focused upon her lips as they spoke his name.

She held her breath, the heat from his body extending to hers, warming her from top to bottom, her spine tingling as she edged half a step closer to him. His head bent a bit and his mouth opened a fraction. As though in a trance, Augusta tilted her chin, the better to watch that mobile arrangement of lips that lured her in a foreign, forbidden way.

The edges of his teeth showed as he smiled, white beneath his dark mustache, and he bent inches closer. Almost close enough to touch her mouth.

"Dinner's on the table." The words echoed in her mind as the screened door opened and Pearl stepped onto the porch.

"Yes." Augusta's eyes closed for just a second, ruing the loss of...what? Had he been about to place those firm, chiseled lips upon hers? Such a thought did not bear pondering, she decided quickly. Pearl had interrupted but a moment of flirtation on his part.

The urge to shake her head in denial of that thought was strong. She considered the man a gentleman, far above stealing a fleeting kiss in broad daylight, in full view of any passerby who might glance in their direction.

Her own gaze flew to the empty road in front of the house, and she blessed the porch roof and the sheltering hedge of bushes that hid them from the boardinghouse next door.

"We'll be right there, Pearl," she said quickly, sending a smile in the woman's direction. "We've just finished the final touches on this shutter."

"Yeah, I see that," Pearl drawled, backing into the front hallway as she cast a mocking grin at Cleary.

"She thinks we were…" Flustered and at a loss for words, Augusta backed off.

"We were, ma'am," he told her softly. "I was about to place my lips against yours, and now I'm regretting the interruption."

"I can't have you saying such things to me, sir," Augusta told him with a haughty glance. "I am not available for a dalliance, no matter that I owe you my thanks for the work you've done on behalf of our shelter."

"I've been happy to donate my time and limited talents, ma'am," he told her as he reached for his vest. "And I have no intention of *dallying* with you. My intentions have never been less than honorable where you're concerned. It just happens that I almost fell prey to your sweetness a moment ago." He turned, meeting her gaze, and his eyes burned with a warmth she knew was intended to disarm her. As were his final words. "I regret if I've caused you any distress," he murmured.

She watched as he rolled down his shirtsleeves, sorting through his words. Losing track when she recalled *dallying* and *honorable,* she managed to recall another phrase, words that sounded like an apology. He'd called her sweet, in a roundabout way. And that thought made her blood hum in her veins. She'd never been described as *sweet,* not by anyone in her life.

But this man, this strong, handsome man whose very presence made her heart beat just a bit faster, thought she was attractive enough to spend his niceties upon. Her smile wobbled as she took another step toward the door, and her words were proper and ladylike, even to her own ears, as she invited him to join the household for dinner.

And if there was a sudden look of relief on his face, she chose to ignore it, setting aside the small disagreement they'd sorted through. He followed her into the house and down the hallway to the kitchen at the back. As he soaped his hands in the pan provided, she poured additional warm water over them from the reservoir at the side of the stove.

It was moments later, as they sat around the table, that she realized his words had held a note of promise she would do well not to ignore.

I was about to place my lips against yours. And now I'm regretting the interruption.

In order to succeed, her shelter must remain first and foremost in her thoughts. Mr. Cleary, with his dark eyes and neatly trimmed mustache, was a distraction she could not afford.

He'd been called out of town. The note was short and to the point. And Augusta was filled with a sense of desolation. One she quickly worked to obliterate, plunging into a cooking lesson as if it were of utmost import this morning. The minister's wife had cried off again, and Augusta was beginning to recognize that she alone, of the original five ladies who'd met to organize this effort, was left to do this sort of thing.

Her ladies watched her warily, and she gathered herself together. It would not do for them to recognize her *attachment* to Mr. Cleary. Indeed, she had no business even thinking about him. The shelter was her first obligation. That and teaching her ladies in order to make them eligible for marriage or a life of their choice beyond the doors of this place.

"I'll never get the hang of gravy," Honey said, stirring

the lumpy concoction she'd managed to devise from bacon drippings and flour.

"When it's browned nicely, you'll add a cup or two of water, and be amazed at what occurs," Augusta said, doing her best to encourage the girl.

"I know what *occurred* last time I did this," Honey told her, her mouth turning down in discouragement. "I ended up with a pan full of paste. Lumpy paste."

"Well, my bread didn't rise the way Bertha's does," Beth Ann said sadly. "I think it'll only be good for toast. Or maybe to feed the chickens."

"That's one good thing about having chickens," Augusta agreed. "Although a pig might be even better at getting rid of our mistakes."

"You don't make mistakes," Beth Ann said, lifting her gaze to Augusta, as if she beheld a woman beyond reproach. "You always seem to know the right thing to do and say, and you've even got Mr. Cleary hanging on your every word."

"Mr. Cleary?" Augusta repeated the name as if it were foreign to her. "What on earth are you talking about?" It would not do to have the ladies thinking she was carrying on with the man, and if Pearl had made untoward remarks after seeing them together on the porch, she'd have to speak to her.

"He's sweet on you, ma'am," the girl said shyly. "I never had anybody look at me the way he looks at you. Never even had any man act like I was fit to spit on." Her mouth drew into a moue, and she sighed deeply.

"Well, by the time we get finished with you, you'll be a fit companion for any man out looking for a wife," Augusta determined. "You'll be able to cook and sew a bit and keep house with the best of them." Deep within, she doubted the total truth of that bold statement, but lest Beth

Ann see her doubtfulness, she smiled widely and patted the girl on the shoulder.

Keeping house was an accomplishment all of the women were able to attain, and the inside of the place was as neat as a pin these days. Floors shiny and windows spotless, it had taken on the appearance of a home. A home such as Augusta hadn't had in several months. She cherished each room, adding to the furnishings gradually as pieces became available through the lady at the general store, who advised her of folks willing to sell various items at a good price. Nothing matched precisely, but it all began to blend with a homey charm that pleased her.

"I think we've accomplished enough today," she said as Honey surveyed her gravy, stirring in vain to dissolve the lumps. "Bertha will fix a new pan for dinner," she told the girl. "Next time will be better."

"My cookies came out good," Honey said quietly. "Maybe I can find a fella to marry who has a sweet tooth." Her smile was trembling, and Augusta's heart went out to the girl who would soon be a woman with a child, and with no husband in view.

"Where's Mr. Cleary gone to?" Pearl asked idly, glancing up from her task of cutting out biscuits. Her eyes were sharp, her query far from idle, and Augusta hesitated a moment, forming a reply.

"He was called out of town on business," she said, wiping the table with a damp cloth and preparing it for dinner. "He'll be back in a few days, I suppose."

"He didn't tell you?" Pearl asked.

August sent her a glance meant to subdue her curiosity, but Pearl was not to be deterred from her purpose.

"I'd think a man as smitten as he is would be here tellin' you goodbye, not just sending you a note." Her eyes lit with humor as Pearl leveled her remark at Augusta.

"He's not *smitten*," August said sharply, "and I don't

appreciate your innuendo, Pearl. Mr. Cleary has been more than generous with his time, helping us do the outside work and supervising the building of the chicken yard and coop. He doesn't, however, owe us an explanation for his absence.''

"Whatever you say, ma'am,'' Pearl replied, her submissive tone at odds with the grin she made no attempt to conceal.

Augusta halted midway across the kitchen and turned to Pearl, her lips pursed, her eyes flashing. And then she let out a deep breath. For the first time in years, she was being teased, and by a master. Pearl meant no harm, she realized, only poked fun. The sight of Augusta and Cleary on the porch had given her a tool, and she was wielding it with a skill Augusta could only admire.

She was a part of a family here, she realized. These women, with checkered backgrounds, unlike her own luxurious beginnings, had joined forces to give her the security of a sisterhood, something she'd never enjoyed.

"Gracious, I don't even know the man's first name,'' Augusta said.

"Jonathan,'' Beth Ann said quietly.

"Jonathan?'' Augusta swung to face the girl, her eyes wide with surprise. "How did you know that?''

"He told me. He saw me pulling weeds in the garden and he came over to lend a hand, and he said my name was pretty. So I asked him what his was, and he told me. I didn't do anything wrong, did I?'' Her blue eyes filled with tears and Augusta was stricken as she watched Beth Ann's mouth tremble.

Her arms surrounded the young girl and she held her closely. "No, of course you didn't do anything wrong. It was kind of him to help you, and even nicer to share his name with you.'' She set her away and met the teary gaze.

"Maybe it's you he's sweet on, Beth Ann, and not me, as Pearl believes."

A flush crept up the wan cheeks and Beth Ann protested, her head shaking, her words spurting forth in a quick denial of any such thing.

The women halted their work and gathered around the girl, and even Pearl touched Beth Ann's nondescript hair with a kind hand as they assured her that Augusta was only teasing. Bertha watched from the stove and flashed a look of understanding, nodding wisely as if she condoned the development of this clutch of women into a family.

A sharp rapping on the front door caught Augusta's ear and she hastened down the hallway to answer the summons. Her footsteps lagged as she set eyes on Roger Hampton, hat in hand, peering through the screen. "What do you want, Mr. Hampton?"

"I thought I'd stop by since your handyman seems to have taken a hike out of town. Thought you might enjoy a gentleman's company."

"And you consider yourself as such?" Augusta asked, a haughty note coating each word. She stood back from the door and slid her hands into her apron pockets. "Did you come for any particular reason? Or were you just riding through the neighborhood?"

"I suppose my visit is to ascertain your reasons for staying here instead of coming with me back to Dallas," he said quietly, apparently deciding to present his better side.

"I have a home here, and responsibilities," she told him firmly.

"And a man chasing after you," he added with a frown. "A man who is operating in a most secretive manner. Even the sheriff is checking up on him."

"And what makes you think that concerns me?" she

asked, her mind spinning as she wondered again where Cleary had gone.

"There's been a rash of robberies—train robberies—lately. The gang is hitting shipments of cash and gold in an area surrounding Dallas, and your Mr. Cleary seems to be spacing his out-of-town trips to coincide with each event." He rocked back on his heels and his features formed a smug grin. "Just thought you might want to chew on that bit of information while you're awaiting his return."

"Well, I certainly appreciate your coming out here to fill me in on all the latest news. But I doubt very much if Mr. Cleary's business has anything to do with bank robbers. He is a gentleman of the first order."

"Is he, now?" Roger's mouth tilted in a smile that did little to increase his appeal in Augusta's eyes. "I heard that he was taking liberties with you, right here on the front porch of your place, just a few days ago."

"Liberties?" she asked, thinking furiously of the kiss she'd almost received. "I'm sure I don't know what you're talking about, Mr. Hampton."

"Don't you?" He smiled, his mouth a taunt. "Well, I just wanted you to know that I'll be leaving town before long. My work in Dallas will no longer wait for my appearance there. If you change your mind, I'd be delighted to purchase a ticket for you to accompany me." He stepped back from the screened door and placed his hat on his head.

"I'd think the atmosphere there would be more conducive to a woman of your stature, Miss Augusta. In fact, I'll be willing to marry you here, before we even got on the train together. And I'll warrant that's a better offer than what you'll get from your Mr. Cleary."

"I told you I wasn't interested in your offer before I left Dallas, sir. I haven't changed my mind." Scathing words spun in her mind, but she set them aside, simply bowing her head and speaking one last phrase as she backed away from the door. She could not help but recognize that her inheritance was more appealing to Roger Hampton than she, herself, was. And that thought galled, tainting her final words.

"I wish you well, Mr. Hampton. Good day."

His mouth was grim as he narrowed his eyes, peering through the screen as she turned aside. "When you discover what a scalawag you're tangled up with, I'll expect to hear from you, Miss Augusta."

She heard his footsteps as he clattered down the steps, and her mind clung tenaciously to his words as she stood facing the flowered wallpaper in the hall.

...a rash of train robberies lately...spacing his out-of-town trips to coincide with each event. Even the sheriff is checking up on him.

She been trusting all of her life, certain of her instincts. Learning that she was the child of a woman of ill repute should have made her more wary of her intuition, yet she'd accepted Jonathan Cleary's appearance on her doorstep and refrained from questioning him about his circumstances.

The man had almost kissed her. *Good grief!* And she'd been more than willing, had he but bent a bit closer, had Pearl not interfered with her call to the table. Apparently she'd lowered all her barriers to him, and all but given him permission to ply her with his attentions. She shook her head at her own foolishness and stiffened her spine.

Just wait until he reappeared. Just wait.

The fourth day came and went, and still there was no reappearance of the man she yearned for. Cleary. *Jonathan* Cleary, Augusta reminded herself, a tinge of hurt creeping into her thoughts as she reflected that he'd not deemed her worthy of such a confidence. She looked from her bedroom window, scanning the starry horizon.

It was almost a mile to his house, she mused. Perhaps

he'd returned already and was even now readying himself for bed. As if she cared, she thought, tossing her head.

And yet, he crept further into her thoughts and she closed her eyes, visualizing his muscular form. Maybe he was undressing, freeing himself from the constriction of shirt and tie, for surely he would be dressed as a gentleman to pursue his business.

Whatever his business was, it was sure to be something refined, she decided, no matter what Roger Hampton's veiled accusations had implied. Maybe he was in charge of…she inhaled deeply as her mind balked, and her thoughts churned with various occupations the man might be involved with.

Cleary didn't appear to be a businessman, although his manners were impeccable. He was adept with tools, and his intelligence could not be disputed, but his talent seemed to lie in getting things accomplished. Like the chickenyard and coop. And like repairing the shingles on the roof, supervising the men from the boardinghouse next door as they worked to his specifications.

She opened her eyes, leaning her forehead against the upper windowpane. It was warm, holding the heat of the day, and she lifted from it. A movement beneath a tree in the front yard caught her attention as a figure stepped from under the low branches. A man, tall, wide through the shoulders, his hands at his sides.

It was Cleary. How she knew for certain was not important. Maybe it was his size, or the broad expanse of his shoulders, his stance seeming taut as he looked up at her window. Whatever inner message filled her mind with the knowledge, it was the beating of her heart and the quickening within her body that made her aware of his presence. She stepped back from the glass and bent to peer through the lower half of the window, where the screen kept night bugs from her room yet allowed soft breezes to enter.

The man watching lifted his hand in a salute of greeting, or perhaps a gesture willing her to come to him, then tucked it neatly in his trouser's pocket. And waited.

She turned to the bed, snatching her wrapper and sliding her arms into the sleeves. He'd seen her, beckoned her with his uplifted palm, and her head swam with the knowledge that he'd come to her. No matter his reason. Whatever the cost, she ached for his presence, for the sound of his voice, for the touch of his hand. Her feet were silent on the steps as she flew down the curving staircase to the front door.

It closed without a sound behind her, and she stood at the edge of the porch as he approached. She leaned heavily against the upright post beside her, and his name was a whisper on her lips. "Cleary?"

He stood below her, as if to approach nearer would be a blemish on her reputation. One hand lifted his hat and held it against his thigh, and still he watched her, silent and sober in the shadows. And then he spoke, the words quiet in the night, touching her heart like the song of a nightingale.

"I needed to see you." Music to her ears, the message he sent vibrated through her mind. *I needed to see you.*

Her reply seemed prosaic, witless and drab, yet she could not speak above a whisper, in a breathless, timid voice. "Whatever for, Mr. Cleary?" She should have called him Jonathan, she thought, ruing her formality. He'd have lifted a brow and smiled at her with delight and…

"I missed you," he said after a moment. His hat moved as he touched it against his leg and then shifted it in his hand. "I wasn't sure you'd see me out there. Or that you'd come down to speak with me."

She yearned to ask where he'd been. Wanted desperately to wonder aloud at the occupation that sent him hither and yon without notice, needed to hear an explanation for his absence. But mostly she ached to greet him warmly, and only the essential dignity she possessed forbade her to extend a hand and allow him the steps to where she stood, perhaps sit beside her on the swing that hung in the shadows at the end of the porch.

"We've missed you, too." It was a pale imitation of what her heart yearned to speak. But it would suffice, she decided, deliberately including the other occupants of this house in her words.

"We?" he asked. "And *you*, Miss Augusta. Did you miss me most of all?"

She saw a smile touch his lips, noted the lowering of his eyelids until only a faint gleam revealed his attention focused on her. The moon touched his hair with silver and the stars attended his smile, bringing to light the white, straight edges of his teeth. He was all male, powerful in his masculine beauty, and she sensed the disintegration of her defenses, if, indeed, she'd ever possessed any where this man was concerned.

"Yes." It was a single word, spoken quietly, accompanied by a small nod that reminded her of her dishabille, her hair falling past her shoulders to wave against her back. She'd taken the pins out, then shaken her head to loosen the locks. Now they tumbled where they would and she was stricken with embarrassment.

A lady did not allow her hair to be seen by a gentleman in such a manner. A fact her mother had dutifully listed, along with several other such rules, all of them written in stone. There were some things a lady definitely did not do.

Augusta feared that one of them surely included standing in the dark with only her nightwear on while a gentleman watched with knowing eyes. Especially when that gentleman had the ability to stir the lady's emotions with only a look or touch.

Cleary's smile held a hint of satisfaction as he heard her soft admission.

Yes. The single word hung between them and he inhaled swiftly.

"I'll be here tomorrow," he said. "Do you have a number of things for me to do?"

She shook her head. "None that I can think of right now." Her mind was blank, all but his image before her having faded to oblivion.

"I'll come anyway," he promised. "There's nothing in my cupboard for breakfast. Perhaps Bertha will allow me to join you."

"I'm sure," she whispered.

He stretched out his hand, his palm open to the moonlight, and her gaze flew to rest there, where she knew calluses hardened the skin. "Step down here with me, Gussie," he said quietly. Her hand twitched at her side and she doubled her fingers into a fist. Yet it would not obey her command, not even when she forced it into her pocket and clutched at the fabric there.

It trembled in her pocket, her fingertips tingling as she considered resting them on that open palm. "Why don't you step up here?" she countered, her head tilting to one side.

As if he had been waiting for the words of invitation, he lifted a foot to the porch, touching the upright post for balance, and, eschewing the stairs, stood before her. She backed from him with haste, but he was immobile, only the rise and fall of his shirt with each breath he drew marring the statue he became.

"You really missed me?" he asked, his voice taking on a husky note that stirred her heart into a more rapid pace.

"Yes."

"Then show me."

Chapter Four

"**S**how you? I don't understand."

She lied, he thought smugly. Though her wide eyes were confused, her body arched, leaning toward him as if she yearned to be in contact with his own solid frame. Escaping the pocket where she'd thrust it, her hand rose, fingers clenched tightly. And then they unfolded and her fist was no more, having become a narrow palm whose trembling fingers lifted toward his wide chest.

"I think you do," he said quietly, denying her words. "Shall I help you?" he asked.

Her gaze was shuttered by drooping eyelids now, as if she concentrated on the movement of her fingers as they brushed against his leather vest. "I thought you'd wear a suit in your pursuit of business. A white shirt and tie, perhaps." And then, as if his words penetrated her mind, she glanced up at him and he saw heat in the depths of her blue eyes, a warmth she was unable to conceal.

"Help me? What do you mean?" Her lips trembled and he fought the urge to cover them with his own. He'd almost done that very thing, less than a week ago, there at the corner of the house as she held the shutter for him. An unnecessary task he'd invented for his own pleasure.

"Like this." He bent his head, and one wide palm lifted to cover her hand as it pressed finally against his chest. She was warm to his touch, her slender hand more than capable of bringing him to a state of arousal with barely a whisper of pressure against his clothing. And what he would do next would perhaps thrust him beyond that initial state of yearning.

Her eyes closed as he surrounded her waist with his other arm, tugging her gently against himself. Lest he frighten her with the evidence of his longing, he allowed only their upper bodies to touch, and that just enough to feel the soft curves of her breasts against the back of his hand.

She inhaled, a deep, quivering breath, and he rested his lips against hers, barely brushing the soft surface. They trembled at his touch and he pressed more firmly, wanting the further intimacy of tongue and teeth exposed to his own. But not tonight, he realized. She kissed like the innocent she was, and so he was dutiful in his behavior, only whispering a soft word of pleasure as he lifted his head.

"Nice," he said quietly. "Your mouth is soft and sweet, Miss Gussie."

"Gussie?" she inquired, as if she'd only now realized his use of a derivative of her name. "You said that a few minutes ago, didn't you?"

"Yes," he agreed with a nod. "I think it suits you."

"My brother called me Gussie," she told him. "A long time ago."

"I won't call you that in front of others," he promised. "Only when we're alone."

"I hadn't planned on us being alone, *Jonathan,*" she replied, using his given name for the first time, emphasizing each syllable. Her eyes met his with a direct gaze that demanded a reply.

"Beth Ann told you, didn't she?" His smile was gentle as he thought of the ungainly young woman who had caught his attention and inspired his gentleman's instincts. "She needed to feel special that day, Gussie. I told her she had a lovely name, and…"

"She told us. And you succeeded at your task. You made her feel good, just by paying attention to her."

"You don't mind? Not only that I told her my name, but that I didn't tell you first. I didn't intend it, but she's a needy female, Gussie. I just thought…"

She shook her head, effectively halting his words. "Every woman needs to know that there is something about her that is attractive to a man. Beth Ann has never felt worthy of anyone's attention. I think now she recognizes that she may have something to offer one day. In fact, I think we're attacking that problem in the proper fashion now."

It was not the way he'd wanted these few moments to be spent, speaking of another woman, yet Augusta went on, and he allowed it, easing himself a bit as he held her against his body.

"We're showing her how to fix her hair. Pearl's good at that, and she has her using lemon juice to rinse it with to bring out the gold. Janine is fixing her clothes a bit, making them fit better, and showing Beth Ann how to stand up straight with her shoulders back."

"And what are you doing for her?" he asked, his voice amused as her earnest words told of her plan.

"I'm helping her to read better and teaching her how to write more clearly. She is sadly lacking in schooling, I fear."

"You have a kind heart, Gussie."

"I have a need to help, Jonathan." As if she tasted his name on her tongue, she pronounced the syllables slowly. "Someday I'll tell you about it, when I'm brave enough."

Brave? Did Augusta need to gather her courage to confide her reasons for what she did here, in this place, with these women? "Someday soon, I'll remind you of that promise," he said quietly. And then pushing all else aside, he bent to her again, catching a whiff of sweet scent he could not identify, mixed with the warm aroma of her flesh. "I think I must leave," he told her, pressing his lips against her forehead. "I don't want anyone to see us and think badly of you."

"I missed you." She repeated his words and her smile was tremulous as she tilted her head to look up at him. "I've never been kissed before," she confessed. "In all my days, no man has ever gotten this close to me."

"Not for lack of trying, I'll warrant," he said quietly. "You are an appealing woman, Gussie." His mouth touched hers, a fleeting caress.

"Appealing?"

"I'm not going to make a list of your charms, ma'am. You've already chastened me on that score once." He softened the words with another quick touch of his mouth against hers. "Besides having lovely hair—" His lips brushed like fairy wings against the wispy curl that lay against her temple "—and beautiful eyes—" He kissed the lids, carefully, with butterfly touches. And then his words were wistful, clinging to her ears like honey dripping from the comb. "Augusta, my love, you have a bountiful supply of attributes which could easily bring a man to his knees."

"My hair is down," she blurted out, as if unable to respond to his elaborate descriptions of what she obviously considered rather ordinary features.

"I noticed," he murmured. "I feel privileged to see it revealed. I'd lay odds that no other man has had such a viewing." His hands yearned to tangle in its golden waves and he forbade himself the intimacy. *Next time.*

"You'd win," she admitted with a sigh. "My mother would roll over in her grave if she saw me here with you. She taught me to be a lady."

"She did a good job of it," Cleary said. "You are every inch a gentlewoman."

"Even with my nightclothes on and my hair in disarray?"

He nodded. "Especially in such a state. Your womanhood does not depend on what you're wearing or your hairpins remaining in place. Right now, you're every bit a lady, and I respect you as such."

Even as I yearn to lay you down and make you a woman. The thought raced through his mind and he inhaled deeply, stepping away from her, releasing her from his embrace, lest he frighten her with his barely controlled desire.

She backed a few steps, coming up against the door, and her fingers groped for the handle. Her face was in shadow and he heard her whisper a soft farewell, watched as she slid within the narrow opening she allowed, into the hallway, where she stood like a wraith beyond the screened door.

"Good night," he said, turning to step down from the porch, making his way to where his horse awaited his return, there beneath the widespread limbs of the tree at the front of her yard. He heard the faint click of the latch as she closed the door, and he led his horse from concealment. With a lithe movement, he mounted, groaning at the firmness of the saddle against his throbbing arousal.

With a last glance at the dark house, he lifted the reins and traveled a roundabout route to his home.

To the house that seemed less a home than the one he left behind.

"Thought I saw somebody out in the front yard last night," Pearl said from behind her as Augusta stood at the back door. Morning had been a relief, her sleep broken by dreams of Cleary. The sun was just above the chicken coop now, almost time for breakfast. She'd thought herself alone in the kitchen, until Pearl's words made her aware that her midnight foray to the porch had not gone unnoticed.

"Did you?" Her voice was quiet, the words deliberate as she turned her head to face the other woman's gaze. "It was Cleary, as you well know."

"Is he leadin' you down the primrose path?" Pearl asked, and Augusta sensed real concern behind the casual query. A crease drew her brows together as Pearl spoke her mind.

"He's not what he seems, Miss Augusta. I've been around the track a few times, and I've known men like him. I think he's a good man, deep down where it counts, but I don't think he's being honest with you. With anybody, for that matter."

Augusta digested the woman's words, reluctantly agreeing with her theory, and then shrugged. "Maybe not. But I know he's done a lot to help us here. And until I find out otherwise, I have to trust him not to do harm."

"Don't go losing your heart to a man who can't make you any promises," Pearl advised. "I'll lay odds he has other fish to fry, and we're just helpin' him mark time while he does whatever it is he does."

"And what do you suppose that is?"

Pearl grinned. "We're both probably better off not knowing. The only difference is that you're the one likely to get hurt before this is over. Now if you were like me," she paused and laughed aloud. "I'm tough as old boots, and I lost my heart in the shuffle a long time ago."

"To a man?" Augusta asked with a smile. For the first time she began to see through Pearl's tough exterior, into the woman's heart she'd just claimed to have forfeited along the way.

"There's always a man," Pearl said with a laugh. "The thing is, you gotta learn how to keep yourself clear of the loving part." Her head cocked to one side as she examined

Augusta's face, and her smile faded. "Damn if I don't believe you've already got in over your head, Miss Augusta." She shook her head and her eyes mourned Augusta's loss of innocence. "Damn."

"I'm not in over my head," Augusta denied quietly. "He's a gentleman in every way. And he didn't molest me last night."

"I didn't think he had," Pearl said agreeably. "But he'll either marry you quick as he can, or take you to bed and tie you to him in ways you've never imagined. And then you'll be…" Her eyes narrowed as she watched Augusta. "He'll answer to me, does he hurt you. And you can bet your bottom dollar I'll tell him so."

"No." The single word resounded like a rifle shot in the room. "No. I won't have anyone interfering in this. I've already been warned, but for the first time in my life, I've found a man I'm willing to trust with everything I have to give, and I won't let anyone else be involved. I need to do this on my own."

"Well, you'd better know I'll be watching him," Pearl said grudgingly. "And so will a couple other people I know."

"It's time for breakfast," Augusta said with a glance at the kitchen door. If she knew anything at all, it was that Bertha would be strolling through that doorway in minutes, and the conversation of the hour didn't need to include another living soul.

"I'll get out the milk," Pearl told her, turning to the icebox, bending to retrieve the bottle from its depths. "Here," she said. "You start the biscuits and I'll get stuff from the pantry."

Within minutes the fire was crackling with the addition of kindling and a few stout pieces of wood. The bacon was sliced and in the pan, and Augusta was demoted to finding a biscuit pan while Bertha made it her business to cut out the pale rounds of dough and place them on the greased surface.

"I heard y'all out here talkin'," she grumbled. "Seems like we could've had another half hour to sleep. Sun's barely up."

"It's just as well we get organized early," Pearl said cheerfully, shooting a wry grin in Augusta's direction. "I have a notion we're gonna have company for breakfast."

In fact, it was barely ten minutes later when a faint rapping at the back door caught Augusta's ear. Jonathan Cleary stood to one side of the door, seeking her gaze through the fine wire mesh as she reached to unlatch the screened door.

"Thought I'd stop by and see if there was a chance of cadging breakfast," he said cheerfully.

"Do you suppose you can find something to do to earn it out?" Augusta asked him, as if she were not fully aware that his mind was no doubt already swarming with tasks to be accomplished.

"I'll manage," he said, his words droll. Walking to the sink, he washed his hands and then turned, seeking a towel.

"Towels are in the pantry," Pearl said shortly. "And there's need of a few more shelves in there, if you're of a mind to nail up a couple of boards."

"I could manage that," he said, his glance mocking as he met the woman's gaze. "Anything else you think I need to tend to?"

Pearl's eyes took on a gleam that warned Augusta she'd best be stepping between the two adversaries. "I've got a short list of things," she said quickly. "We can talk after breakfast."

The short list involved using a lawn mower, a new one Augusta had ordered from the Sears, Roebuck catalogue. "Am I the first one to use it?" Cleary asked. "It'll be a far sight easier to push than the one I used back home as a boy. I well remember having to rake up the clippings to feed the goats.''

"Why didn't your father just stake the goats in the yard and let them do the work?" Augusta asked with a grin. Looking at Cleary beneath the hot sun, his forehead wearing a handkerchief to halt the pouring of sweat into his eyes, was a treat.

Now he halted, midway in his rounding of the yard and eyed her boldly. "You think you're smart, don't you, lady? All cool and crisp while I'm sweating like a horse, doing your chores. And for your information, when I was growing up, the other ladies in town would have thought we were peasants had we tied the goats in the yard."

"Where was home?" Augusta asked quietly, her gaze resting on his strong body, outlined by the dampness of his clothing. Another time, with another man, she might have considered her thoughts forward, would have looked anywhere else but at the flex of muscles in his arms as he reached for the glass of lemonade she held. But not with Cleary.

After last night on the porch, she'd become aware of him in a new way. She knew that he wanted her, as a man wants a woman, and that knowledge made her brave, bold in her scrutiny.

He took the glass, and she reveled in the touch of callused fingertips against her finer skin. Tilting his head back, he drank, his swallows readily draining the glass. And then he held it out to her. "We lived not too far from here, as a matter of fact."

Perhaps she hadn't expected his honest reply, and yet, somehow she'd known that when he could, Jonathan Cleary would be honest with her. "Do you see your folks?" she asked, looking up at him.

He shook his head, and his words held a ring of harshness she had not expected. "They're gone." And that seemed to be all he would say on the subject as he glanced up at the sky. "Might as well get this job done. I think we're in for a good rain before nightfall." His grin was quick, as though his moment of brusque behavior was forgotten. "And that will only make it grow quicker."

Augusta looked upward, where clouds gathered at the western horizon. "Well, you'll have to come back for breakfast next week then, won't you?" she heard herself saying.

His laugh rolled forth and she looked at him warily. "Go get me some more lemonade, sweetheart, or a glass of water from the well. Any sort of liquid will do. I'm still dry."

She turned to walk away, and his words were a whisper in her ear. "I'll be back for breakfast, all right. You won't be getting rid of me, honey."

Sweetheart. Honey. The simple endearments clutched at her heart as she hurried to the house, hearing the mower's blade spin behind her. He'd called her names she'd only heard before from her father when he spoke to the woman he adored, in those times when her parents thought their children were abed and out of hearing. Words she'd cherished, knowing how deeply her mother loved him, and how devoted her father was to the woman he'd married.

A woman whose passions she seemed to have inherited.

In the house, a letter awaited her on the kitchen buffet, and a stranger sat, stiffly upright in a chair at the table, a cup of tea before her. "This is Glory," Pearl said, nodding at the woman who looked as though she were in need of a hiding place. "Came in on the morning train from Dallas."

"Hello again, Glory," Augusta said quietly. The new resident had looked healthier the first time Augusta had laid eyes on her, a couple of weeks ago. Now she bore fresh bruises and a bandage on her forehead.

"Ma'am." Glory's gaze was fleeting, touching Augusta's face, then over her shoulder. "Am I still welcome here?" she asked quietly.

"You can share a room with Beth Ann," Augusta told her, casting a silent request in Pearl's direction.

"I'll take care of getting you settled, Glory," Pearl said. "Miss Augusta's kinda tied up right now, giving orders in the backyard. And I'm thinking you could use a nice long nap, anyway."

She picked up the letter from the buffet, and handed it to Augusta. Addressed in a scrawling hand, it was simply sent to Miss Augusta McBride, in care of the postmaster in Collins Creek, Texas. "Bertha brought this from town," Pearl volunteered. "I was just about to bring it out to you, when I saw you heading for the house. And then I thought maybe you'd like to say hello to Glory here."

"You were right. And we'll talk more at dinner, when Glory's had a chance to recuperate from her travels."

She glanced down at her letter. "I wonder..." Augusta turned the missive over, as if the sender might be revealed by looking at the back of the soiled envelope. "It looks as though it's gone through a great number of hands to arrive here, doesn't it? And some of them none too clean, I'd say."

"You'll probably find out more if you just open it, ma'am," Pearl said dryly.

And if her barely concealed curiosity was anything to go by, the woman would no doubt be peering over her shoulder, Augusta thought. Her index finger slid beneath the flap, and she carefully tore at the sealed edge. The paper was wrinkled, the ink smeared, and she opened it with care. Only a few lines met her eye, but they were filled with portent.

"My brother..." she began, seeking Pearl's concerned face.

"Where's my water?" came a call from the back stoop, and an audible gasp sounded from Glory's lips.

"Fill this for Cleary," Augusta said, lifting the empty glass from the table and handing it to Pearl. To her credit, the woman took it and did as she was asked, opening the back door to give the waiting man his drink. He downed it and Augusta watched from the middle of the kitchen, her mind filled with the message she'd just read.

"Thanks," Cleary said. "Where'd Augusta go?"

"Inside," Pearl said briefly, accepting the empty glass and backing from the door.

"Tell her I want to talk to her," Cleary said, peering now past the screen door.

"She's busy." Pearl's voice left no room for discussion, but Cleary would not be foiled in his purpose.

"Augusta!" His calling of her name was loud and clear and she cast a glance at Pearl as she stepped to the door. He smiled at her. "I need you out here to tell me which green things along the edges are flowers and which are weeds."

"Yes, all right," she told him, folding the letter and tucking it into her pocket.

She faced him on the stoop and his eyes narrowed. "What's wrong? What happened to make you look like you've just lost your last friend?"

"I may have," she told him quietly. She felt her eyes fill with tears, and through the mist was aware of his hands lifting to cradle her cheeks.

"Tell me, Gussie," he said quietly. "What's happened?"

His callused palms lent comfort and she stifled a sob, lest she lean her head on his shoulder and cry aloud for the loss she felt. Reaching into her pocket, she drew forth the envelope and unfolded the single piece of paper it contained. "Shall I read it to you?"

He shook his head. "No, I will," he said, taking it from her hand, his fingers long and tanned against the white paper. "'Dear Sis,'" he read aloud, and she winced as she braced herself for the next words. "'I've escaped from prison in Colorado. I won't bring shame on you, but I have to see you one last time. I'm on my way to Texas, but it may take a while, as I'm on the run.'"

A muttered oath escaped Cleary's lips and his voice was brittle as he read the closing line. "'I love you, Sis. Wilson.'"

"Did you know he was in prison?" he asked.

She shook her head. "He was working on a ranch in Wyoming last I heard. But that was months ago. I assumed—"

"Never assume. It'll cause trouble every time." His voice was harsh, its timbre unfeeling as he set his jaw in an uncompromising fashion. "How old is he?"

"Twenty-one."

"When did you see him last?" His hands crumpled the letter and she reached to take it from him, lest it be destroyed.

He looked down, as if unaware of his hands folding into solid fists, and muttered another phrase. Twice now, she'd heard him curse, and her hands rescued the missive quickly, smoothing the paper and folding it carefully.

"It's been well over a year," she said. "Since he left home to go west. He said he'd send for me when he found a place and bought a piece of property. I got one letter that told me he was working as a cowhand, and he stood to come into a decent amount of cash."

Cleary's head lifted, his gaze shooting to meet hers as she spoke. *"A decent amount of cash?"* he asked. "From where?"

"He didn't say. Maybe he'd had his boss hold his wages until they mounted up to an appreciable amount," Augusta offered, even as she eschewed the idea. It simply didn't sound like Wilson to do such a thing.

"Didn't he have a *decent amount of cash* when he left home?" Cleary asked quietly. "What do you suppose he did with it?"

Augusta was at a loss for words. She'd wondered the same thing herself, and deep inside knew that Wilson had probably gambled away his share of their parents' legacy. He was not a strong man, and her mother had spoiled him. And yet, Augusta had let him go with her blessing, hoping that somehow he would grow up, that his travels would teach him the values he'd ignored during his youth.

"He's in trouble with the law, Gussie," Cleary said bluntly. "You can't afford to harbor him if he shows up here."

"You think I should turn him away?" The idea was reprehensible, and she shuddered as she considered closing her door against her only living relative.

"I think he'll take advantage of you."

"Maybe. Maybe not. But if he shows up here, I'll open the door to him, Cleary. He's my blood kin. And if I can take in a whole houseful of women and give them refuge, I can't deny my own brother. He can sleep in the attic, or in the yard if need be."

He turned his back and she recognized the anger he would not reveal to her face. His broad shoulders stiffened and his dark hair was ringed with a line of perspiration as it lay against his neck. The back of his shirt bore a wide, damp patch down its center and she thought suddenly that his labors had been on her behalf, and all she'd done was argue with him.

"Don't be angry with me," she said quietly, reaching a hand to touch his back. He jerked and she wrapped her fingers inside her palm, allowing it to drop to her side. "I'm sorry. I shouldn't have touched you."

He turned and his eyes burned with a dark fire she'd seen before. "You can touch me any damn time you want to, lady. Just know that when you do, it sets off a jolt of lightning inside me and I'm hard-pressed to keep my own hands where they belong."

"Lightning?" Was that akin perhaps to the tingling sensation his fingers imposed on her when he gathered her close? When his lips touched hers and a flame arced from that spot to the depths of her body.

"Yeah. That's what I said. I missed you for four days, Miss Augusta. I dreamed of you every time I crawled into bed. Spent some damn restless nights, in fact. And you're such an innocent you don't know what I'm talking about, do you? I couldn't even tend to business the way I was supposed to, what with thinking about the kiss I almost snatched before I left."

It was just as well she not dwell on his revelations, she decided, and focused instead on the last admission he'd spoken aloud. *"Business."* Something about tending to business. He'd made the opening and she forged ahead as Roger's visit came to mind. "What business called you away?" she asked.

He frowned and his words were slow, as if he chose them carefully. "I got a telegram notifying me that my presence was required in several places over the past four days," he explained. "Three towns, including Dallas, where problems have occurred lately. I'm working on—" He halted, glaring his frustration.

"What sort of problems?" she asked, plunging beyond his explanation, determined to pin him down.

"Having to do with the banks I represent," he told her, softening his tone. "Including the one here in town." And then his brow lifted and he slid his hands into his back trouser pockets. "Why the sudden interest in my travels, Gussie?"

She shrugged, looking past him to where the grass grew thick beneath the blue sky. He'd begun on the edges and mowed in a huge square, and now only a patch the size of the parlor remained, tall and unkempt. "I just wondered," she said. "And it's not really sudden, as you well know. I'm aware that the topic of your occupation is off-limits in our conversations." Her gaze returned to his chest, then moved upward until his dark eyes narrowed again as she spoke a challenge. "I have to wonder at your reticence on the subject."

"There are some things I can't discuss with you right now," he said. "I thought I'd made that clear, and now you're intent on digging for information. And my good sense tells me there has to be a reason." He was even more persistent than she, and like a dog with a bone, he pushed for her reasons.

"Who set you to thinking and wondering?" And then his eyes sparked and glittered and she caught a glimpse of fury she could only hope was not to be directed at her. "Did the sheriff come out here and ask about me?"

"The sheriff?" She was astounded that he would fear the sheriff's interest, and yet knew in her depths it was not fear that fed his anger. "No, I haven't seen the sheriff. Although I heard that he was making inquiries about you and your secretive travels."

"Did you, now?" His hand cupped her chin in a quick movement and he held her firmly in place, tilting her head back, the better to look into her eyes. "And who brought you that information?"

"Roger Hampton."

"Roger Hampton," he repeated slowly. "Your erstwhile beau from Dallas. The one who wanted to marry you." His fingers tightened their grip and she winced, fearful he would leave a bruise. "Did he tell you I'm a criminal of some kind?"

She felt the loosening of his hold, as if he'd only now become aware of the strength that long-fingered hand possessed. "No," she denied hastily. "Nothing of the sort." And felt a flush suffuse her cheeks as she spoke the lie.

His smile was chilled by the dark glitter of his eyes, yet his words touched her ears as softly as a sigh. "You're too honest for your own good, Augusta McBride. You don't lie well. This is the second time."

"The second time?" She searched her mind for the first, not willing to compound her sin by adding another untruth upon the last one.

"The first was on the porch, just last night, when you said you didn't know how to prove you'd missed me."

"I wasn't sure," she said, dithering as she recalled that moment when she'd been so close to reaching for a man for the first time in her life.

"Maybe not, but you're lying now."

"He said—" She halted abruptly, not willing to repeat the accusations Roger had spewed forth. "He mentioned train robberies in the area surrounding Dallas."

His mouth twitched, and then he laughed aloud. "He thinks I'm a train robber? And you believed him?"

"No," she said, denying the words he spoke. "I didn't. I knew better than that."

"And what do you think now?" he asked, his laughter ceasing as he released her chin to wrap her waist in his hands.

"I don't know what to think about you, Jonathan Cleary." The words burst forth, accompanied by a sob of frustration, and her hands rose to clench into tight fists against his chest. "You have me totally confused."

"Well, that probably makes two of us then," he admitted, his fingers flexing on her slender waistline. He released her suddenly, then nodded at the patches along the border of the property, where taller grass grew.

"I need you to tell me how far to mow. If there are flowers there, I don't want to cut them down. Go take a look, and I'll make my way in that direction as soon as I finish the middle of the yard. It won't take five minutes. You'll be able to sort it out by then."

"All right," she agreed, backing up from the overgrown area he'd left until last.

It was shady beneath the overhanging branches of the maple trees that edged her property, and she walked along the borders he'd pointed out. Several of the leaves were familiar to her, including a patch of hollyhocks that appeared to be volunteers from last year.

"I'll weed this area," she told him minutes later as he pushed the mower toward her. "If you run that mower through here you'll make a mess."

"All right," he said agreeably, leaning against the closest tree. "I'm willing to watch you work for a while, just as soon as I put this contraption in the shed." He was gone only minutes, then found shade beneath the tree once more, sliding down to rest his back on the rough bark, and she saw his eyelids flutter a bit.

"You're tired, aren't you?"

"A little. I rode a lot of miles over the past few days, and I haven't caught up on my sleep."

"I'll go fill up your glass," she offered. "Why don't you just lean your head back and rest?"

The pump in the kitchen sink produced clear, cold water from the place deep in the ground where the well had been drilled, and Augusta substituted a quart canning jar for Cleary's glass, carrying it back to where he waited. It was cooler beneath the maple trees and she blessed the breeze that wafted through the branches.

He'd slid to the ground, and his hat covered his forehead. One knee was bent, the other leg stretched out, and his chest rose and fell with a regular rhythm as she watched. Propping the jar of water close at hand, she bent to the weeds that cluttered the bed of flowers next to the hedges.

And watched him as he slept.

Chapter Five

Although his eyelids never fluttered, Cleary was well aware of the woman who kept guard over his supposed slumber. She'd pressed him beyond expectations, goaded by her erstwhile suitor from Dallas. And that man bore looking into, he decided, examining his memory for a trace of the meddlesome gentleman. *Roger Hampton* was not a common name, but he could not recall it. However, his momentary glimpse, that first day, brought to mind a fleeting memory of the face of the man in question.

The story of Augusta's brother was another thing altogether. Cleary's recent activities included his infiltration of a gang of rustlers in Wyoming. A risky business, one in which he'd almost lost his life, he recalled. There at the last, when things had come together with a bang, he'd come close to hanging up his gun.

But justice in Wyoming had prevailed, and the rustlers were now sitting in cells in that state's prison. All but one of the men, Gus, who ended up being shipped off to Colorado to prison. The judge had listened to testimony, and had given him a more lenient sentence than the rest of the gang, due to his help on Cleary's behalf when the chips were down.

Reading the letter from Augusta's brother had brought back that particular memory, and his shoulder twitched as he recalled his days of recovery from his injury. He'd watched as the men were hauled off to Laramie; the man named Gus, whose change of heart had given him a better chance for early release, was sent south.

To Colorado to serve his sentence. Cleary flinched inwardly. The chances of such a coincidence being possible were slight, yet his instincts were on alert.

Being a U.S. Marshal was an occupation that made a man old before his time. And Cleary was feeling the effects of his job choice. He'd worked with the Wyoming Cattlemen's Association on his last assignment. Here in Collins Creek, he was operating directly with the local banker, plus a couple of others in nearby cities, under the guise of being a gentleman on hiatus from his usual employment.

Hampton had come too close for comfort with his veiled accusation of Cleary being a bank robber. Seeking out the leader of the group involved working undercover, and Cleary was gaining ground with his infiltration into the network of men who worked outside the walls of respectability.

And Augusta, bless her heart, had made him cringe with her pointed queries. He'd hoped to keep her at a distance until this whole mess came to a head. But his own needs managed to get in the way, and he'd been mixing business and pleasure. A volatile mixture, indeed, he'd discovered. Especially when a woman such as Augusta McBride was involved.

He watched her from beneath lowered lashes, his gaze warm on the line of her back as she bent to her task. She sat upright, casting aside a handful of weeds, and inhaled deeply, looking upward with one hand shading her eyes. Probably wishing for the rain clouds to move more rapidly in this direction, he thought. Though her grass was green and the kitchen garden flourished, Augusta's avowed theory was that if a little was good, a lot was better when it came to watering her growing vegetables.

Her breasts rose with each breath she took, and he watched, feeling not a twinge of guilt, only the pleasure a man took in observing the woman he'd chosen as his mate.

And wouldn't she be surprised, when all was said and done, and he'd accomplished his purpose, freeing himself for the enjoyable pursuit of his lady love.

Wouldn't her blue eyes widen with astonishment when he finally was able to offer her his name in marriage, and take her out of the environment she'd managed to get herself involved in.

And then he pondered that very idea more closely. Getting Augusta out of this house and into his own might be more involved than he'd first supposed. She was closely entangled in the lives of these women. The little innocent, golden-haired woman he'd decided to claim as his bride might be more deeply mired here than he'd first thought.

He watched as she lifted her forearm to wipe a line of perspiration from her brow, suppressing a smile as he took note of the large garden gloves she'd donned before she began digging in the dirt. They engulfed her hands, making her task awkward, but she persevered. As she did in her every endeavor.

Her gaze lowered and drifted to where he lay, and he caught a glimpse of a smile curving her mouth, saw her tongue touch her upper lip. Watching her, he felt himself a bit of a voyeur as her eyes swept his lengthy form. Her nostrils flared and her bosom lifted as she caught a deep breath, and her mouth was soft and damp.

It would never do for Augusta to observe his growing arousal, he decided, impatient with his lusty response to her innocent surveillance of him. He mumbled a bit, rolling to his side, and with a great show of awakening, opened his eyes.

Her head was bowed over the pile of weeds she'd accumulated, and with a smile, she noted his heavy-lidded attention on her person. With a quick movement she rose, stepped to where he lay and uncapped the canning jar of water she'd carried from the house for his benefit.

He drank deeply from it, then offered it to her in silence, watching as a rosy hue developed on her cheeks at the gesture. Her fingers curled around the jar and she lifted it to her lips. He watched, veiling his hunger, as she tilted her head back and drank thirstily. A trickle of water touched the corner of her mouth and a drop fell on her dress, forming a circle and staining the fabric over her right breast.

His gaze touched the spot as he reached for the jar, taking it from her and returning it to his own lips, pleased when she gave the gesture her full attention.

"I couldn't have slept long," he said, wiping his mouth with the back of his hand, a gesture he hoped was nonchalant. "The water's still cool."

"Only fifteen minutes or so," she said agreeably. "Long enough for me to clean up that whole area." She pointed to the flower bed she'd rescued from the encroaching weeds, turning her face away from his regard.

"You do good work, Miss Gussie," he said lightly. "Now, as a reward for your diligence, how would you like to get rid of those gloves and join me for supper at the hotel restaurant?"

She glanced down at her oversize gloves with a grin, then nodded slowly as her brow furrowed a bit. He could almost see the wheels of her mind moving as she considered the ramifications of such a thing. "Yes, I'd like that," she said finally. "But first I'll need some time to get acquainted with our new guest."

"You have a new woman in the house?"

"She arrived the same time as my letter and, I fear, she got lost in the shuffle. I met her in Dallas. Her name is Glory, and from the looks of her, she's had a tough row to hoe in order to get here."

"By all means, take time for that," he said quickly. "I won't interfere in your work, Gussie."

"And then I'll have to speak to the ladies about my letter before I can leave the house, don't you think?"

"Wouldn't be a bad idea. You don't want your brother knocking on the door some day when you're not here, and them not know about him coming."

Augusta looked at him as he rose from his resting place beneath the tree. She thought his voice was neutral, neither approving nor disapproving, yet she sensed that they were miles apart on this thing. "I can't contact him, Cleary," she said sharply.

"No, you sure can't," he agreed. "But you need to be thinking about what you'll do when he shows up. And your ladies need to know what they're letting themselves in for if they allow him to hide out here."

"Hide out?" She was defensive now, and her hands clenched as she recognized that her anger was unfounded. Cleary was right, but still she owed Wilson her loyalty. "I'll give him shelter until he can decide what to do next. I won't be providing a criminal hideout."

"Well, let's not argue the point, honey," he said mildly. "I doubt we're going to come out on the same side of the fence on this one."

"I need to go inside." She turned away, frustrated at the quarrel they'd become involved in. "Are you sure you want to take me out for supper?"

"One thing has nothing to do with the other, Gussie," he said quietly. "Yes, I want to take you to the hotel and sit in the dining room there with you. I think you need to be certain you want to be seen with me, since your friend

Mr. Hampton has been dragging my name through the dirt.''

She turned around and shot him a look, and he held up his hands in abject surrender, his smile beneath the lush mustache he wore teasing her out of her mood.

''I'll be ready at six, Mr. Cleary,'' she said primly, lifting her skirt to climb the step to the stoop.

He bowed in a gentlemanly manner. ''I've taken care of the lawn mower, and you've done some weeding. Tomorrow, I'll rake the grass. In the meantime maybe on our way home from the hotel this evening we can search out a goat to eat our greenery.''

''Ma'am, I'm ever so grateful.'' Glory's eyes were swollen from the tears she'd shed, yet a look of relief shone from those same drenched orbs as she reached out a hand to touch Augusta's. ''I thought I was a goner for sure when Miss Josephine sent out her big bruiser after me. I didn't know I could run so fast. And once I got in the train station, I think he feared to snatch me up in front of the rest of the passengers.''

''I told a nice gentleman that I was on my way to Collins Creek, and he escorted me on board the train.'' Her face turned crimson as she recalled the event. ''Turned out he was a man of the cloth, and he wouldn't even let me pay my fare. Found me a seat and when the train got here, he made sure I got off.''

''You were indeed fortunate,'' Augusta said quietly. ''Had the *bruiser,* as you called him, gotten his hands on you, you might not have survived. It's been my experience that most madams do not allow their girls to escape, for fear they set a bad example for the rest of the women in the house.''

''How much experience have you had at this sort of thing?'' Janine asked, leaning forward as if she would hear a juicy tidbit from Augusta's mouth. "I mean, have you been in a lot of whorehouses?"

"Houses of ill repute, I prefer to call them, Janine." Augusta sent a glance of warning at the woman whose needle seemed to fly through the dress she worked on. "I don't consider you ladies as *whores,* only women who've been caught up in situations you could not escape by yourselves."

Janine shrugged. "Whatever you say, ma'am. I only know I'd rather be here than at Lula Belle's place." She bit off the thread next to the knot she'd fashioned in the seam of her latest project. "By the way, I may have a chance to work for Miss Clarinda, that dressmaker over by the bank. She told me to bring some of my work over, and she'd take a look at it."

"I'll bet she'll put you in the back room," Pearl said glumly. "Women like us don't sit up front where the decent folks can see us."

"Her other seamstress sits in the back room," Janine said sharply, "and she's a farm girl from west of here. I don't mind settin' there with her, not one little bit. At least I'll be makin' money and helpin' out with things here."

"Yes, and once you get established, you may be able to afford a place of your own," Augusta said quietly. "That's our goal for each of you."

"I'll do whatever you say, ma'am," Glory said, digging in her pocket for a well-used handkerchief. "I'm just glad to be here."

"We'll talk about your duties in the morning," Augusta told her. "In the meantime, you'd better let Bertha take a look at your bruises. I'm assuming there are more beneath your dress."

Again Glory's face turned a bright pink. "Yes. I fell down the stairs, trying to get out of Miss Josephine's place. And then got my arm pretty near yanked off when I was almost at the train station. That horrible fella caught hold of me and tore my sleeve, but I couldn't let him catch me.''

''Well, you're safe and sound with us. Beth Ann has made room for your things in her dresser.''

Shamefaced, Glory shook her head. ''I haven't got any things to speak of. Just a sack I scooped up some stuff in. Maybe somebody can loan me a dress so I can wash mine out.''

Augusta's heart wrenched as she thought of living in such a state of uncertainty. ''We'll find you clothes, Glory. Janine will sort through the things from the missionary barrel the church ladies dropped off.

''Now I have something else to speak to you about,'' she said, her gaze touching each of the women who sat around the kitchen table.

The restaurant held a decent crowd, considering that this was a weeknight. Yet, there was a table reserved by a window, and a young, fresh-faced waitress led Cleary and Augusta to be seated there. He held her chair, then moved to sit across from her.

''I'll have coffee,'' he told the waiting girl, and then looked inquiringly at Augusta.

''Tea, please,'' she said, smiling at the young woman, her gaze remaining on the crisp white apron over a starched black dress as the waitress walked away.

Cleary held a single piece of paper and offered it for Augusta's inspection. ''They've just come up with a menu here,'' he told her. ''They used to have a chalkboard inside the door. But someone decided they needed a touch of class, and they had Walter Dunnigan over at the newspaper office print these up for them.''

''I see the special for Thursday is roast beef,'' Augusta said. ''That sounds good to me.'' She handed the menu back to Cleary, and he felt her attention on him as he read quickly through the list of offerings.

"That makes two of us then," he said, placing the menu on the table. He glanced up and took his napkin from the table as their waitress returned. "Here comes our coffee and tea," he told Augusta. "If you like, I'll order for both of us."

She nodded, and he placed their order quickly. "I haven't been here before," she admitted in a low voice. "In fact, I haven't been in a restaurant since my parents died."

"Lost your appetite?" he asked. "Or were you too busy to take the time?"

"A little of each, I suppose," she said, looking out the window to where a few stragglers occupied the sidewalk. "Everyone seems to have gone home. Town's almost empty," she said. "It makes me sad to see the lights go out in the establishments up and down Main street, and then only those with nowhere to go are left to wander."

"You have a tender heart, Gussie," he told her quietly, bending to speak across the table. "I'd take your hand in mine if I could without compromising you in public. You make me want to do more than that, to tell the truth. Maybe when we get you home, we can talk about it."

She looked up at him, her blue eyes curious. Her mouth, pink and luscious, opened a bit and she touched her upper lip with the tip of her tongue. "I'm not sure what you're saying," she said in a whisper.

Her cheeks took on a rosy hue and Cleary made fists of his eager hands, ruing his rampant enthusiasm for the woman. He hadn't meant to say such a thing to her. A man his age should certainly have more control than he was possessed of these days.

"Forget I said anything," he told her. "Let's talk about

your news. You said you'd learned something exciting from one of your ladies.''

She brightened immediately and in moments had given him chapter and verse of Janine's opportunity. "This is our first success story," she said, beaming at him. "And Beth Ann has written her parents, asking to be allowed to come home. I sent along a note with her letter, assuring them of her good intentions.''

"Will she fit in back home?''

"I hope so.'' Her words were fervent. "Now to find some nice man for Honey.''

Cleary inhaled a drop of coffee as Augusta sweetly announced her next goal. He choked for a moment; then, wiping his mouth with the linen napkin, he shook his head. "Are you saying you believe some young fella from around here will take Honey—baby and all?''

"I think she's a deserving young woman," Augusta said.

"That may be. But most men want to raise their own children, not a nameless…''

He halted, unwilling to speak aloud the word most children in those circumstances were known by.

"The right man would do it," Augusta said firmly. "I just need to locate him.''

Their meals were delivered then and Cleary thought it was just in time, since words could not describe his feeling about that particular sentiment.

They ate slowly, quietly, enjoying what passed for elegance in the hotel dining room. And then, as Cleary paid the bill, Augusta looked around the room, aware of more than one pair of eyes on her and the man who'd invited her here. Two of the ladies who'd been instrumental in establishing the shelter sat with their husbands and smiled timidly at her.

That some of the men in town saw Augusta's place as just another house of ill repute, no matter that male visitors were not welcomed through the doors, was a fact she'd tried to overlook. Now, as Cleary took her arm and led her from the room, she wondered what she had done, placing him in the position of escorting a woman whose reputation might not be white as the driven snow.

It was a position he didn't seem to mind, his hand warm in the center of her back as he ushered her through the door onto the sidewalk. She relished the warmth, regretting its loss as he offered her his arm. The cool of the evening surrounded them as she tucked her hand into the crook of his elbow, and they walked at a steady pace toward her home.

"I don't want you to suffer any loss of respect because of your association with me," she said as they left the sidewalk to stroll past picket fences and flower gardens.

"Do I look like I'm suffering?" he asked, his brow lifted, his grin insouciant.

"No," she admitted. "But I'm sure you know what I mean."

"Yes, I do," he told her. "In fact, I've been thinking about that very thing lately."

She looked perplexed. "What very thing?"

"There is one solution to the problem we face that you may not have considered."

"I didn't know we were facing a problem," she said, slowing her steps. The sun was settling behind a cloud bank, and brilliant hues of pink and blue painted the sky above the thunderheads that held the promised rain.

"Just look at the sky," she told him, coming to a halt. "I've never seen such colors right ahead of a rainstorm."

"Let's move along, Gussie," he said, urging her to pick up her pace. "I don't want to be caught under a tree if it starts to rain before we get to your house."

"Pooh," she said, admonishing him. "We have hours before the clouds arrive overhead."

"I'd still rather be on your porch," he told her. "I've taken a fancy to your swing."

Several of Harriet Burns's boarders were on the front steps as they passed by, and two of them lifted hands in greeting. Augusta nodded a response, and Cleary lifted his own hand in a salute before opening the new latch on the front gate. He allowed Augusta to precede him, and, latching the gate behind himself carefully, he followed her.

"Where's your horse?" she asked as they gained the shelter of the porch.

"I walked over this afternoon. Decided I needed the exercise, and I thought you'd enjoy a stroll."

"Oh, I did," she said quickly. And then she looked at the swing that hung invitingly at the far end of the porch. "Will you have time to sit a while before the rain begins? I hate to think of you walking all the way home in a downpour."

"I'll sit." He steered her to the swing, waited as she settled herself at one end, then joined her, placing himself almost in the middle. "Scoot over here a little, Gussie," he told her. "I want you right beside me. The swing works better that way."

His foot touched the floor and the wooden swing moved at his bidding.

"Now, about the solution to our problem," he said. And at her puzzled look, he lifted a brow. "I mentioned it on the way home, and you said you didn't know we were facing a problem."

"Are we?" Her skirt was tucked nicely next to his trousers and her toes barely brushed the porch as the swing obeyed his command.

"I'd say so, ma'am," he said. "You're worried about my reputation, as I recall."

She ducked her head. "Well, yes. I'm feeling vibrations from some of the husbands, and though their wives are still contributing to the effort here with a bit of cash and boxes of foodstuffs, they're starting to make themselves scarce.''

Her hands twisted in her lap, and he was reminded of the first time they'd met, when those fingers had done that very thing. Augusta was upset over the withdrawal of moral support the ladies in town had offered at first through their physical presence.

"I understand how their husbands may feel, Gussie," Cleary said softly. "Did you ever consider that some of those men may have been customers at the Pink Palace? They may not want their wives to hear such rumors from your ladies, should any gossip take place here."

"Do you think so?" Her face paled, then flushed at the thought, as though such a thing being possible was beyond her limited experience. "The men who go to church every Sunday? You really think some of them visit the..." She apparently could not mention the Pink Palace in the same breath with such dignified gentlemen.

Cleary smiled, nodding his reply. "It's a worldwide condition, sweetheart. Men are what keep women like Lula Belle in business."

"Do you go there?" she asked, and then her hand flew to cover her mouth. "I already spoke of that, didn't I?"

"You asked me if any of your ladies would recognize me, honey, and I told you they wouldn't." For which he was exceedingly thankful. "And no, I don't go there."

"Do you have a lady friend?" Her hand dropped from her lips and made a fist in her lap.

"A *lady* friend?" He felt a grin stretch his mouth and lifted his hand in a casual gesture to brush his index finger beneath his mustache. "Only you, Gussie."

Her blush deepened. "I'm just a friend, Cleary. Not a *lady* friend."

Tilting his head to one side, he surveyed her with a long,

calculating, heavy-lidded look. "I'd say you look like a lady to me."

"I *am* a lady." Exasperation emphasized every syllable, and she rolled her eyes at his obtuse observation.

"Well then," he said patiently, "what's the problem? You asked if I have a lady friend, and I said I have, and then identified her as Miss Augusta McBride. Who, by the way, is the most ladylike lady I know."

"You're teasing me," she accused him, jaw upthrust, eyes narrowed, and her mouth pinched as tight as an old maid's.

His thought halted abruptly at that. She might be considered an old maid by virtue of her age and unmarried condition, but Gussie was far from being on the shelf.

He reached for her, ignoring her defensive position, her hands swatting at him, her mumbled imprecations about good taste and broad daylight. "It's almost dark, sweetheart," he murmured, grasping her shoulders and drawing her stiff, arching body toward him. "And even if it *were* broad daylight, I'd still be kissing you."

Her hands dropped, her eyes opened, crossing a bit as she peered closely into his. Their faces only inches apart, he could smell the scent of tea, and the sweet aroma of the lilac soap she used. And then he leaned forward, his mouth taking aim with precision, hers opening to protest.

It was a handy thing she'd done, he thought as his mouth touched the soft inner surface of her lips. He was right where he wanted to be, where his tongue could taste the alluring flavor of Augusta McBride's mouth. He slid it inside her upper lips and she squirmed. From there it moved to skim the surface of her teeth and she inhaled sharply.

"Wha—?"

Ah! He slid home, between pure white enamel into a hot cave, where her pliant tongue resisted his efforts to tangle with its length. She whimpered, her hands lifting to grip his shoulders as his own found the curves of waist and hip, moving the length of her back. She gasped, and he slid his tongue against hers, gently nudging, agile as he suckled it into his mouth. Her fingers tightened, her body slumped against him, and she tilted her head a bit as her lips relaxed their rigid stance.

And then she moaned, a quietly despairing sound of surrender, her hands sliding to encircle his neck, her fingers delving into his hair, then gripping as if she must somehow anchor herself to him.

Her back was narrow, her clothing restrictive, when all he wanted to do was touch her skin. For tonight he'd be satisfied with caressing her through the crisp linen of her dress, one hand seeking the rounding of her hip, his fingers pressing into her resilient flesh, the other pressed against her waist, holding her fast against his needy self.

Satisfied? Not until he had her flat on a bed without a stitch of clothing between them, he thought desperately. Not until he had the right to touch her curves. Not until he was given the privilege of blessing each and every inch of her pliant form with a string of kisses that would...

He released her mouth, inhaling sharply as he recognized his loss of control. She'd gone limp in his arms, and he pulled her against his chest, aware of the rapid heartbeat where his nose nuzzled her throat. His lips touched the spot and she murmured a wordless sound that made him feel like soaring beyond the moon and stars.

"Gussie?" His whisper made her gasp and press her fingers into his shoulders, squirming to sit upright.

"Oh, my," she murmured, peering up at him, her hands shifting to cover her cheeks. "Oh, my," she repeated, struggling to move from his grasp.

"Shh—" As though he would comfort her, put her at ease with his shushing sound, he repeated it. "Did I frighten you?" he whispered. "I wouldn't do anything to cause you distress, Gussie."

"Cause me—" She looked into his eyes accusingly. "You weren't treating me like a lady just now, Mr. Cleary. You had your *tongue* in my—" Her lips clamped tight as if she could not speak the word.

"You didn't seem to mind there for a moment, Gussie," he reminded her.

"No one, absolutely no one in the world has ever done such a thing to me," she whispered, brushing with frantic fingers at the front of her dress.

"Well, I would hope not," he told her judiciously. "Only a man intent on marrying you would have the right to such liberties, I would think."

Her head lifted and her gaze smacked his with the force of a bullet from a gun. She opened her mouth, then closed it abruptly, as if the words she wanted to speak were not available.

"Did you hear me?" he asked politely. "I want to marry you, Gussie."

She nodded, an abrupt movement of her head. And then she stood suddenly, catching him off guard. "You want to marry me," she repeated, as if she had not heard aright.

He nodded solemnly as he stood to face her. "That's my firm intention, ma'am."

"I have my hands full with my project here, sir. I cannot take on the additional responsibility of a husband, even if I were tempted to marry."

"Don't you like me, Gussie?"

"Of course I like you. I just don't want to marry you."

"Not tonight? Or never?"

"Well, *certainly* not tonight," she said firmly. "And never is a long time, but the whole idea of getting married is preposterous, anyway."

"Well, I'm not prepared to haul a preacher out of bed

tonight," he said agreeably, "but I certainly have plans for a wedding not too far in the future."

"Well, you'd better find yourself a bride, then," she said tartly. Abruptly she turned to the door, jerking it open with a harsh movement, then stepped inside, allowing it to bang shut behind her. She closed the heavy inner door and leaned back against it.

Tears slid down her cheeks and she muffled the sobs that begged to escape her lips. He'd treated her as if she were…her thoughts spun. As if she were her mother's daughter. The daughter of a woman named Little Dove. A woman who'd come from a life of degradation to that of a respectable wife and mother.

But any man who claimed Augusta McBride as his wife would have the right to know who her mother had been, and from whence she had come. The disgrace of her beginnings brought hot blood to Augusta's face, bringing heat to every part of her.

"I'm not ashamed of you, Mama," she whispered. "Truly, I'm not. I just could never bring myself to tell any man about you. And I'd have to, did I want to marry him."

A vision of her mother's sweet smile appeared before her closed eyes, and Augusta slumped against the door behind her, sliding to the floor in a heap of abject despair. "I'll never marry," she murmured, the words a vow she intended to keep.

Chapter Six

"We got enough extra eggs to sell, Miss Augusta," Bertha said, wiping the last gathering of hen fruit with a damp cloth. "Those pullets are doing good."

"If they didn't smell so bad, I could like them a lot better," Pearl said glumly.

"No one ever said a chicken coop was akin to a rose garden," Augusta told her. "And if it gets cleaned regularly, it won't be nearly so odorous."

"Well, that's easy fixed," Pearl said bluntly, looking around the breakfast table. "Whose job was it to shovel chicken poop yesterday?"

Honey looked up, her mouth pinched tightly. "It was mine, but I kept throwing up, and I quit before I barely got started." Shamefaced, she turned to Augusta. "I'll do most anything you tell me, ma'am. I truly will. But when my belly starts churnin' I just can't abide the stench of that place."

"It's not that bad," Beth Ann said quietly. "I've cleaned worse back home. I'll take Honey's turn at it."

"Could you do it this morning?" Augusta asked nicely. "And perhaps Honey will take over one of your chores in exchange."

"Anything," Honey said, her voice fervent with appreciation.

"I'm supposed to iron the linens for Harriet Burns's place," Beth Ann told her. "It's hot work, Honey."

"I can sweat like a trooper, and it won't make no never mind," she answered. "I'll get the irons on the stove soon's I finish breakfast."

"How many extra eggs do we have?" Augusta asked, pleased at the outcome of this morning's minor hassle.

"Couple of dozen for now, twice that many by tomorrow, probably." Bertha held up a specimen. "They're lookin' good-sized, too. I'll warrant you'll sell every one of them right next door. I'll ask Harriet myself."

And that would eliminate Augusta carrying eggs to the general store. She was relieved at that thought. There'd been a change in the air, even from the ladies who'd begun this project with such enthusiasm. Perhaps Cleary was right in his perception of the situation. The husbands in town might not like their wives so involved in the shelter.

Augusta stiffened her shoulders. It mattered not, she decided. They were getting off the ground, with Janine working at the dressmaker's shop. Now, with enough extra eggs to sell, money would be in better supply. Perhaps she could cut down on her withdrawals from the bank. And, by the time the garden came in and they filled the pantry with canned vegetables, things would indeed seem more prosperous.

She looked on as Honey put the irons on to heat and dragged the ironing board from the pantry. A breeze from the kitchen window kept the heat from the stove under control, and with a laundry basket of rolled, dampened sheets and pillowcases, Honey would be busy for a couple of hours.

Raking the yard was next on her list, a task Cleary had promised to complete today. Perhaps after last night… She considered the last part of the evening carefully, aware that she'd spoken harshly and with finality to the man. Probably, he wouldn't even show up today. Not that she'd blame him.

She walked to the back door, looking out on the dried grass that lay atop the lush green growth beneath. The cuttings were too heavy to let lie, and she'd better locate the rake and do the job herself. The door to the shed stood open and she caught her breath, trying to remember if she'd left it ajar yesterday. And then she saw a man step from the shadows into the sunlight.

Cleary. As tall and handsome as he'd been on her front porch just hours ago. As if her words had not penetrated his ego to any degree, he'd come to complete the task he'd begun. She stepped back from the screen, lest he find her gaping at him, and turned to find Pearl's gimlet gaze on her.

"That man's not gonna be happy till he gets his hands on you."

He's already had them on me. All up and down my back, in fact. He no doubt could have shifted them to my front and I wouldn't have lifted a finger to stop him. The words were alive in her mind as Augusta sorted through a reply. "He looks pretty happy to me," she said finally, pleased at the tart tone she managed.

"You know what I mean," Pearl told her, casting a glance at Honey, whose own gaze was fixed on Augusta.

"Miss Augusta, don't let any man take advantage of you," Honey advised solemnly. "Especially when you're not even gonna get paid for it."

"Wives don't get paid," Pearl said dryly. "And I think our handyman out there is planning on turning Miss Augusta into a married lady."

Honey's eyes filled with tears. "What will happen to us?"

"You'll have a home here for as long as you need it,"

Augusta said quickly. "And don't listen to Pearl. I'm not getting married."

"I don't advise it," Bertha said glumly. "Even to a man as easy on the eyes as that fella out in back. Men are a pain in the arse, if you don't mind my sayin' so. They make fancy promises and then—" She turned aside, her thought unspoken as she dumped a kettle full of hot water into the dishpan.

"Well, we'll keep this one around so long as he comes in handy," Augusta told the women surrounding her. "And enjoy his company while he's here. We just won't expect too much from him, will we?" Her smile felt glued to her lips as she finished her small speech, and only Pearl offered a reply, a sharp burst of laughter that denied Augusta's theory.

Now, while the man was occupied with a rake and lending his encouragement to Beth Ann, who worked doggedly in the coop and chicken yard, would be a good time to take a short jaunt into town, Augusta decided. It had been overlong in coming, this trip to speak to the sheriff and to the banker, in whose hands her funds were being held. She freshened up before her looking glass and adjusted her dress, smoothing out the skirt as she prepared for the walk into town.

Whether or not Roger Hampton knew what he was talking about, she needed to get her mind settled as far as Cleary was concerned. Before she got too entangled in his web, she must find out for herself if he was as open and aboveboard as he would have her believe. And if there were answers to be had, the banker and sheriff were the ones to give them to her.

A faint sense of unease followed her down the stairs and through the hallway as she peered into the kitchen. Cleary would be angry, should he discover her purpose this morning. But a woman must look out for herself, she decided.

Glory and Pearl were up to their elbows in soapsuds, washing the linens from the hotel, and they'd gotten a promise from Cleary to tighten the clothesline for them, insuring his preoccupation for the next little while.

Augusta set off at a fast clip, nodding a greeting to ladies who watched her progress from their porches, speaking nicely to those she met on the sidewalk as she neared the bank. And then she was inside the cool, high-ceilinged lobby of Nicholas Garvey's financial establishment.

The man was handsome, she decided, measuring him against the male she'd left in her backyard. Perhaps not as appealing as Cleary, but fit and well put together, nonetheless. His smile was broad as he left his desk to welcome her, his hand cool against hers as he shook it with discretion, two small pumps of his elbow being the accepted greeting.

"What can I do for you this morning, Miss McBride?" he asked jovially, as his eyes scanned her in an indulgent manner.

"I came to make inquiries," she said primly. "May we have a bit of privacy?"

"Certainly," he said, escorting her to his inner office and closing the door behind them with a gentle click of the latch. He offered her a chair and settled behind the big, mahogany desk, tugging his vest in place, then placing his elbows on the spotless ink blotter. "Now, what seems to be the problem?"

"I'm here to inquire about Mr. Jonathan Cleary," she said bluntly, alert to the change in his position as he sat upright and straightened a stack of papers.

"Well," he said after a moment, smiling at her so that his teeth gleamed whitely, impressing her not at all. "What would you like to know about the gentleman? Not that I can tell you much of anything, you understand. He is a customer here, but beyond that I'm not at liberty to gossip about our investors.''

A faint flush rode his cheekbones, and Augusta eyed it suspiciously. The man was lying. As surely as she knew her own name, she knew somehow that Nicholas Garvey was not being honest with her.

"Does he work with you?"

Mr. Garvey looked out into the lobby through a window in his office, where two tellers tended to customers and another man sat at a desk shuffling papers. "Do you see him out there?" he asked, his mouth twitching as if he suppressed a smile.

"That's not what I'm talking about, and you know it," Augusta said firmly, ignoring his hand that waved at the elegant lobby. "I mean is he working with you on a series of…" *How to say it?* "Does he work for the banks or the government or…" She shook her head. "You know what I'm asking, Mr. Garvey."

"And do you think I would give you an answer, ma'am, even if I had one to offer?" The man's jovial, easygoing facade slipped, even as Augusta watched, and a firmness touched his jaw that had not been apparent before. His eyes narrowed and fixed her with a piercing look that seemed to see beneath her composure.

"Perhaps not," she said. "But someone—that is, I've heard some gossip, and I want to be certain that my association with him is not likely to land me in trouble of any sort."

"Who?" he asked shortly.

"Who mentioned him to me?" She lifted a brow, amazed at the change in Nicholas Garvey's demeanor.

"Yes. Please be honest with me, ma'am. This may be important."

Augusta clenched her hands in her lap. She shouldn't

have come here. She had no business inquiring about Cleary, not even here, where she was assured of Mr. Garvey's discretion. "From a man I knew in Dallas. He's been in town for a few weeks." She looked up at the man across the desk. "Perhaps you know him? Roger Hampton."

He nodded. "I've heard of Mr. Hampton. Spoken to him once or twice. I'm not sure I'd put much credence in his word, ma'am."

Augusta felt a blush rise to cover her cheeks. "He said the sheriff had been making inquiries about Mr. Cleary, and advised me not to be associated with the man."

"Why didn't you ask the sheriff?"

"I intend to," she said stoutly.

Mr. Garvey leaned back in his chair, his scrutiny beginning to make Augusta uncomfortable. She resisted the urge to squirm in her seat. "Is Mr. Cleary interested in you?" he asked quietly.

"Interested?" Augusta almost choked on the word.

"You surely know what I'm asking, ma'am," the banker said kindly. "Does he have intentions where you're concerned?"

"I'm sure I—" Augusta halted. Yes, the man had intentions, but none she was willing to share with the banker. And then she saw the man's eyes shift, his gaze narrow as he looked into the lobby beyond his office. He rose abruptly, and at that, the door opened and someone entered the room behind her.

Cleary. She caught his scent, inhaled the aroma of dried grass and sunshine, and the smell she'd come to associate with the man. A blend of honest masculine sweat beneath clothing that had been exposed to the heat of the day. He hadn't taken time to change before he followed her here, she thought.

He followed me here. She stiffened in her chair, at once embarrassed and, at the same time, aggravated.

There was an edge of anger in the words he spoke. "I thought you were going to help me rake the grass, Miss McBride."

It wasn't at all what she'd expected, yet he'd seldom done as she'd thought he might, throughout their whole relationship.

She rose on unsteady legs and turned to face him. "I had business with Mr. Garvey," she said quietly.

Cleary's gaze shot to fix Nicholas Garvey in place, and his uplifted brow asked a silent question.

The banker cleared his throat. "Miss McBride asked about you."

Cleary's eyes never faltered from the man's face. "Well, why didn't Miss McBride come to me with her questions?"

"I think you'll have to ask *her* that."

Augusta blew out a mighty breath of air and lifted her chin for battle. "*Miss McBride* came to you with questions, sir. And you put me off with nice words and…and…"

"Do you think I'm a train robber, Augusta?" he asked quietly, turning his attention to her face, repeating the question he'd asked once before. His eyes lit with tenderness as he watched her and she knew, deep in her heart that he was remembering the things he'd done to put her off track. The kisses, the warm embrace, the words about marriage.

She shook her head. "No, I suppose I don't. I'm not sure what I believe, Mr. Cleary."

"Can you trust me?" he asked, standing before her with none of the accoutrements of a gentleman to plead his case. He wore no suit coat, no hat, no tie or any semblance of prestige except for the simple dignity of the man himself. His eyes dark with a plea she could not deny, he waited for her verdict.

"Yes, I suppose I can," she said finally. "I don't see that I have a choice, sir. Mr. Garvey has not denied your reliability." She shot the banker a sour look. "Of course, he hasn't assured me of it, either. Only wanted to know what your intentions toward me consisted of.''

"He what?" Cleary's voice rose with the question, and his dark glare pinned Nicholas Garvey where he stood. "You're treading on shaky ground there, Garvey."

"I suppose I was wondering how centered you were on the project you've undertaken," the banker answered, his jaw firm, his eyes shuttered as if he would nudge Cleary into anger.

"I've never failed before. I don't intend to now," Cleary told him. "My personal life is my own. Miss McBride is none of your concern."

"She made herself my concern when she walked in that door." Garvey sat down in his chair, leaned back and smiled. "She's a lovely lady. If your intentions aren't honorable, I'd like to know."

Augusta's face felt like molten fire as she backed from the men who'd chosen to speak of her as if she were not present in the room. "I don't think I want to hear any more of this conversation," she whispered, wishing with all her heart she'd never initiated her early morning mission.

"You'll hear it," Cleary snapped. "You won't know everything you set out to discover, but Mr. Garvey here will assure you of my trustworthiness. And I, in turn, will assure him of my *honorable* intentions where you're concerned, ma'am."

Augusta clapped her hands over her ears. "I've heard enough already. I told you last night I don't intend to get married, ever. And I meant it. Honorable intentions or not, if that's the reason you've been working around the shelter, you're wasting your time, Mr. Cleary."

"Ever, or never, however you say it, is a long time, ma'am," Mr. Garvey said, his look solemn though his eyes sparkled with humor.

"Oh!" The sound exploded from her lips, and her skirt

swirled around her legs as Augusta spun in place and then turned to the door. She opened it with a rattle of glass, rocketing through the portal like a ship with sails unfurled. Her shoes made unladylike noises on the marble floor as she headed for the tall front doors of the bank, and she totally ignored the sidelong looks of two customers who watched her progress across the lobby.

The heat hit her like the blast from a cannon as she found herself on the sidewalk. Flustered, she stood looking across the street to where the sheriff's office sat, its door open to catch any wayward breeze. And then, with a sharp toss of her head, she turned back to her house. The visit with the sheriff could wait, she decided. And whether or not he would be of any assistance was doubtful.

It seemed that Jonathan Cleary had the banker in the palm of his hand. What assurance was there that the sheriff would not be in the same location? Indeed, Cleary seemed to have tied the banker up in a neat package and tucked him in his pocket. She stalked rapidly down the sidewalk, and then, as her feet touched the sandy path beyond the edge of town, her paces slowed and she began breathing more deeply.

If the banker was to be believed, Cleary was on the up-and-up. She'd been wrong, perhaps, to doubt his word. Yet exactly *what* had he given her to go on? Only a few half-truths and some sweet talk that had curled her ears and made her heart turn over in her breast.

And a mention of marriage, surely an honorable proposal.

"Wait for me, Augusta," a voice called from behind her, and her steps halted. He grasped her arm as he reached her side, and she was hustled unceremoniously toward home. "We need to talk," he said, his voice rough, his fingers holding her as if he had no intention of losing his grip anytime soon.

"If you didn't trust me, you should have made it clear," he said, his voice grating like two pieces of iron scraping together. "My work here is dependent on secrecy, Augusta, and half the town just watched me burst into the bank like a bat out of hell."

"What was your rush?" she asked pertly. "I might have been going to see Mr. Garvey for a draw on my account."

"Not likely. I knew you were up in arms last night. Then, this morning, when you didn't come out in the yard and no one knew where you'd gone, I had a notion you were sticking your nose in where it didn't belong. I saw you going into the bank as soon as I left your front yard. I had to hustle to catch up."

"My nose doesn't belong in anything to do with you, I take it," she said quietly.

"I didn't say that. It's just that there are certain areas—" A sound of exasperation halted his words, and he growled beneath his breath, a phrase she ignored, considering it beneath herself to pay any mind to foul language.

Her gate swung open easily under his hand, and she was escorted with a firm touch onto the front porch. He'd pushed her just about far enough, she figured. Enough was enough. Turning to him, she jerked from his grasp.

"Are we having a confrontation right here in front of the whole neighborhood?" she asked, glaring at him, taking note of his flaring nostrils and ruddy cheeks.

"Wherever you'd like, lady," he told her. "But for your own sake of propriety, I think we need to go indoors." Hands on hips, he nodded at the screened door. "Lead the way, Miss McBride."

She opened the door, hearing the spring expand, and marched into the hallway. Behind her the door slammed closed and a warm hand pressed against her back, squarely between her shoulder blades. "Into the parlor, please,"

Cleary said, his words sounding as if they were forced between clenched teeth.

She walked through the arch, across the room to where a window looked out upon the side yard, and lifted one hand to brush at a speck on the glistening glass surface.

The parlor door closed, the latch catching firmly. And then he spoke. "Turn around and look at me."

She shivered at his words, aware of his body inches from her back. He would not hurt her physically. Of that she was certain. But pain might come in a variety of forms, and she was more vulnerable to this man right now than to any other human being in her life.

Jonathan Cleary had the ability to break her heart, and that knowledge stunned her even as she accepted it as truth.

He didn't wait for her obedience, but, instead, placed his hands on her shoulders and spun her to face him. She would have toppled to one side, but his firm grip held her steady, and she felt the flex of strong fingers against her flesh. He was angry. More than angry, she decided. Fury filled him to overflowing, and her heartbeat was heavy, causing her body to shudder beneath his touch.

"I've spent long weeks in this town, recuperating from an incident that should never have happened. During those weeks, I made up my mind that *nothing* would ever again take my mind from the job at hand." He loosened his grip and the touch became a caress.

"I've hurt you, haven't I?" he asked, and she could only shake her head in a silent denial. "Yes, I have. I forget how fragile you are sometimes. The way you work around here and carry the load of this house and its occupants is too much for a woman on her own." He looked upward at the ceiling, as if he searched for words. "Damn it all to hell, Augusta. You're a little bit of a thing, taking on the cares of the world, and I've spent too much time thinking about you, and too many nights walking the floor because you haunt my dreams.''

"Me?'' she asked, unable to accept his words as truth. "I've never haunted anyone's dreams in my life. I'm an old maid, Cleary. I'm a woman past her prime, with more responsibility than I bargained for. But I'm not a quitter. I'll handle whatever comes my way, and I don't need you worrying about me.''

As if his mind snagged on one phrase in the midst of her diatribe, he snatched at her again and lifted her, until her toes barely touched the floor. "Past your prime? What fool ever told you that?'' he asked. "Did that horse's arse from Dallas feed you that story?'' His eyes searched her face. "You're about as far from being an old maid as any woman I've ever known. Hell, Augusta, I want to marry you. Doesn't that mean anything to you?''

She nodded and, then in a swift change of mind, shook her head. "Yes, well, no,'' she said quickly. "Of course it means something to me. And no, Roger didn't say anything of the sort.'' She dangled there, fearing the onset of weeping if she didn't manage to escape him. Totally mortified by the sum total of the past half hour, she knew that tears were on their way, and crying in front of a man was the last thing on God's green earth she wanted to do.

"Please put me down on the floor,'' she whispered, holding her eyes wide to halt the onset of moisture.

He looked stunned at her words, and glared down to where her toes touched the faded piece of carpet. "Yes, of course,'' he muttered, lowering her carefully to stand on her own. And then he slid his hands into his pockets and bent his head to meet her gaze. "Are you going to marry me, Gussie?''

She thought he held his breath as she formed a reply. Yet, surely, a man like Cleary would not die of a broken heart should he be rebuffed. He could seek and find another woman faster than she could murmur her denial of his proposal. Well, maybe not quite that rapidly, she thought, but certainly a man as handsome and appealing as he would never have to spend time alone unless it was his choice.

"I told you last night, Cleary," she said quietly, her insides trembling as she prepared to tell a blatant lie. "I don't want to marry you."

His lips curved just a bit and she wondered at his humor. Surely the man had heard her aright. Rocking back on his heels, he shook his head, and his words were mocking as his hands slid from his pockets and lifted to circle her waist.

"Gussie, Gussie," he said, admonishing her as if he scolded a child. "I told you before, you don't do well at telling falsehoods. And the words you just spoke were about as far from the truth as anything you've ever said in your life."

"Well, I don't," she said sharply. "I have too much to do right here to be spending my time on a husband."

"Maybe so," he said agreeably. "But what you said was that you don't want to marry me. And honey, you may not know it, but marrying me might be the best thing for you right now." He inhaled deeply. "You need me, Gussie. And I need you. And I'm not about to walk away from you."

Thank you, God. Cleary was right. She needed him and, selfishly, she couldn't bear the thought of him leaving, never to return. And if Cleary said he wasn't walking out the door, she could bet her bottom dollar he'd be back tomorrow. She just couldn't face the thought of what marrying him would entail. Of what she must tell him before she accepted his suit.

Oh, yes, by the way. My mother made her living in a house of ill repute until my father bought her freedom and married her. I'm the daughter of a whore. And wouldn't

he disappear like a late April snowstorm in New York when
the sun comes out?

"Are you listening? Did you hear me?" he asked, bending to peer into her face. His brow was furrowed, his words
emphatic, and she nodded quickly.

"I hear you," she said sharply. "And if you want to
hang around, I'm not about to send you on your way.
You've come in right handy, as you very well know. And
I'm wondering if that wasn't your intention from the beginning. To make me dependent on you. To make me need
you."

"And do you?" he asked.

"You know very well I do. I wouldn't have known
where to begin with all the projects you've had a hand in,
right from the first day you came to call." She made a
subtle attempt to move away, but his grip on her waist only
tightened.

"Please remove your hands from me," she said quietly,
biting her lip as he shook his head and drew her closer to
himself.

"No, Gussie. I want you to admit that you have feelings
for me. And I don't know any other way to do it than force
the issue."

"Of course I have feelings for you," she said politely,
turning her face to the side as he would have touched her
lips with his. "I like you, and I admire your skills. I appreciate the help you've been to my shelter, and I've decided that, even though you're involved in something that
frightens me, I'll leave it alone for now."

"Now that," he said flatly, "is about the worst recom-
mendation I've ever had from anyone, man or woman. You
could say all those things about the handyman at the hotel,
and I know for a fact he's involved in messin' around with
half the women at the Pink Palace."

"You know what I mean," she told him. Her face

flushed at his reference to Joey Waters's predilection for the women who filled Lula Belle's place.

"You mean, you'll allow me to lend a hand here, so long as I don't expect you to consider my suit for your hand in marriage."

Put that way, in blunt language she could not misinterpret, she could only feel shame wash over her. "Do you think I've taken advantage of you?"

"I've allowed it," he said quietly. "But then, I've taken advantage of you a time or two. Like I'm going to right now."

"Now?"

He nodded, and she held her breath, anticipation rising with every beat of her heart. One long arm slid to rest just below her waist and she bent her upper body back a bit, as if she would escape. He laughed, a dark sound, and his other hand lifted to her throat, where white mother-of-pearl buttons began a line that ended several inches below her waist.

A long finger flipped the first button from the neatly stitched hole that contained it, and she caught her breath, looking down at his tanned, scarred hand against her pale skin.

He repeated the action on the next button, and a triangle of flesh was exposed. "I don't think—" she whispered, and then her voice halted abruptly as a third button met that marauding finger, only to lose the battle.

"Don't think, Gussie," he said quietly. "Just feel. Feel my hand holding you against my body. Feel the warmth of my fingertips against you, here at your throat."

Warm? They were hot, surely burning her flesh where they touched the edge of her collarbone. She bent her head to watch as he smoothed the front opening of her dress to either side, setting loose another button in the process. The chemise was edged with fine lace, and he lingered there, as if he tested the dainty ruffle and found it engrossing.

"You shouldn't be doing this," she whispered.

"Shouldn't I?"

Glancing up, she met his gaze, and realized he was watching her face. "I won't be seduced, Cleary," she said, her voice not quite as firm as she'd have liked. "Especially not in broad daylight, right in front of the parlor window."

"No?" His hand left her back and he pulled the heavy drape over the window behind her. "Is that better?"

"There are women in the kitchen," she said. "Don't shame me in front of them."

"The door is locked, Gussie."

"You locked it?"

He nodded. "When I followed you in here." His mouth twitched, and then he whispered a suggestion she shuddered to hear. "If you scream, the ladies will come running to your rescue."

"You know I won't do that." And she wouldn't. Not for the world would she put herself into such a situation. Augusta McBride's reputation had been unblemished for her entire life. Not until she'd bought this house and filled it with women who needed a haven had she faced anything but smiles and approving glances from the people surrounding her. Her ladies thought she was without fault. All but Pearl, she amended silently.

His hand moved, jarring her from her thoughts, and she looked to where long fingers slid inside the opening of her dress. An opening that had expanded to include seven buttons, exposing the sheer batiste of her chemise and revealing a good share of the pink circle that adorned the crest of her right breast.

She gasped, her shock doubled as his fingers proceeded to loose the buttons on her chemise. They were small and dainty, yet he seemed to have no problem with them, his fingers agile at the task. If she knew anything at all about it, this appeared to be the seduction he'd threatened.

"Are you going to scream, Gussie?" he asked, his low and husky voice coming from deep inside his chest.

"No." The single syllable was whispered on an indrawn breath, and she found herself holding the air within her lungs as his fingertips slid inside the soft fabric. They touched her skin, and a hum of satisfaction escaped his lips.

"Please, Cleary," she said softly.

"Please don't?" he asked. "Or please touch me. Which is it, Gussie?"

"Yes. I don't know," she whimpered. "I'm afraid."

"Of me?" His fingertips pressed against the soft curve of her breast and as she watched, the pink crest grew taut and firm.

"Yes."

His hand was still, his fingers unmoving. "I won't hurt you," he said quietly. "I'll never hurt you, Gussie."

And if she pulled away, he'd let her go. In the depths of her heart, she knew she need only draw away and his hand would drop to his side. He would allow her to button herself together, and...and what?

Never know the touch of a man? Not just the tempting, gentle movement of callused fingertips against her maiden flesh, but the knowledge that for once in her life a man desired her. *Her.* Augusta McBride, spinster.

His head bent and his mustache brushed the skin just beneath her collarbone, his hand holding the chemise aside to make way for the pressure of his lips as they moved in a slow dance to where puckered flesh throbbed with every beat of her heart.

And then he paused, and his hand cupped the weight of her breast, his breath hot against her. He kissed her there, less than an inch from the small nub, and she felt her breath leave her lungs in an audible sound.

"I'm sorry, Gussie," he whispered, lifting his head to look into her eyes. "I took advantage of you, and I apologize. I had no right to touch you." His fingers were skillful as they redid the series of buttons, both on her chemise and the bodice of her dress.

"I'm sorry," he repeated, smoothing the fabric of her collar and brushing the back of his fingers the length of her cheek and jaw. "Forgive me." His mouth touched hers, and she felt his lips move to enclose hers, suckling gently for just a moment before he released her lower lip reluctantly. Warm and damp, his kiss felt more of a reassurance than the promised seduction he'd put into effect.

And the only thought in her mind was that he had stopped too soon. That now she would never know the pleasure of a man's mouth there, where even now her breast was swollen with desire.

Chapter Seven

"Beth Ann got a letter." Pearl waved the envelope in the air, and the women assembled around the dinner table greeted it with a certain amount of apprehension. If Beth Ann's parents would accept her back into the fold, it might be the best thing for her; and yet, the opposite reply might be contained in the missive Pearl held in her hand.

"Would you read it to me, Miss Augusta?" Her eyes wide and woebegone, Beth Ann seemed breathless, and Honey reached to place her arm across the girl's narrow shoulders.

"No matter what it says, you'll not be without a home," Augusta told her firmly. "And if your parents can't find it in their hearts to welcome you...well, you know you're at home here with us."

"Yes, ma'am," Beth Ann said, nodding politely. "But it surely would be nice to see my ma again." She looked down at her lap where her hands rested, and her voice was a murmur in the silence surrounding the table. "Could you read it now, please?"

August took the missive from Pearl and slid a fingernail beneath the flap, then took the single piece of paper from within. She unfolded it and perused the first line silently, then began to read aloud.

"'Daughter,'" it began. "'Your mother and I have decided to allow you a second chance at making some sort of success of your life. If you will agree to obey the rules of this house, we will take you in.'"

A concerted gasp from Janine and Glory drew Augusta's attention and she frowned forbiddingly in their direction, then looked at Beth Ann's flushed cheeks. "It's signed simply with your father's name. He is Gunther Jacobson, I take it?"

Beth Ann nodded and looked up, her eyes damp with tears. "It doesn't sound very welcoming, does it?"

"Under what circumstances did you leave?" Augusta asked.

Beth Ann's cheeks turned even rosier than before. "My pa caught me out behind the barn with a neighbor boy. We were kissing, and Pa whipped me. He said I was only good for one thing, but as long as I lived under his roof, I wasn't gonna be doing it on his property."

"So you left?" Honey asked, patting Beth Ann's shoulder as if she would give what comfort she could.

"I left the next day, soon as I could gather up my things. I thought Doyle Webster, the fella who wanted to kiss me so bad, might be interested in marrying me, so I walked to his pa's farm and asked Doyle right out, did he want to." She inhaled deeply and looked up directly into Augusta's eyes. "He told me he was just practicing on me. He'd decided to marry one of the town girls, and he wanted to be real good at all the kissing and loving stuff before he set out to court her."

"Did you consider going back home?" Augusta asked.

"Oh, no, ma'am. Pa woulda killed me, had he found out I'd left and then come back. I just went into town and bought a ticket on the train and headed west till my money ran out." She frowned as she remembered her jaunt. "That was right here in Collins Creek, and when I walked down the street and asked for work, nobody needed any help. One man said to go to the Pink Palace. So I did."

"Do you want to go back home now?" Honey asked softly. "Will your pa hurt you, do you think?"

"Maybe I've changed enough to make a difference," Beth Ann said hopefully. "I can read pretty good now, and my hair looks better and my cooking is comin' along somewhat. I'd like to give it a try. I miss my ma."

"We'll buy you a train ticket," Augusta told her. "You decide when you want to leave, and I'll take care of the rest." She spoke with confidence, but her heart ached for what the girl would face when she returned to the man who had fathered her.

"Now," Augusta said brightly, "what else do we have to talk about today before we begin our lessons and chores?"

"Who's gonna clean the chicken coop when I'm gone?" Beth Ann asked, slanting a sympathetic look at Honey's stricken features.

"I will." Glory spoke quietly but firmly. "I'll do anything y'all need for me to do. I don't have any family waitin' to take me in. I'm afraid the bunch of you are it for me." Her smile was sudden, and Augusta was cheered by the change in the girl since her arrival. "I don't mind dirty chores. I just won't lay on my back for a man ever again. That's worse than cleanin' chicken poop any day of the week."

"Depends," Pearl drawled. "Some men make it downright worth your while."

"That'll be enough," Augusta said quickly.

"How about your Mr. Cleary?" Pearl asked with a grin. "I'll bet he was mighty persuasive behind that locked parlor door the other day."

"This is not a matter for discussion," Augusta said firmly, rising from the table. She felt her legs tremble as she walked to the sink with her empty plate, and in an instant her mind drew her back to those moments when Jonathan Cleary had stripped away her inhibitions and drawn her into a web of seduction she'd been unable... perhaps unwilling, she amended silently, to escape.

As if the mention of his name was enough to summon him, a rap at the screened door next to the pantry drew the eyes of the women in that direction. Cleary stood on the porch, hat in hand, and Augusta knew a moment of anxiety as he peered through the screen toward the sink where she stood. The sun overhead caused his dark hair to glisten with a sheen that brought to mind those moments they'd shared in the parlor, when her fingers had slid so readily against his head. Augusta propped herself on the edge of the sink, fearing her legs would not hold her erect as she felt her stuttering heart slam against her ribs.

Cleary was the one. The one her mother had told her she would recognize one day. The man who could steal her heart or break it. Who might walk away and never look back, leaving her empty and forlorn.

Yet, he'd said he wanted to marry her. And he was back today, obviously seeking her company. *If only—*

"Miss Augusta?" he said quietly. "Would you mind coming out into the yard? I have something for you."

"Go ahead, ma'am," Glory urged her, rising to gather the empty plates. "I'll tend to this." Her eyes glowed as she considered the man beyond the portal, then she winked as she met Augusta's gaze. "You just visit with your...your friend," she finished nicely.

"Yes, all right." Her legs moved rather well, after all, she thought, walking to the door, her gaze on Cleary's hand as he drew it open, her ears aware of the spring as it stretched. And then she was on the porch, the door having closed behind her, and all was quiet in the kitchen, where six women were amazingly silent.

Cleary took her elbow and placed his hat atop his head. He escorted her from the stoop, then across the yard to where a small stack of lumber awaited her inspection. It appeared to be leftovers from the chicken coop project, with only three or four new boards added to the pile.

"What are you planning?" she asked, aware of his grasp against her arm, where long fingers held her firmly, as though he feared she might attempt to escape. And then, as they paused to inspect the pile of wood, his hand released her and his arm slid to circle her waist.

She shivered and looked up at him. "The women can see us," she whispered. Yet, if he moved that bit of support she might crumple where she stood, she thought, her legs once more unsteady beneath her.

"Naw. The chicken coop's in the way," he told her, his eyes touching her face, then roving lower to rest approvingly on her bosom. "I haven't been able to sleep," he admitted quietly. "I keep thinking about you, Gussie."

She had to clear her throat, finding herself unable to speak as his words brought to mind the feel of callused flesh against her skin. "I can't imagine why," she said sharply, ruing the quiver in her voice. "I would think you've had your way with more women than I can count. I don't know why my..." She looked down at herself and her shoulders drew forward as if she would hide the effect his attention brought into being.

"I know why," he whispered. "Because you're very special to me. You're the woman I want to marry, Gussie."

He lifted her chin, and her mouth trembled as she spoke. "You must think I'm loose to allow you such liberties," she murmured, feeling the painful blush cover her face.

"As I recall, I didn't give you a lot of choice," he reminded her. "I was not a gentleman that day."

"No, you weren't," she agreed, a bit more firmly. "But I must accept my share of the blame, since I didn't fight off your advances."

"There's no blame to be assumed," he told her. "What two people do in their private moments is just a part of the process of loving. I meant you no harm, sweetheart. I only wanted to show you that your body is a part of what draws me to you."

"What's the other part?" She tilted her head and lifted her hands to rest against the broad expanse of his chest.

His grin was wide and he shook his head. "Ah, Gussie. You don't mince words, do you?" He bent to place a quick kiss against her forehead, then brushed his lips to the tip of her nose and just a bit lower to press them warmly to hers. "That's what I like about you, sweetheart. I know where I stand. You're quick-witted, your tongue is a bit like a two-edged sword sometimes, and you sure don't pull your punches."

He leaned back to look her over approvingly. "I like that about you. Not just your curves and the way you hold your head so high and your back so straight, but the way you shoot from the hip." Then he grinned again. "So to speak, ma'am."

She blinked in astonishment at his words, and then her modesty forced her to change the subject. "What's my surprise?" she asked, wondering that her head didn't expand as he listed the long list of attributes he'd blessed her with. She'd feared that shame would possess her in his presence, but it had not come to pass. Instead, for the first time in her life she felt a degree of confidence in her own person.

"Changing the subject, are you?" He sighed, then released her and turned her to face the pieces of lumber he'd deposited here, close to the back of her property. He was warm and solid against her back and she subdued the urge to lean against him. It would not do to press herself against that long, firm body.

"Ma'am?" His hands met at her waist and she looked down in surprise as he drew her back, fulfilling her longing. His voice was filled with amusement as he continued, as if he read aright her vacillating and had taken the responsibility upon himself to bring them into physical contact.

"I suspect I'd better let you be the judge of this," he said. "I thought you needed a dog, Miss Augusta. This is the material for his house."

"A dog." She repeated his words, stunned by the idea. "I've never had a dog."

"Well then, I'd say it's about time you did," he murmured, leaning to speak the words into her ear. "There's a fella just outside of town with three pups more than ready to leave home. Thought you might like to take a ride and choose one of them for a watchdog."

She looked back over her shoulder at him. "You think we need one?"

He shrugged. "You never know. And so long as he knows me, I can come visiting whenever I want without him causing a ruckus."

"You cause enough ruckus on your own, without any help from a dog," she said dryly. "And I suppose we could use a dog." Her pause was long and then she repeated her earlier statement, the words soft and filled with a degree of longing that made her shiver. "I've never had a dog."

Cleary felt a tug at his heart that made him want to envelop this woman in a more intimate embrace, one that would fill all the empty places in her life. Imagine never having a dog. Imagine never knowing the power of being a woman. For he knew, without a shadow of a doubt, that until just days ago, Augusta McBride had never recognized her own body as being worthy of a man's attention.

But she knew now, and he planned to enlarge her knowledge by increments, until she could no longer refuse his suit. If only he were able to spend more time with her, persuade her more quickly. But the message from Nicholas Garvey in his pocket meant his departure this very evening.

"Tell you what," he said quickly, deciding to move on his instincts. "Let's take a buggy ride and you can pick out your dog, and then I'll build him a house this afternoon. What do you say?"

"I have responsibilities here this afternoon, Cleary," she said quickly, looking aghast at his suggestion as she removed herself from his embrace. "I'm going to work with my ladies on some elementary recipes, those that need more instruction in cooking. Janine has the afternoon off, and she's teaching some rudimentary sewing skills to the others."

"They won't miss you," he said quietly, and then at her swift look of reproach, he revised his statement. "You can set things up and let them work on their own. They won't always have you to lead them around, Gussie. They need to be given the chance to be independent."

She looked thoughtful at that idea, and nodded agreeably. "You may be right. And if I'm to have a dog, I'll want to choose it myself. And you understand, I can always change my mind, if what this gentleman has doesn't suit me."

"Absolutely," he said, and then, with a sigh signifying the end of the discussion, he grinned. "Well, that's decided." He turned her toward the house and marched her quickly across the grass. She looked over her shoulder at the stack of wood and frowned, her expression dubious.

"Are you sure you can build a doghouse in one afternoon? It looks like a mishmash of lumber to me."

"I can do anything if you stand by to cheer me on, ma'am," he told her, his eyes savoring the look of rosy cheeks and sparkling eyes she wore so well. "I'll be back in thirty minutes. That should be long enough for you to set things in motion here.''

He opened the door for her, nodding at the ladies who stood in various positions around the kitchen, as if they'd been leaning to look out the window and door just moments since and had scrambled to move from their observation points.

''Good afternoon,'' he said politely, tipping his hat at them before he rounded the back corner of the big house and headed for the street.

The pups were spotted, black and tan on white, with legs too long and feet too big for their pudgy bodies. ''Don't know who the daddy was,'' Carl Wilson said with a cheerful grin. ''But the mama is about wore-out trying to keep up with these rascals.'' He bent to pick up the nearest pup, and it dangled from his hand, obviously not afraid of heights. ''My younguns play with them a lot,'' he said. ''They're friendly little fellas.''

Cleary watched as Augusta reached for the pup, her movement impulsive, her mouth curving in a smile. ''May I hold him?'' she asked, even as the farmer placed the wriggling creature in her outstretched hands.

''Don't put him near your face,'' he warned. ''He'll lick you to death if you give him the chance.''

And as if he'd been given permission to do that very thing, the pup leaned toward her and Augusta's arms bent to ease the youngster against her bosom. He lifted his head, propping his oversize feet against her, and a long tongue went into action.

Augusta laughed aloud, a sound that brought an amused grin to Cleary's lips. ''I think he likes you,'' he told her, reaching to ruffle the short hair atop the pup's head.

''You want to take a look at the others?'' Carl asked.

''Maybe,'' Augusta said, looking down at the frolicking,

spotted creatures who were taking hold of the hem of her dress. A ferocious growl from one caused her to erupt with laughter again, and she bent to tug her clothing from his mouth. Off balance, she tumbled backward as he released his hold, and Cleary found himself squatting beside her.

"You all right?" he asked, peering down into her face.

"I'm fine. Just clumsy," she told him, her grasp on the puppy in her arms still firm. She tucked her skirts under her knees and placed the pup on her lap, where he was joined within seconds by his littermates. They bit and chewed on each other, climbing to lick at her rosy cheeks, falling from her lap to the ground and then regaining their chosen spot with a great wriggling of hind legs and wagging of tails.

"You want all three, ma'am?" Carl Wilson asked, leaning on the hitching rail. "Looks like they've taken to you in a big way." He exchanged a glance with Cleary, and his approving nod was silent sanction of Augusta.

"Oh, no, I couldn't," she exclaimed. "One is more than enough. I have to admit to a total lack of knowledge when it comes to training a dog or doing much other than feeding it."

"Not to mention allowing it the privilege of making itself at home on your lap." Cleary's observation brought a resounding laugh from Carl, and that in turn brought two young boys running from the barn.

"You givin' away the pups, Pa?" one asked, panting to catch his breath as he squatted next to Augusta.

"This is Miss McBride," his father said. "She'd like one of your pups. Which one do you think would work best for her?"

Deep brown eyes surveyed her where she sat, and the youngster bit at his lip. "I think Henry likes her real well, don't you, Joey?" He touched the pup who'd remained on

Augusta's lap, while the other two tumbled to the ground and wrestled in the dust.

His younger brother watched for a moment and then nodded wisely. "Yeah, I'd say so." He reached to the chosen one and his fingers scratched beneath the wrinkles on the puppy's throat. "He's a good dog, ma'am. He pret' near always comes when you call him," he added as a final inducement.

"Henry?" Augusta said in a level tone of voice. It was obviously not her first choice as a dog's name, Cleary thought, but she nodded wisely and looked up at the brothers. "He will do very well, I think." She lifted him and handed him to the smallest boy. "Will you hold him while I get up?"

"Yes, ma'am," the lad said, clutching the puppy against himself and bending to kiss the top of his head.

Cleary reached quickly to lift Augusta to her feet and stepped aside as she brushed at her skirts. "Can I help?" he asked politely, and found himself the recipient of a warning glare from her blue eyes.

"I don't think so," she said firmly. And then she turned to regain possession of the chosen pet. He climbed within her grasp to lay his head against her shoulder and, with a sigh of obvious contentment, closed his eyes.

"What do we owe you?" Cleary asked Carl, and was waved away with an uplifted hand.

"Nothing. We're glad to find good homes for them. The boys may be by to visit someday when we take a trip to town, ma'am, if that's all right with you."

Augusta shot a look at Cleary, then nodded politely. "I live in the large house next to Harriet Burns's boarding-house," she said primly. "The boys are welcome anytime."

"Next to Harriet's place?" Carl's brow furrowed a moment and then his eyes lit. "Ah, yes. I know the place. I've heard about your project there, ma'am. Hope all goes well for you. If you can use some extra tomatoes and cucumbers for the house, feel free to help yourself from those on the porch.''

Cleary held his breath. Augusta looked on the verge of tears at the offer, and he hesitated, lest he cause her to lose the rigid control she placed upon herself.

''Thank you,'' she said, her chin held firmly, her smile properly appreciative. ''That's more than kind of you. My ladies will appreciate it.''

Carl nodded, and with quick movements provided a basket from the porch, filling it with the vegetables he'd offered. The oldest boy took it from his hands and slid it onto the floor of the buggy, then stood back, eyeing the pup Augusta held with a wistful expression on his round face.

Cleary lifted her over the wheel and onto the seat in an easy movement, his hands firm around her waist. He tucked her skirts in and resisted the urge to run his hand the length of her calf as he did so. Touching Augusta was at the back of his mind, it seemed, no matter what else he was occupied with. She was addictive, her scent luring him close, her smile bringing her lips to his attention, and he found himself craving her presence.

Marriage was the answer. Now to convince her of the notion.

The doghouse went together well, once Cleary got his mind off Augusta and onto the pile of lumber. She sat on a quilt beneath the nearest tree and watched as he sorted through the lengths of wood. ''How about putting it in the shade?'' she asked, absently petting the pup who'd taken up what looked like permanent residence in her lap.

''Whatever you want, honey,'' Cleary said obligingly.

The ladies had all trooped out to inspect the pup, and he'd given each of them his approval with a tongue that seemingly never wearied of tasting feminine skin. Even Bertha took her turn holding the newcomer; then, as if she must draw a line, gave an ultimatum, limiting his presence in the house.

"I won't have a dog begging at the table," she said firmly. "He stays outdoors."

"What if it rains?" Honey asked beseechingly, bending her head to nuzzle the damp, black nose that had sniffed out her plush bosom.

"He'll have a fine house to stay in," Bertha told her. "Mr. Cleary here is building a house big enough for two dogs, it looks like to me."

"We aren't sure how large he'll get," Augusta said.

"Well," Pearl said wisely. "From the size of those feet, you'd better plan on a monster. We had a pup once when I was a youngster. Fella who sold it to us said it came from two small dogs, and he guaranteed it to be not more than a foot and a half tall, full grown. Ended up with a shepherd, longhaired at that, with feet like saucers."

"We have a big yard," Augusta said defensively. "I don't care how big he gets."

"For a woman who wasn't at all sure about this whole thing, you sure are singing a different tune," Cleary said, lifting a length of two-by-four.

The ladies had drifted back to the house, deeply involved in their projects for the afternoon, and Cleary had bent to his task. Now he sorted the widest boards and placed them on the ground.

"Is that the side?" Augusta asked.

"Hmm," he answered, his mind figuring the measurements he'd planned. There was enough ten-inch stock to put together the sides and rear of the house, and pieces to form the roof. He glanced up at her, aware that his reply had been vague, unwilling to ignore her presence, lest she wander off to the house. It had taken some fancy footwork to persuade her to remain with him, and he wasn't about to ruin his afternoon by neglecting her.

"I'm thinking, Gussie. Help me here. I don't want to go to the lumberyard unless I have to. There should be enough wood here to piece things together."

She rose quickly, placing the pup on the quilt and petting him a moment to encourage the continuance of his nap, then moved to where Cleary squatted. "How about this?" she asked, lifting and rearranging several pieces of lumber to form a rectangle. "I think there's enough to make two this size, and they can be the sides. Then the ends can be a bit narrower and you can just put on a sloped roof. What do you think?"

"Smarty," he said accusingly. "You let me think you were sitting over there playing with that dog, and all the time you had this thing figured out." He tugged her down on the ground beside him and bent to drop a kiss on her cheek. "You'll come in handy once we get married and start looking for a place to build our home," he told her.

"Married." She stilled, and he felt her shiver.

"I've already told you, sweetheart. I'm planning on marrying you. We'll work things out in the next couple of weeks or so. You'll see. Everything will be fine."

She lifted stricken eyes to meet his gaze, and he felt a pang of remorse at whatever he'd done to cause her pain. "I can't marry you," she said quietly. "I told you that before, Cleary. I don't know why you're interested in me as a wife, even with all the folderol you spouted earlier today. I have a commitment here, and things in my past that make it impossible for me to marry."

"Has someone hurt you?" he asked, smitten with the thought that somehow, somewhere, a man had caused her to feel less than worthy of his proposal. "Did anyone force themselves on you, Gussie?"

She shook her head. "No, nothing like that. Just a family

background that will not bear exposure. And I won't say more than that.''

"Your brother?'' Should her scalawag brother be causing her to hesitate over his proposal, he'd set that right in moments.

Hesitating, she bit her lip and then, in a gesture that implied having made a choice, she shook her head again. "Not Wilson, although his being in prison doesn't say much for my background, does it?''

"You're not responsible for his actions, Gussie.'' And he thought of the man he'd sent to prison in Colorado, his mind accepting the possibility that there might be a connection with Gussie.

The young man's name was Gus, back there in Wyoming where a bullet from one of the band of rustlers had almost put Cleary in a grave. He'd considered the idea before and dismissed it as too much of a coincidence. Now, it struck him with the force of a blow. She'd never be able to forgive him if he turned out to be the man who'd jailed her beloved brother.

"I'm only responsible for myself,'' she agreed. "But when there are things in the past that rise up to haunt you, a choice must be made. And I've made one in this case.''

"Can you talk about it?''

She was so vehement yet so quietly determined, he felt the same cold chill run the length of his spine as she shook her head and tears sprang to her eyes. "Not now, Cleary. Not today. Maybe another time.''

He would not argue. The doghouse was yet to be built, and he was scheduled to leave town by dark. "Whatever you say, sweetheart. Let's get this thing put together. What do you say?''

"All right,'' she agreed, and set to with a will, placing boards and handing him nails as he hammered the pup's new dwelling together.

Supper was cold meat, bread and thick slices of cheese, with cool glasses of lemonade to sip as they leaned against the tree trunk and took stock of their miniature mansion. Working together, they'd put it together in less than two hours, and with a piece of old carpet inside and a metal ring for Henry's rope, the place was ready for occupancy. Tar paper applied with a generous hand would keep the roof from leaking until Cleary could pick up some stray shingles, and now they faced the task of acclimating the dog to his new abode.

"It's getting late," Cleary said, glancing at the sun, just above the western horizon.

"Do you have plans for the evening?" she asked, trying to sound nonchalant and succeeding not at all. She wiped her mouth on a linen napkin and folded it judiciously as she awaited his reply.

"I'm afraid I'll be gone for a couple of days," he said quietly.

Her mouth opened, then closed. Her head bent to examine the bits and pieces she'd left on her plate, and her voice was without expression. "I see."

"No, you don't," he told her. "And I can't help that." He reached to tilt her face up, daring her to struggle against his firm hand. "It won't be long, Augusta. I'll tell you everything soon."

"I'll still be here when you get back," she said, her eyes flashing her frustration.

"I don't understand you," he told her, his own level of aggravation fast approaching the boiling point. "You don't want me, yet you get angry when I stay away. I don't know what you expect of me."

Tears rushed to her eyes and she pressed her lips together, trying to curb the flow that threatened to reveal her weakness. She could only shake her head. If she spoke even a single word, the tears would be released and she would be mortified.

"Do you care for me?" he asked roughly. "I won't ask if you love me. I know better than that. But you must care a little, Gussie, or you'd not have allowed me to touch you and kiss you in the parlor the other day."

She nodded, a silent reply, and bit at her lip until surely it would bleed beneath the pressure of her teeth.

He apparently would not have it. Reaching for her, he set aside the plates they held, placing the glasses on the ground carefully, lest they spill. And then she was on his lap, her face buried in the crease of neck and shoulder, and she felt the tears beneath her cheek and knew they soaked through his shirt to dampen his skin.

"I love you, sweetheart," he said, his lips moving against her temple. "I want to take you home with me and put you in my bed and never let you loose."

"That's what Pearl said you wanted," she mumbled against his skin.

"She did, did she? Smart lady, that one."

Augusta lifted her head to peer into his eyes. "If you really want…that is, when you get back—"

His hand over her lips halted the offer she would have made, and he shook his head. "Not on your life, Augusta McBride. I won't take advantage of you. Not without your promise to stand before the preacher and say the vows with me."

"I mean it, Cleary. I won't deny…" Her voice trailing off, she repeated the offer, yet stopped short, unable to speak the words that would deliver her soul into his hands.

"I do want. But only when I can call you my wife. You're a lady, Gussie. I won't turn you into a whore. Your mama would roll over in her grave if she knew you'd made such an offer."

"You don't know the half of it," she said mournfully.

"But thank you for turning me down. I don't know what I was thinking of." And if that wasn't a lie, she'd never told one.

The thought of spending nights in Cleary's bed brought forbidden dreams to her mind, and she yearned to know the reality of those visions that plagued her nightly. She knew. Oh, yes, she knew what she'd been thinking of. But it was not to be. No matter how seductive his kisses were, how tender his hands and lips.

Fate had decreed that she would never be a bride.

Chapter Eight

Beth Ann set off with a new dress, Augusta's valise stuffed full of remade clothing, and high hopes for her future back home with her family. Augusta, on the other hand, watched with an aching heart as the girl climbed on the morning train, heading for Saint Louis and stops in between. One of which was Beth Ann's hometown.

A quiet settled over the big house as its occupants went about their duties throughout the day, as though they mourned her departure. And indeed, they did. She'd become a part of their lives, and had only begun to shed her cocoon, emerging as a young woman capable of making a place for herself. To return to a father who might again be abusive could destroy Beth Ann, and that knowledge cast a pall over the ladies she left behind.

Augusta went to bed with a heavy heart. Not only had she waved a final farewell to Beth Ann, she also missed Cleary. There was no getting around it. He'd woven a web and she'd fallen headlong into it. And now she would pay the price for her foolishness. She lay beneath the sheet, hands folded beneath her breasts and thought of what words she might use to explain herself insofar as Cleary was concerned.

I'm the daughter of a whore. Well, that was direct and to the point, all right, and she laughed, a stifled sound of despair as she considered it. *My mother was called Little Dove. My father took her out of a house of ill repute and married her.* Now that might sound a bit better, she thought. Not quite as forthright, but again, to the point.

And either route would earn her his scorn. No, not scorn, for Jonathan Cleary was a gentleman, for all his secrecy and down-to-earth ways. But at least he would look at her with new eyes, casting aside the layers of respectability she'd assumed, and recognize that she had come from a woman whose living had been earned in a whorehouse.

She rolled to her side, covering her mouth with an open palm, lest her mournful sobs be heard through the walls of her bedroom. It was only here she could let down her guard, only in the silence of the night hours that she could allow herself to grieve for the future she was denied.

Sleep came late and morning early. The rooster in the chicken yard greeted the dawn with his usual chant. Three times in a row, echoed by another rooster a few houses away. Augusta pulled her pillow over her head and groaned, then set it aside. It was no use. She had responsibilities and looking at the ceiling would not accomplish a thing.

Breakfast was nearly ready by the time she reached the kitchen, and Bertha shot her a concerned look. "You all right, Miss Augusta? You're lookin' kinda peaked this morning."

"Didn't sleep well," Augusta admitted, reaching for a stack of plates from the buffet. Glory took them from her and placed them on the table before the assembled chairs. The table had gained the use of a leaf, with the coming of another occupant of the house, and with Cleary's frequent visits. It was no longer round but oval.

"If there's time, I'll go out and feed the chickens while y'all put the food on," Glory offered.

"Take the basket along and gather up the eggs while you're at it," Bertha told her. "We'll wait for you. Janine ain't outta bed yet, I'll warrant. I heard Pearl yatterin' at her a minute ago."

Glory nodded agreeably and snatched up the egg basket, then opened the back door and inhaled deeply. "Sure smells like morning out there," she said cheerfully, leaning to look past the chicken coop. "That's a dandy doghouse Mr. Cleary made."

"Where's the dog? I don't hear him." Augusta moved to the doorway, peering over Glory's shoulder to catch a glimpse of Henry. If he stretched his rope to its furthest point, he should be visible, yet there was no sign of him. And as Glory set off for the chicken coop, she was not greeted with puppy sounds of welcome.

"The dog's not out there," Bertha said, shooting a glare at the direction of the back stairway. "Somebody went out and hauled him in the house last night. I heard the door open and a few minutes later, somebody took him upstairs."

"I didn't hear anything," Augusta said.

"You were too busy cryin' into your pillow," Bertha told her.

"No such thing," Augusta denied, and then was silent as Bertha turned the full force of her disapproving look in her direction.

"Honey had that dog in her bedroom all night," Pearl announced from the kitchen doorway. "She said he was howling and she didn't want the neighbors to complain. Now she's kneeling on the floor mopping up a puddle."

Augusta didn't have it in her to admonish Honey as she carried Henry into the kitchen minutes later. She looked shamefaced as it was, shooting an apologetic smile in Augusta's direction as she hurried out the back door to tie Henry to his house. By the time she returned, Glory was at her heels, egg basket half full of good-sized eggs, and Bertha had the food on the table.

Augusta trailed across the yard, aware that her half-eaten meal had gained the notice of all the occupants of her house. But Henry was properly grateful for his morning repast, barely sniffing at the leftover sausage gravy and biscuits scraped from everyone's plates, before he dove into the pie pan half full of food. His water bowl was an old washbasin, and Augusta filled it with well water as he ate, then took the pie plate back to the house.

All mindless tasks, she realized, all designed to keep her mind from Cleary and what he was doing, wherever he might be this morning.

By suppertime, she'd managed to put him out of her mind, sitting down at the table with a list of accomplishments she'd made note of throughout the day. Between bites of Bertha's cold offering of leftovers and a bowl of fresh potato salad, she praised the work the ladies had accomplished. And then made plans for the garden, which was overflowing with tomatoes.

Bertha had looked askance at the basket from Carl Wilson's farm, muttering about "carrying coals to Newcastle," which went completely over the heads of most of the women gathered around the table that day. Augusta had nodded agreeably, not for the first time aware that her house mother had hidden depths.

Now a trip to the general store to purchase canning jars was in order, and Augusta made note of the requirements for the next day's chores. Too late today to accomplish the trip, but early morning would be better anyway, she decided, before the sun was overhead.

It wasn't until bedtime that she allowed herself once

more to consider Cleary's whereabouts, and then only in a perfunctory manner. She must rid her mind of the man, she decided, punching her pillow and setting her jaw. And then she heard the puppy begin to howl, and she rolled to her back, heaving a sigh of aggravation.

It would never do, she decided, after a full minute of listening to his plaintive carrying-on, and she sat on the edge of the bed, reaching for her slippers and robe. It was dark on the back stairs, the kitchen even darker, and she stubbed her toe on a chair as she passed the table. Limping, she headed out the back door, shushing the noisy dog as she went, wishing for the moon to come out from behind a cloud to light her way.

She had rounded the chicken coop when she became aware that Henry had stopped his noisy serenade and her steps slowed. Perhaps he'd given up and she could return to bed. Maybe…she peered ahead, only to see a tall figure standing near the doghouse, Henry in his arms. He slumped against the structure as she watched and she stepped forward again.

"It's me, Gussie." Cleary's voice sounded strained, his posture uneven, leaning a bit to one side and she approached him with caution.

"What's wrong?" Her intuition might be working overtime, but she sensed disaster as she neared him. "When did you get here?"

"A few minutes ago," he said, his voice sounding hollow. "I was riding past the house and I heard Henry raising a fuss out here. Thought I'd take a look and see if I could calm him down." And then with a quick look at her, Cleary slid to sit on the ground, the dog still clutched against his chest.

"Are you all right?" Augusta asked, crouching beside him. The odor of blood rose from his clothing, acrid in her nostrils, and she bent closer. "You've been wounded. Where are you hurt?"

"I'm fine, just a bit groggy," he said, his voice wavering on the words. "I guess I could use a hand, honey."

"What can I do?" All of her dithering had come to naught, she realized, for the reality of Cleary before her negated her every thought about putting him from her mind and life. "Are you bleeding now?" she asked.

He nodded, a barely perceptible movement of his head. "I need to be home, Gussie, in my own bed. I didn't want you involved in this, but I don't think I have a choice right now." He sighed deeply and his breath shuddered. "Help me get home, will you, sweetheart?"

"I'll take the pup," a voice said quietly from behind them, and Honey strode into sight from the shadows of the chicken coop. "You go on and do whatever you have to, Miss Augusta." She approached Cleary, arms outstretched, and he allowed her to take Henry from his grasp.

"Thank you, Honey," Augusta said quietly, and then turned back to Cleary. "Can you walk?"

"Well, if I can't you're gonna have a tough time getting me on that horse." His words were slurred, but as though he would reassure her, he tried to inject a note of humor. Leaning on the roof of the doghouse, he attempted to rise, and Augusta moved quickly to place her shoulder in his armpit for support. His long arm draped across her and his hand clutched at her as she turned him toward the shelter of the trees alongside her property line, where his horse blended into the shadows.

With a great deal of shifting and lifting, he was in the saddle, and Augusta placed a hand on his thigh, unaware of the intimacy of her gesture. All she knew what that Cleary needed her and she could not fail him.

"I'll go in and put on my clothing and find my container

of bandages and medicants," she told him. "Wait right here for me, will you?"

He nodded, and she turned away, her steps hurried as she crossed the yard and entered the house.

In less than five minutes she was at the door, taking her leave, when Pearl spoke from the back stoop. "Everything's quiet out there, Augusta. You watch your step, you hear? Honey told me what's going on, and I don't want you gettin' into a peck of trouble over any man. If you want me to, I'll go instead. My reputation's already about as plastered with mud as it can get."

"No, Pearl," Augusta said quietly. "I'll be back before sunrise, and I'll be sure no one sees me. You just take care of things here."

She ran the length of the yard and was breathless by the time she reached Cleary. "Slide your foot from the stirrup," she said, "and I'll climb on behind you."

He nodded, slumping over the saddle horn as if his strength was almost at an end, and she handed him her satchel, then clutched at his arm as she managed to gain the horse's backside. Her arms circled his waist and she leaned her head against his back as they rode in a roundabout route to his home on the other end of town.

He slid with a groan from his horse's back to land on his knees. Augusta almost collapsed, his weight dragging her with him as she attempted to keep him from landing fully on the ground. A muttered imprecation gave notice of his pain and she whispered encouragement, battling to catch his arm across her shoulder and lift him to his feet. The scent of blood, both dried and fresh was stronger now and she recognized that somewhere he had begun to bleed anew.

They'd ridden as close to the rear of the house as possible. Leaving the horse there, his reins touching the ground, Augusta hauled Cleary up the two steps to the stoop. The back door was unlocked, as she had expected, and they struggled through the doorway into the kitchen. This was new territory to her and she squinted through the darkness to find a doorway leading to the rest of the house.

It was not to be. Cleary fell to his knees and then, with a groan, sprawled facedown on the floor. Augusta was drawn with him, his arm around her neck hauling her to lie beside him, and she was careful as she slid from beneath its weight, lest she cause more trauma to his body than he'd already suffered.

The darkness altered as she became accustomed to it, and in the shadows she caught sight of a lamp hanging over the kitchen table. Her hands searched blindly on the surface of the furniture as she went from table to buffet to a cabinet against the far wall. There a pasteboard box met her fingertips. "Thank you," she whispered, sliding it open to find a supply of matches.

One rasping swipe against the rough texture on the side of the box brought a blaze of light that made her blink. The match glowed steadily and she stepped to the table, lifting the globe from the lamp and lighting the wick. It flared brightly and she turned to look finally at Cleary's body, sprawled across the middle of the floor.

A dark stain on his backside met her gaze.. The stain became more red in hue, as fresh blood gathered on the already matted fabric of his trousers. Dropping without heed to her knees, she discovered he'd tried to stanch the flow with a light jacket folded and stuffed inside his trousers.

Her hands slid beneath his stomach, where she undid his belt and the buttons of his pants, then tugged them down his hips, the better to see the site of his wound. His drawers slid to rest on his bottom, and the site of a bullet's path was exposed. It rode his hipbone, blood oozing from the long gash, but from what she could tell, he suffered more from loss of blood than the shock of containing a bullet within his body.

For that she was grateful and a long sigh of relief left her lips as she stood looking around the room, searching for a clean towel of some sort. The pantry was in darkness, but she lit another match and moved inside its cavernous interior. A supply of candles was on one shelf, an assortment of canned goods on another. And there, at eye level, was a stack of clean towels. She snatched them against her breast and reached for several candles, carrying her loot to the kitchen table.

The reservoir on the side of his cookstove held tepid water and she poured a dipper of it into his washbasin, scrubbed at it with a soapy cloth, then refilled it with clean water. A towel soaked it up quickly and she wrung it hard before placing it over the wound.

Her satchel sat beside her on the floor and she opened it, sorting quickly through the various jars and tubes of ointments. "Cobwebs," she whispered. "If I just had some cobwebs."

"Hell, the parlor's full of 'em," Cleary grumbled, his eyes closed, his face ashen in the lamplight.

"The parlor?" Augusta repeated. She bent closer, her nose almost touching his cheek. "You have cobwebs in your parlor?"

"Yeah. Haven't cleaned it since I moved in. Look up in the corners." One eye opened and he shifted position, an involuntary moan protesting his action. "Whadda you want with cobwebs, Gussie?"

"They'll stop the bleeding," she said, stifling the urge to press her lips against his cheek. He wouldn't bleed to death at least, not if she could disturb his cobwebs and apply them to the wound. "I'll be right back," she whispered, and was satisfied as he nodded.

A clean cloth from her satchel, tied to the end of his mop

handle did the trick, and she carefully carried her haul back to the kitchen. For once she'd been pleased at someone's scarcity of standards of cleanliness.

Cleary lay where she'd left him, and his eyes were closed again. The towel was stained beyond its limits to absorb the flow of blood and she frowned. Perhaps sending someone for the doctor would have been a better plan. If the cobwebs didn't work, she might have to go searching for the gentleman's house herself. It was in a mood of desperation that she found another clean towel and removed the bloody one, sopping up the residue of blood to reveal the open wound. A silent prayer wafted upward as she applied the gob of gossamer film to the shallow trench on Cleary's hip.

Folding a piece of clean, soft linen into a thick pad, she placed it atop the wound, holding it with one hand, trying to decide how to keep it there. A roll of bandage, torn from an old sheet nestled in a corner of her satchel, and she placed it over the pressure bandage and began wrapping it around his body.

As though he recognized her plan, Cleary lifted his lower body, pulling his knees beneath him as she circled his belly with her other arm, bringing the bandage fully around him. Aware of the bare skin she leaned against, she felt a blush warm her cheeks. If ever she'd thought of being this close to a man's body, with only her own clothing as a barrier to his masculine flesh...

And yet there was no help for it, and it obviously wasn't bothering Cleary. Again she wrapped the length of bandage around him, and he cursed beneath his breath, a profanity she excused, given the pain she knew her action was causing him.

"Just once more," she said quietly. "It has to be tight enough to hold it." He lifted again and she completed the third circling, then tied the bandage off in a knot.

"I'm going to try to get you to your bed," she told him, and was rewarded with a scathing look from dark eyes as he lifted his head and turned it fully toward her.

"I hate to spoil your plan, sweetheart," he growled, "but a pillow and blanket here will do just fine." He rolled halfway to his side, one arm cradling his head. "My bedroom's at the head of the stairs. I'll never make it there, not tonight anyway. You'll have to bring down what I need."

Augusta hesitated, then bowed to his determination and, lighting a candle, she left the kitchen to find the staircase leading to the second floor. Near the front door, as she expected, it rose in a half circle and she climbed it quickly, her eyes on the closest door. It opened with a squeak of hinges that needed oil and she entered Cleary's room. Unease gripped her, as if she had trespassed on his privacy, and she scanned the area quickly.

It was neat and tidy. Apparently his sloppy housekeeping did not extend to his bedroom. A dresser stood against one wall, a chair beside it. The bed was neatly made, the quilt folded at the foot. She caught a hint of his scent as she scooped up both pillows and grasped the bulky quilt beneath her arm. And scolded herself that she could think of the male aroma he exuded, now when he lay helpless on the kitchen floor.

Her feet barely brushed the treads as she sailed down the stairs and hurried to the kitchen. On her knees beside him, she lifted his head carefully and slid one pillow beneath it. The quilt unfolded with a snap of her wrists and she covered him, tucking it against his back and across his shoulder. A wisp of hair fell to cover her right eye and she blew at it futilely, then glanced down to find his gaze trained on her face.

"Thank you, Gussie." He slid his arm from beneath the quilt and touched the wayward lock, tucking it behind her ear. "Bend down here and kiss me, sweetheart," he told her with just a hint of pleading in his tone. "I need some loving."

Her heart squeezed within her chest and she gave way to his urging. Rising, she lifted the globe from the overhead lamp and blew out the light. The glass chimney settled with a clink of glass against metal and she stepped back to kneel beside Cleary. The extra pillow fit nicely beside him and she carefully tucked her clothing around her as she placed her head beside his.

"Gussie? I won't keep you here if you feel you need to go home," he said softly. "I wouldn't do anything to put you to shame, you know that."

"You won't," she answered, lifting the quilt and tugging it to fit over her shoulder. She faced him, the covering tented over them, and her hand lifted to rest against his chest. "I can't leave you, Cleary. If you should begin bleeding again or if you start a fever during the night, I need to be here with you."

"Can you do something for me?" he asked, his voice rasping, as if he swallowed pain and found it hard to digest. "Will you call me by my name? Not around the others, but when we're alone."

"Jonathan?" she asked, her palm flat against him, feeling the rise and fall of his breathing. "Can I call you Jon? Has anyone ever...?"

"No one," he said, the words spoken on a breath that sighed between his teeth. He was silent a moment, then his arm rose from his side to slide to her waist, then to her back, drawing her closer. "Say it again, Gussie."

"Jon." She tasted it in her mouth, knew a moment's pleasure as she recognized the intimacy of speaking a name none other had given him. "Jon." Again she whispered it, tipping her chin to look through the darkness to where his face was barely discernible. He was close, close enough to touch and she stretched the small distance to place her lips against his. It was an intimacy beyond the speaking of his name, perhaps a shameless move on her part, yet she could not resist the temptation he offered.

''Do that again, sweetheart,'' he said, his words slurring with the effort to speak.

And she could not resist his plea. She kissed him again, felt his lips soften and open as did hers. It was a gesture of love, without the heat of passion in the blending of their mouths. It was comfort, an assurance that she would be with him throughout the night hours. And he sighed as she drew away to settle her head once more beside his.

''We just gotta get married,'' he murmured, his voice raw as he moved beneath the quilt. A groan signified his pain was not eased, and Augusta bit at her lip, finally gathering the courage to suggest a solution she'd been trying to put aside.

''Do you have any liquor in the house?'' she asked. ''Would a drink ease your discomfort?''

''Yeah, I expect it would,'' he said. ''In the pantry, behind the sack of flour, there's a bottle of whiskey.''

In moments, she'd poured a dollop into a glass and offered it to him. He lifted on one elbow and she held it to his lips, allowing him to sip it slowly. And then he groaned. ''All of it,'' he said harshly, and she tilted the glass, hearing him swallow as he drank the final mouthful. ''Thanks.''

They lay beside each other, and Augusta lifted her hand to press against his cheek, then upward into his hair. The need to touch him was almost overpowering, and she bit back tears as she considered how close she had come to losing this man.

''Did you mean it?'' she asked quietly. ''About marrying me?''

''Yeah, I meant it,'' he told her.

''All right.''

''All right? Just like that?'' With a lurch, he attempted

to lift again to his elbow, but she halted his movement, shushing him and pressing him back against the floor.

"As soon as you like," she said. "When you're better. When your wound is healed."

"Hell, I feel better already," he said. "Damn, I feel downright—"

"Miserable, is what you feel, Cleary. Now just close your eyes and we'll talk about it tomorrow." She snuggled close, inhaling deeply of clothing holding the scent of his horse, the leather of his saddle and the clean male aroma of his chest and throat, rising from his skin to tempt her.

She'd left his trousers undone, so that the bandage would not be bound by the denim fabric, and his skin met her palm as she skimmed it the length of his side. She felt the bandage, deemed it dry and rested her fingers above it, where his hipbone was firm beneath her touch.

If they married, as she'd promised, she would touch him in just this way every day, anytime she wanted to. And that thought sent a shiver along her spine as he murmured her name against her temple.

"Gussie…" And then his breathing slowed a bit and he relaxed beside her. A whisper from his lips caught her ear and she held her breath, lest she miss his words. "Tomorrow. Promise."

"Yes, tomorrow," she said. "Tomorrow."

"You've really done it now," Pearl said glumly, standing aside as Augusta packed a basket with food.

"Really? Because I took care of a man who needed help? And now I'm taking him something to eat?"

"You know what I'm talking about, girl. You spent the whole live-long night with the man. And I'd be willing to lay odds that more than one of our fine, upstanding citizens saw you leave his house this morning."

Augusta reached for the side of bacon and began cutting

thick slices. "I walked the back way, and I arrived here at dawn." She looked up at Pearl, noting the woman's frown and the concern written on her face. "We all do what we have to, Pearl. You should know that as well as anyone. Yes, I stayed with him all night, and I'll probably stay there all day today. Somehow I have to get him into a bed and change his bandage and get him fed."

"There's a perfectly good doctor right smack in the middle of town," Pearl said stubbornly. "You could stop by his office and give him the job to handle." She lowered her voice and leaned closer. "Unless there's a good reason why nobody's s'posed to know that your fancy friend got shot in his hindquarters."

"Don't say such a thing," Augusta told her sharply. "The wound is across his hipbone, not his fanny."

"And you're gonna pull down his britches and put on a fresh bandage, are you?"

"I put on the first one." Augusta wrapped the sliced bacon in a dish towel and placed it in the basket, then counted out six eggs and enveloped them in another towel.

"There's a fresh loaf of bread," Pearl said grudgingly. "Bertha baked enough for an army. You might's well take a loaf along with you. And some butter to go with it."

Augusta peered into the basket, surveying her supply of food. "Have Janine carry a jar of soup over on her way back to work at noontime," she said. "Pearl...there's a lot I can't tell you, but you need to know that Cleary is on the up-and-up. He's an honest man, and even if he can't explain his actions to us right now, I believe in him."

"You got it real bad, ma'am," Pearl said sadly. "I'd say he's got you on a short leash, and you're not even thinking about getting loose, are you?"

"Well, that's an interesting way of putting it, I suppose," Augusta said. She lifted the basket and turned to the back door. "You might as well be the first to know, Pearl. Cleary and I will be getting married before long."

"Am I supposed to be surprised? We've been thinking that very thing since the first day he showed up here, sweetie. The man settled in for the long haul, right off. I knew he was dead serious."

"Well then, you knew a lot more than I did," Augusta told her with a short laugh. "In fact, I'm still not dead certain how I'm going to get past a wedding ceremony without being totally honest with the man."

"I always said you don't need to tell everything you know, right off," Pearl said. "It's a good thing for a woman to have a little mystery about her. Makes a man stick close."

"Well, when Cleary hears what I have to tell him one of these days, he may walk out the door and leave me holding the bag."

Pearl snorted, laughing aloud. "Not likely. He's besotted with you, girl. It'd take a team of horses to drag him away from you, once he gets you in bed and puts his mark on you. You don't stand a chance."

"We'll see," Augusta said quietly, stepping over the threshold. "I'll speak to Bertha before I leave. I see she's out in the garden already."

"She's after a batch of beans for dinner. Honey got real puny looking this morning and Bertha told her to take a lay-down on the bed."

The screen door slammed behind her as Augusta stepped from the stoop. She paused to speak with the housekeeper, then walked the back way to Cleary's house. If she could bring down a mattress, she'd put him in the parlor and then attack his collection of dust and the rest of the cobwebs.

The mattress slid down the staircase easily, and Augusta released her hold as soon as it was apparent that she might meet disaster should she attempt to guide its downward plunge. Hauling it into the parlor took her breath, but in moments she had it covered with a sheet and the pillow she'd slept on last night.

In the kitchen, she found Cleary beneath the quilt, grumpy and grimly determined to climb the stairs. "There's not a reason on God's green earth why I can't go upstairs and sleep in my bed," he told her, shoving the pillow to one side as he sat upright. His face paled with his effort and Augusta knelt beside him.

"There's every reason in the world," she told him. "In the first place, I've already toted your mattress into the parlor, and I'm not about to carry it back upstairs."

"That probably wasn't the brightest thing you've ever done." His mouth was set in a mulish pout.

"No one ever said I was the smartest woman in the world."

He looked subdued, reaching for her hand. "I'm not being very nice. Especially not after you took care of me all night."

"Especially since I'm going to feed you the best breakfast you've had all week, just as soon as I get you out of my way."

"I wondered what you brought in that basket." His eyes closed for a moment and then he looked up at her, and an embarrassed grin touched his lips. "I may not be up to finding out if the preacher's available today, sweetheart. Maybe tomorrow. Will that be all right?"

Augusta nodded. "I'm more concerned with getting you into the parlor right now. Help me, Cleary." With care, he rose, clutching the back of a kitchen chair with one hand, grasping her shoulder with the other.

A groan escaped his lips as they began the trek, and by the time the parlor doors were behind them, he was clammy with perspiration, trembling as if he had a case of ague and muttering beneath his breath. With a sigh of relief, he lowered himself to the mattress and edged carefully to lie on his side.

"You going to change the bandage?" he asked, arching a brow as he looked up at her. "If you're planning on stripping off my trousers, you'd better have at it while I'm still able to help."

Her eyes were intent on him as he began the task of sliding his denim trousers down his thighs. "That's far enough. Just turn a bit more to your side and I'll cut through the bandages." She'd gotten to the heavy padding over his wound when a sharp rap on the front door caught her attention. Her sigh was deep, and for a moment she considered ignoring the visitor. Yet it might be important, perhaps Nicholas Garvey come to check on Cleary.

"Don't move," she admonished him. "I'll see who it is."

Outside the beveled glass insert gracing Cleary's front door stood the figures of a man and woman, starched and prim, meeting her gaze solemnly. She was tempted to turn tail and run, scoot out the back door and make tracks for her house on the other side of Collins Creek. But it was too late.

A look of disapproval, mixed with disappointment, formed a mask, turning Penelope Young's face into stone. Beside her, the Reverend Young took a deep breath, his chest seeming to rise to his throat, where a tie was tied firmly in place.

Augusta opened the door.

Chapter Nine

"We've come to set a rumor at rest."

Well, Augusta thought despairingly, that was clear enough. She forced a smile and opened the screened door, inviting the visitors inside.

"Gussie, get in here and do your stuff." From the parlor, Cleary's voice was impatient, and Augusta closed her eyes, a rare feeling of helplessness enfolding her.

"Your *stuff*?" Penelope repeated, her voice rising on the final word, imbuing it with a whole new meaning. "What on earth—"

"Mr. Cleary really isn't up to having visitors right now," Augusta said quickly, moving to shield the open parlor doors from the minister's sharp gaze.

"What's wrong with him? Can I help?" His forehead wrinkling with concern, the man brushed past Augusta's firm stance and came to a halt beneath the lintel of the parlor door. "Well," he said uneasily, "I'd say you have a situation here."

"I'd be glad to lend a hand," Penelope said, striding from the open screened door to where her husband stood.

"Get back, Pen," he said abruptly, turning to grasp her

arms, turning her aside before she could catch sight of Cleary's bare skin exposed below his waistband.

Augusta closed her eyes, weaving where she stood. "This isn't what it appears to be," she said faintly. "Mr. Cleary has a problem—"

"I can see that," Mr. Young said sternly. His steely gaze met Augusta's eyes just as Cleary turned his head toward the door.

"What the—" Cut off in mid-thought, he glared at Augusta, then in turn at the minister and beyond him to where Penelope stared wide-eyed at the man whose pale skin held a large, rectangular bandage. "Why don't we just charge admission while we're at it, Augusta?"

It was too much. Considering the long night with little sleep, and a mountain of worry keeping her company, then the rush home in the darkness before dawn to find food for Cleary, and change her own clothes, she decided she was worn-out. Now to be faced with the most dignified couple in town, with Cleary's bottom almost exposed in the middle of the parlor...

It was indeed too much. Augusta felt the first tears begin their slow slide down her cheeks, and heard Cleary's choice curse words as he struggled to get to his feet. One hand clutched at the waistband of his trousers, the other leaning heavily on the back of a leather chair, as he stood with dark hair hanging over his forehead, his eyes like black marbles.

"Don't you dare cry, Augusta McBride. Tears never solve anything."

"That's easy for you to say, young man." Penelope's judgment was stern, her mouth drawn in a firm moue as she faced Cleary. "A bad reputation doesn't mean much to a man like you, but to Miss McBride it could be the end of her world as she knows it."

Cleary stood as upright as he was going to get, at least for now, and his jaw jutted forward as he buttoned the fly of his pants. "Well, I'd say the world as she knows it could be improved upon mightily. Trying to make a home for women who need a champion is a thankless task, as far as I can see, and Augusta is about worn-out, working herself to death for their benefit."

"You don't care about her reputation?" The Reverend Young ran his gaze over the cluttered parlor, where dust and furniture had formed a firm relationship.

"Of course, I do," Cleary said. "If I weren't laid up with this sore hip, I'd have been on my way to the church this morning to arrange for a wedding. As it is, it was handy of you to show up at my door."

Penelope touched Augusta's hand, and her eyes were filled with sympathy. "We got no less than four messages early this morning that you were seen making your way home from this place, *before dawn*." Her voice trembled as she spoke the final words, and Augusta waited expectantly to see the woman's eyes roll back in her head at the very idea of such a thing happening.

"I was here to help Mr. Cleary," Augusta said quietly. "He was injured and I stopped the bleeding and applied a bandage."

"On his…" As if the words could not be uttered aloud, Penelope only gestured in Cleary's direction.

"Yes, on my hip." His mouth was thin, his eyes narrowed as he faced the visitors. "If you would like to do the honors in my home, instead of at the church, Parson, you can have a ceremony, here and now, for Miss McBride and myself."

A nod of agreement was exchanged between the two men and Cleary held out a hand to Augusta. "Come here, Gussie. You're about to become a wife."

"I didn't plan…"

"Neither did I," he said quietly as she crossed the floor to stand before him. "At least not today, not this way. But it doesn't matter. What counts is that I get to call you Mrs. Cleary, and you get to wear a wedding ring and belong to me." He leaned heavily on the chair beside him, and his eyes held hers with a look of pleading she could not resist.

Augusta was torn as she faced the prospect of a wedding that held all the elements of a shotgun situation. Her heart ached as she recognized the potential harm to her ladies and the haven she'd created for their benefit, should gossip spread throughout the town.

"Reach into my trouser's pocket," Cleary said, his eyes fastened on Augusta's face. "There's a small box there."

"A box?" Her fingers slid timidly to his pocket opening and he shook his head.

"The other side."

"Oh, all right." Again she forced herself to press her hand into the length of his pocket, until her finger touched the square container he carried. "Where did this come from?" She turned it in her hand, a small, green velvet box, worn on the corners.

"It was my grandmother's ring. She left it to me, and told me I should be very choosy about the woman I gave it to. I was going to show it to you last night." A crooked smile curved his lips, and he covered both her hands with one of his. "She'd be pleased with you, Augusta."

The words of his approval brought quick tears, and she brushed them away impatiently. "Are you sure?" she asked softly, searching for some sign, some magic moment in which she would know and recognize love in his voice and eyes.

He nodded. "I'm sure. I told you the other day that this was what I wanted for us. I haven't changed my mind."

"Well," the minister said, clearing his throat and adjusting his waistcoat. "I don't have my book with me, but I think I can recall from memory most of the ceremony."

He turned to his wife. "Stand over here, Pen. We'll need a witness."

Cleary had never paid much attention to the vows spoken during the few weddings he'd attended or been a part of, usually forcing himself to be patient as the words droned on and on. The dancing with pretty girls and the drinking of punch, usually spiked by some friend of the groom, were first and foremost on his mind.

Today he listened, and if the Reverend Young missed any of the essential parts, Cleary did not recognize the loss. He repeated his vows, watched Augusta as she spoke promises on his behalf, and then attended to sliding the ring over her knuckle to be clenched in place as her fingers curled to secure it. He lifted her hand and pressed his lips against the place where gold and pearls met pale, smooth skin.

"You may kiss your bride."

The words were welcome, and Cleary circled his wife's waist with one arm, still holding the chair with the other hand to balance himself. His hip throbbed like a house afire, and his leg ached like the worst toothache he'd ever had. And yet a sense of completion, of coming home, filled his heart, and he gathered Gussie to his chest and bent to bestow his kiss against her mouth.

Cool and chaste, his caress touched her trembling lips and drew away. "Hello there, Mrs. Cleary," he said quietly, aware of Penelope's handkerchief coming into play as the lady sniffed and blew with decorum into a lacy square of linen.

"We're really married." As if she could not believe it, Augusta turned to the minister. "Is that it? Will you give us a certificate so we can frame it and place it on the parlor wall?"

"Yes, indeed," he said, smiling brightly now that he'd solved the problem of decency so neatly. "I wouldn't be surprised if the ladies come visiting with gifts one day soon."

Cleary's whisper was soft in her ear. "I wouldn't count on that if I were you. Not until you move in here and live in my house. 'Cause I'm sure not going to park my carcass in that houseful of women on the other side of town."

"I'm married." She'd thought about it all the way home, deciding how best to break the news. Only to decide that the simplest way might be the easiest. And so she repeated the words as five women sat around the kitchen table and stared at her as if they beheld a two-headed monster from the swamp.

"How did that happen?" Honey was the first one to gain her feet and she tugged at her dress as she faced Augusta. "I mean, we didn't know it was gonna be today."

"We were kinda talking about a party for you and Cleary," Pearl said. "But then we decided it might not be too well attended, should we invite any of the townsfolk."

"The townsfolk I care about live in this house."

"Well, you'll have a place in town society now," Janine said. "I doubt the good folks of Collins Creek will appreciate you hanging around with the lot of us."

"This is my home," Augusta said. "Cleary wants me to move into his house, so I'll probably have to do that, but this will always be home to me. I'll be here every day. That much won't change. And we'll still be finding a future for all of you."

"How about a party today?" Honey looked hopeful. "I can bake cookies pretty good, and Bertha already has a big ham ready for the oven for dinner, and maybe we can think of a few folks to invite."

"Cleary's not quite up to a party, yet," Augusta said slowly, unsure how much of the man's situation these women should be aware of. "He's having a hard time moving around, but a couple of days will make a big difference, I'm sure.''

''Did he get shot, Miss Augusta?'' Glory's eyes were huge as she asked the question. ''We only just know that he was hurt and you took him home.''

''Yes.'' It might not be wise to give any more details than necessary to these women, but they were not prone to gossip and, except for Janine, none of them were out and about. ''He got shot, but the wound is shallow and it should heal fast. It just bled a lot.'' Her hands brushed together in a gesture of readiness. ''Well, now, let's get to work. We have a lot to accomplish today. Janine must go to work and some of us will be canning tomatoes from the garden.''

''I'll dust and run the carpet sweeper,'' Honey offered cheerfully. ''And I've got ironing to do for Mrs. Burns.'' She stood and pushed her chair beneath the table, then turned to face Augusta. ''Will you be taking Henry with you over to Cleary's place?''

Honey's wistful expression was a dead giveaway, Augusta decided. The girl had grown tremendously attached to the dog, and it seemed mean hearted to take the pup from here to Cleary's place. ''No, I think this house needs a watchdog and Henry is attached to all of you already. He'll stay here. After all, I'll be here a good share of the time anyway.''

With that matter of business settled, the women scattered in various directions and Augusta followed Glory out the back door. ''I'll take care of the chickens first, ma'am, and then help with the tomatoes.''

''Glory…what do you want to do with the rest of your life?'' The girl was slender to the point of being thin, and her dark eyes held painful memories; yet, there was a hopeful air about her that encouraged Augusta. ''Would you like to marry someday, have a family of your own?''

A crimson stain covered Glory's cheeks. ''I don't think

any decent man would want me to have his children. I'm a fallen woman, ma'am, and that's the truth. About the best I'll ever do is to maybe cook in the hotel or clean up after folks.''

"Oh, no. Don't ever think that. There are good men in this world, Glory. I just know that someday one of them will see you and appreciate your fine qualities.''

"I won't be a slave to a man." Glory's chin lifted defensively. "I'll never let a man hurt me again, or use me—" Her words halted abruptly. "You don't have the least idea about such things, ma'am. Mr. Cleary is a fine gentleman, and he'll treat you right.''

Augusta sighed, acknowledging the truth in that statement with a nod. "Yet, I feel driven to help all of you," she said. "In fact, I've been hoping that the other ladies I spoke to in Dallas would show up here before now.''

"Most of the girls are scared to run off. There's some of them that don't think there's any chance for a different way of living." She lifted her chin and her eyes glittered with pride. "I knew I couldn't live that way the rest of my life.''

Bertha pushed open the screened door and stuck her head out, calling to Augusta. "There's a man in the parlor lookin' for you. Good-lookin' son of a gun.''

"I'll be right in." Augusta smoothed her hair back and brushed at her skirt. "You go ahead and tend to the chickens, and I'll be back to help you pick tomatoes in just a little bit," she told Glory.

The man in the parlor was indeed a good-looking specimen, and Augusta smiled as he stepped toward her. "Good morning, Mr. Garvey. What can I do for you?''

He wore a sober look, and his glance toward the doorway told Augusta that privacy was important. She turned and slid the parlor doors shut and faced the banker once more.

"Is Cleary here?" he asked quietly. "I got word that he

disappeared yesterday, late in the afternoon, and I haven't heard from him. I thought you might know where he is."

"He was here, but he isn't now."

"Is he all right?"

She shook her head. "When I left him this morning he was sleeping, but he won't be up and around for a few days." Her hands were clasped at her waist and she glanced down as her fingers traced the lines of the ring she wore. Nicholas Garvey's gaze touched the glistening gold and the muted gleam of pearls, and his eyes narrowed as they swept up to rest on her face.

"I didn't notice your ring when we met before, ma'am. Is it new?"

"No. In fact, it's a family heirloom, sir. It belonged to Mr. Cleary's grandmother."

"And now you wear it?" His brow rose in silent query. "Is there something you'd like to tell me?"

"I suspect you've already surmised why I'm wearing the ring." Augusta was enjoying this play of words, suddenly basking in the knowledge that she was a married woman. There was a new confidence in her bearing. She felt... *honored* seemed a good word to describe her new position in life. Cleary had cared enough to marry her, had given her his prized possession to wear.

"I have to assume you're a married lady, ma'am. And I'd say congratulations are in order." He slid his hands into his trouser pockets and rocked on his heels, exuding an attitude of satisfaction. "Now if I could locate Cleary, I'd be happy to offer him my hand and tell him what a fortunate fellow he is."

"He's at home. And I'm sure he'd be happy to have you stop by." She considered that statement for a moment. "Maybe not happy, exactly, given his present state, but if you'll open the front door and call out, I'm sure he'll invite you into the parlor."

"Into the parlor. He's sleeping in the parlor?"

"I dragged his mattress down the stairs. It was easier than dragging him up to the second floor."

"I think you're quite an inventive young woman, but I'm not going to ask you why all that was necessary." Nicholas was quite dashing when he smiled, Augusta decided. And she couldn't decide if he were flirting with her, just a bit, or not.

"But do allow me to extend my best wishes on your marriage, ma'am," he said politely. "May I ask how long you've been keeping this a secret?"

Augusta made a great show of looking at her lapel watch. "About three hours now."

"You were married this morning?"

She nodded. "It seemed like a good idea."

His smile faded, replaced by a more serious demeanor. "Did Cleary tell you anything? About his trip? Or the results?"

She shook her head. "Apparently there are some things he doesn't consider his wife should be concerned with."

"He's a good man, ma'am, you can be certain of that."

"If I were not, I wouldn't be wearing his ring, Mr. Garvey."

With a pounding like thunder on his front door, Cleary was made aware of a visitor. He struggled to sit up on his mattress and reached to comb his hair back, his long fingers making tunnels in the dark length. "Yes, come on in." Sounded like a damn bear, he decided, his voice deep and harsh.

"I hear congratulations are in order." Nicholas stood in the parlor doorway and grinned. "How'd you ever manage that, old man?" He strolled past the dusty tables, across the worn carpet and took a seat on the brocade couch. His hat found a spot beside him and he crossed his ankles, leaning back as he quirked an eyebrow at Cleary.

"Augusta is not the sort of woman any gentleman would hold up to ridicule. She spent the night here, and when the minister came to rescue her from my clutches, I thought it an opportune time to take a wife."

Nicholas snagged the pivotal point and repeated it. "She spent the night here?"

"Tending to my bullet wound." Frustration rode each syllable.

The banker sat up straight. "Where? And how?"

"Where? Too damn close to my butt for comfort. As to how, some fuzzy-cheeked deputy with poor aim turned his gun on me while I was riding away. Pretty near shot my horse."

"Were you exposed?"

"Hell, no. The law was after me. That gang probably thinks I've got a record a mile long."

"Well, we're about ready to round up the whole bunch of them, and you'll be out of this altogether. Did you find out their plans for the gold shipment?"

"I gave them the location and told them I'd have a man in the mail car. They won't be expecting a setup."

Nicholas smiled grimly. "Will you be ready to ride by then?"

"It's weeks away. I'll be fine. Couple of days and this thing should be all healed up."

"You haven't told Miss McBride everything, I understand."

"I haven't told her much of anything," Cleary said. "The less she knows, the better off she'll be." He shifted to the head of the mattress and leaned on the overstuffed chair behind him. "And you'd better be putting things in place for the next part of this plan, Nick."

"It's taken care of. The banking community doesn't for-

get the sort of thing you're doing for us.'' He rose from
the couch and picked up his hat.

"You've got a fine wife. Are you planning on living with
her?'' Amusement lit his words, and a grin touched his lips.

"Damn right I am.''

"Here or there?'' Nicholas's smile widened as he
awaited a reply.

"There's more privacy here. She'll be home in time to
cook supper. I'm hoping she'll bring her valise with her.''
He considered that idea for a moment and then looked up
at Nicholas.

"On second thought, how about dropping by the livery
stable and hiring a wagon to go over to pick up all her
belongings. Let her know I sent it.''

With a half salute, Nicholas agreed, and in moments the
front door closed firmly behind him.

Cleary slid down with care, favoring his hip, and con-
templated the evening ahead.

"He don't waste no time, does he?'' Pearl watched as
the burly gentleman from the livery stable carried Augusta's trunk down the staircase. Heavy though it was, he'd
hoisted it on his shoulder and was passing through the front
door on his way to the wagon out front.

"Who? Cleary?'' Augusta was flustered and rosy with
embarrassment generated by the man who'd told her Mr.
Cleary had sent him, and he was to bring her, bag and
baggage, to his home.

"Who else, honey?'' Pearl's eyes gleamed as the tall,
muscular man came back in the house and shot a considering look in her direction. His feet were heavy on the
treads as he climbed back up the stairs, and Augusta hastened to keep up.

He was in the middle of her room, and as she entered

he looked back at her over his shoulder. "Just the valise, ma'am?"

"That and a box of books," Augusta said. "But they can wait until another time."

The man shook his head. "No, ma'am. Mr. Cleary's message was that I was to bring everything you owned over to his place. I'll get the books right now."

The man was bossy, issuing orders from a mattress in his parlor and expecting everyone to bow to his will. And as she bustled down the stairs behind the behemoth carrying the rest of her belongings, Augusta blew out a breath of exasperation. Love, honor and *obey*. That dreaded word had been a part of her vows, and she'd glibly repeated it after the minister without a thought as to how soon it would come into play.

"You about ready to ride along, ma'am?" He'd loaded the final bits and pieces contained in her second best valise, Beth Ann having been given the good tapestry bag. Now he awaited her presence on his wagon.

"You'd best go along," Bertha said placidly. "I fixed a basket for dinner for the two of you. Fried chicken and ham sandwiches and deviled eggs. There's a couple of tomatoes to slice and a jar of beans to heat up."

"If I never see another tomato in my life, it won't be too soon to suit me."

"Well, your mister likes them just fine," Bertha said. "Besides, canning tomatoes always makes you sick of 'em. It's the smell, I think."

"I surely do enjoy a picnic." Cleary picked up another sandwich and fit his mouth around the thick mound of sliced ham it contained. "Maybe we can talk Bertha into coming here a couple of days a week. I'm gonna miss her cooking."

"I'm a fair cook myself." Augusta chose one of Honey's

cookies from the tin box the girl had sent along. And then she sent a wry glance in Cleary's direction. "You sure you don't want to just move in over there? It'd be right handy, having a cook and housekeeper on the premises."

"I'd rather have a wife, and a bit of privacy." His eyes gleamed over the top of his sandwich as he bit into it, and he brushed negligently at a crumb on his mustache as he chewed. "We'll probably both be spending time over there, you especially, but we can have one of the women come here and redd up the place for you every week if you like."

"*Redding up* isn't going to cut it, Cleary. This house needs a top-to-bottom cleaning, and for that I'm going to bring over all the ladies for a day. This carpet is probably lovely underneath all the dust, but it's pretty hard to tell for sure. And those draperies haven't been shaken out in years."

"Well, those ladies of yours aren't coming tonight, I'll tell you that much," he said firmly. "One way or another, we're going to have a wedding night, Gussie."

She felt her heart race as she thought of what a wedding night might consist of, and she leaned to gather up the bits and pieces of their picnic. A stop at the icehouse had provided a fifteen-pound chunk, and the driver had slid it into the bottom of the box for her, making it ready to hold the leftovers from their wedding supper. She'd wash up the dishes quickly. And after that…

She looked at him, noting the lines drawn around his mouth. "What about your wound?"

"Don't worry about my wound. It's just a scratch, anyway."

She laughed aloud. "A *scratch?* You're forgetting something, Cleary. I saw that *scratch* last night. I was the one who washed it and rounded up cobwebs and padded it up so it wouldn't bleed all over the place."

"I haven't forgotten. Not for a minute, Gussie. First time

I've ever had my fanny exposed to a lady in quite that way.'' He grinned at her and reached for her hand. ''You didn't even flinch, sweetheart. You just cleaned it up and did what you had to do. I didn't know how you'd handle taking care of me, and I was sorta thrown for a loop when you just dug in and took over.''

''I didn't look at your fanny,'' she said primly. ''All I saw was that long, bloody gouge in your skin, and I knew I had to stop the blood flow. Either that or go find a doctor, and I wasn't sure you'd let me do that.''

''You're right there.'' He lifted her hand to his mouth and turned it to kiss her palm. ''Your ladies won't tell anyone, will they? That I was wounded, I mean?''

She thought his action was meant to mask the importance of his question. But there was no sense in making him worry over exposure, even if he didn't have the good sense to come right out and ask her to cover up the events of the evening.

''My ladies have been keeping secrets for years, Cleary. They aren't about to go running all over town, telling folks that you were dumb enough to get shot in your backside.''

''It's not in my backside,'' he said, a sulky look invading his features. ''I'd like to have a little dignity left to me. You're supposed to love, honor and obey. Remember?''

''I think I've done my share of obeying for today,'' she said primly. If he was going to pout, there wasn't any reason for her to put up with it, she decided. And Cleary had better find out right off the bat that she would not be dictated to.

''You? Obey? When did this happen?'' He truly seemed puzzled, and yet, Cleary was a scamp. Perhaps his eyes were a bit too wide, his amazement a bit contrived.

''You sent a wagon for me, with orders to pack my belongings and get everything loaded up for a trip across town.''

"Get everything loaded up?" She thought his mouth took on a grim line, his eyes a gleam of leashed anger. "Tell me you didn't lift your things onto that wagon. Or carry one single box or bag down those stairs and out that front door. Except for that sleek little body, I don't want to know that you were responsible for toting one thing from that house to this one."

Her sigh was deep, and she reached to touch his face with her fingertips. "So quickly you rise to my defense. Of course, I didn't carry my things. That giant ox of a man from the livery stable took care of everything." She ran through his words, those terse sentences he'd leveled in her direction.

"I didn't know you were so prickly, Jonathan Cleary." Her hand flattened against his cheek, then curved to enclose his jaw, her fingers ruffling the hair above his ear. "Do you always leap to the aid of the ladies in your care?"

"I've never been married before, Gussie. I've never cared about another woman the way I do you. You durn betcha I'll be *prickly* where you're concerned. Like it or not, I intend to take care of you for the rest of your life."

"Well, that's quite a statement," she said quietly. He'll take care of you, but notice he didn't say he loves you, she thought. Her heart clenched within her breast as she allowed her hand to drop to her lap, and she searched for a fresh note to instill, to somehow bring back the easy flow of their communication.

As if he read her thoughts, he tilted his head and frowned. "Who was the giant ox of a man you mentioned? Sam Ferguson?"

She shrugged. "Maybe so. Just someone from the livery stable," she said. "You should have seen the way he looked at Pearl, and the gleam in her eye when she watched him climb the staircase. I had to wonder if he knew her. You know, if he'd...met her before."

"Well, she knows not to have company while she's in your house, doesn't she?"

Augusta nodded. "She won't allow him to visit. But that's not saying she wouldn't be interested should he be on the lookout for a bride. She told me she's not interested in a man in her life, but her eyes were as shiny as a new penny when she got a gander at him."

"Look at me, Gussie."

"What?" Her mind on Pearl, she turned her head and glanced at Cleary, and then took stock of his expression. "I'm looking," she said after a moment.

"Blue eyes don't shine like new pennies," he said softly. "But once in a while, yours look kinda like a summer sky or a bluebird's wing."

"Do they?" She felt ill at ease, his close scrutiny making her fidget, as though he saw deep inside her and knew the lack of knowledge and total inexperience his bride possessed. "I always thought they were just plain blue." She placed the basket at the foot of the mattress and made a great show of folding the napkins they'd used.

Cleary bent to her and whispered, "They're beautiful, sweetheart. Like the rest of you." He leaned on his elbow then, his uninjured hip against the mattress where they'd had their impromptu picnic. "You know what? I'd like to see your hair hanging down your back. I want to run my fingers through your waves and wrap the whole length of it around my hand. And then I want to spread it over that pillow."

"My hair?" She swallowed, a hard lump seeming to form in her throat. "It's just ordinary yellow hair, Cleary."

"There's nothing ordinary about you, sweet." His gaze touched her, skimming her face and throat, then resting for a moment on her breasts. "Say my name, Gussie. You told me you would."

"Jonathan? You want me to call you Jonathan?"

"That'll work, I suppose. But you called me Jon before. Remember?"

"Yes, I remember." Surely this wasn't her voice, this thin thread of sound that fought to escape past the swelling in her chest that filled her lungs, threatening to take her breath.

"Are you frightened of me, sweetheart?" He lifted his free hand and tugged her to join him, drawing her down to kneel by his side on the mattress.

"No, of course not." There was a demand in his eyes now that accelerated her breathing and sent a shimmering warmth to the depths of her belly. "I'm not afraid. I'm not sure what you expect of me, but I know you won't hurt me, Jonathan."

"Ah, but I likely will, I fear," he said, denying her faith in him.

"I knew I should have asked Pearl about this," she muttered as she tried to decipher his meaning.

He grinned, his eyes glittering, his teeth gleaming, and she was reminded of a wolf eyeing his prey. "I'll answer all your questions." His voice had become rusty, his tone rasping as he soothed her uncertainty.

Her eyes opened wide, her hands twisting at her waist. "Maybe we should wait until you feel a lot better. I wouldn't want you to start bleeding again."

He looked around the parlor, his gaze seeking out the corners where cobwebs still hung in several places, from draperies to the ceiling, from ceiling to wall. "I'd say we have enough in here to cover that problem, should it arise. Probably enough to supply a whole hospital," he told her, grinning as if he found an unbelievable depth of amusement in her words.

"I don't plan on harming myself, Gussie. In fact, I'll bet we can do this without any major damage being done to either of us."

He sobered then and tugged her down to press his lips against hers, a brief, tender caress. And then he looked directly into her eyes. "You have any questions you need to have answered before I take your clothes off, sweetheart?"

Chapter Ten

"Are we going to do this right now?" Augusta waved a hand distractedly toward the window, as if to call Cleary's attention to the fact that the sun was only now setting, casting a pink glow across the western horizon. It would be some time before full darkness descended, and to say that his bride was apprehensive was an understatement.

"I thought we might," he said, his fingers removing white pearly buttons from their moorings in a casual manner. He'd hoped to get a glimpse of Augusta's charms, and unless he missed his guess, she wasn't about to let him light a lamp, even if he felt so inclined. The truth was, the thought of rising from the mattress gave him a definite pain in his backside. Getting her to kneel beside him had been a stroke of good fortune.

How he was going to conduct this wedding night was still a puzzle, but one he was certain he was capable of solving, given a bit of cooperation from his bride. "Your heart is goin' a mile a minute, Gussie," he whispered, bending to brush his mouth against the pale triangle of flesh he'd managed to expose at her throat. Three buttons undone, and many more to go.

"We've already done this, you know, undoing my dress,

once before," she reminded him. "I thought you might just skip this part. I don't mind having my clothes on. Really."

"Naw, I don't think so. I kinda like peeling off your layers and getting down to brass tacks." He watched as she attempted a smile. Her mouth trembled, and he touched it with a fingertip, pressing the plush surface until his finger was taken prisoner between her lips.

She blinked in surprise and he rubbed the inside of her bottom lip, watching as she shivered. And then he drew her head toward him with his other hand, fingers tangling in her hair as he guided her closer. His mouth replaced that wandering finger and he suckled gently there, his teeth touching with care, as his hand moved to curve beneath her breast.

Through the layers of fabric, he felt the definite rounding of firm flesh and heard her indrawn gasp as she responded to his touch. "Cleary? I don't think I can breathe."

"You're doin' just fine, sweetheart. I can feel your chest moving right here under my hand." And as if to prove his claim he formed her breast more firmly within his grasp. His grip slid upward to encompass the firm crest and it pressed against his palm with satisfying speed, as though that tiny bit of rosy flesh welcomed the movement of his body against hers, even through the restriction of fabric.

It wasn't enough, he thought, reining in the desire that blossomed in the wake of her innocent movement. Though he'd had a long dry spell, over a year in fact, without a woman to ease his needs, he'd planned to restrain himself, bring her slowly and gradually to a state of yearning. And when he knew she was ready, was comfortable with his touch, he would take pleasure in easing her introduction to the act of loving.

There would be pain—of that he was certain—for his bride was innocent, a virgin. Though she might be versed in the plight of the women she helped, she knew little of the hard, cold facts of their lives, only that they were used for the pleasure of men. And even that knowledge was limited, since he was certain the ladies had sheltered her from much of the details of their lives.

Gussie was somehow driven to offer a haven to the unfortunates she'd gathered to her bosom. Whatever her reasons, she kept them to herself, where they might remain a mystery for a time. He'd decided from the beginning not to pressure her, but instead use every skill he possessed to gain her confidence. And in doing that, perhaps her love. Because looking into his future, without the vision of Gussie by his side, was not to be countenanced.

But for now, he would be somewhat satisfied to get her out of the layers of clothing she wore. And that might prove to be difficult, given the time of day and the degree of her modesty. Slowly he released his hold on her and thought he heard a sigh escape her lips, as though she rued his retreat. It gave him encouragement, as she peered into his eyes, looking for all the world like a woman in a state of anticipation, awaiting his next move.

Whatever it might be, whatever he did now, would tinge their relationship forever, and he was at sea, unversed in the seduction of a virgin. It was like playing the piano by ear, he decided. You could only plunge ahead, listening for the chords that blended into a pleasing harmony. But none of that could be accomplished until he had her as close to naked as he could arrange. He'd been this far before, that day in the parlor, and thus far she was not protesting his actions. That thought was encouraging.

His fingers slowly completed the process of undoing her dress, and she allowed it without protest, her gaze falling from his face to watch his agile hands as they stripped the garment from her shoulders and lowered it to her waist. Her chemise undone, he opened it wide to feast his eyes on the rounding of her bosom, the pale skin and peaked crests, and found she was even lovelier than he'd thought on his first swift appraisal.

The chemise slid easily down her arms, and his fingers returned quickly to her waist. There he found the strings that kept her petticoat and drawers in place, and with agile movements he untied them. "You'll have to stand up, sweetheart," he murmured. "I want to get these things off you."

And wonder of wonders, she did as he asked, perhaps, he thought, influenced by the vows she'd spoken this morning. *Obey.* His favorite word, he decided cheerfully, especially if that memory made his Gussie this docile and willing to oblige. As she rose, the clothing slid to the floor and he heard her indrawn gasp.

Then he watched as her hands dropped to shield the apex of her thighs. Her slender fingers were tanned, framed by the golden triangle she guarded, where skin that had never known the kiss of sunlight appeared fragile to his eager eyes.

He looked up into eyes that had darkened and held a fearful element. Yet, his lips curved involuntarily, and his voice was a husky groan. "I think you're the loveliest creature I've ever seen." Reaching up, he clasped her hands, his own trembling as he drew them aside, exposing the golden thatch she'd tried to hide.

"That's just a part of your body, Gussie. And I'm prepared to love all of you, from head to toe. There won't be any secrets between us." His fingers brushed across the soft curls and he yearned to delve beneath their cover to where damp flesh awaited discovery. But her hands turned to cover his and she whispered his name.

"Jonathan." Just that, his name, as though she would halt his advance.

"Do I frighten you?"

"Shouldn't I be embarrassed?" she asked softly. "I

don't want you to think I'm brazen, just standing here in front of you.''

A pink tinge colored her face, but an air of expectancy shrouded her and he could not help but chuckle as he shook his head. "No, I know better than that. The thing is, there's just you and me here, sweetheart. We can do whatever we like. That's what marriage is all about.''

"How would you know?'' she asked as she slid to her knees, and he thought it a perfectly logical query.

"Something my father told me once. And then when I stayed in Wyoming a while back I watched a man and woman who discovered the depths of their love while I was working there. I could sense the air of belonging they shared, and I knew it was what I wanted one day, when I found the right woman.''

"And were you searching for a woman when you met me?''

He reached to enclose her waist with long fingers, encouraged by her acceptance of his touch on her bare skin. "No, not really. And to tell you the truth, you weren't what I'd expected to want as a wife.''

He thought a look of disappointment swept her expressive features, and he strove to vanquish it, his words soft and coaxing. "But all I had to do was look at you, Gussie, and I knew. That golden hair and your blue eyes made me lose my breath. I offered you lemonade when you came to call because I didn't want you to leave.'' His laugh was quiet and rueful. "I'd have done most anything to make you stay on my porch that day.''

"You teased me,'' she reminded him. "Unmercifully.''

"I wanted you to remember me, and welcome me when I came by to see you.''

"Really? And here I thought maybe you were laughing at me because I was so mortified…you know, about raising money for my ladies.''

"No, never that. I knew then that I wanted you, Gussie. It just took a while to realize that I wanted you on a permanent basis. In the meantime, I had to make up reasons to hang around until you got used to me and felt comfortable in my company."

"I didn't feel very comfortable when I knew you meant to kiss me, that day you put up the shutters." She bent to touch his hair with her fingertips and her breasts brushed his shirt. "It frightened me, Jonathan. Not because of you, but because I was fearful of the way I felt about you."

"How did you feel?" he asked, hope rising as she gripped his shoulders, then rose above him, allowing her hands to slide to where his buttons awaited her touch. Her fingers slowed, carefully separating buttons and buttonholes, until she had exposed his chest. Her palm flattened the springy patch of hair in the center, and she shivered.

"It was the first time I'd ever wanted a man to touch me. Do you remember how you unbuttoned my..." She bit her lip, shaking her head. "Well, of course you do. How silly of me."

"I remember every time I touched you, sweetheart. I was afraid you might not forgive me for taking advantage that day in the parlor."

She tugged at his shirt, pulling it from his trousers. "I didn't want you to stop, even though I knew I shouldn't be feeling that way." The buttons on his trousers were easily undone, and he felt his male flesh bulge into the opening, needy of space.

She looked down and her gaze fastened there, one index finger unfurling from her fist to touch the hard thrust he could not control. "Oh." A single sound, released on a long breath, and enough to send new life surging to that part of him he most needed to subdue. He jerked, an involuntary movement, and she stiffened.

"It's all right," he hastened to assure her. "Don't ever be fearful of touching me, any part of me, sweet."

Especially that part.

"Is that going to fit where I think it's supposed to?" she asked.

"Well, I suspect it will, but you'd better know right off that it's probably not going to be very comfortable for you this first time." He wouldn't ever lie to her if he was able to be honest. He'd decided that from the first. His trips out of town weighed heavily on his conscience, but there was no help for his duplicity there.

But here, in their marriage bed, there would be only honesty. Honesty and faithfulness.

"It's going to hurt, isn't it?"

He nodded. "I suspect it will. But I think we'll be able to make it easier if you do your part." He thought her eyes held a glow of eager anticipation as she nodded and her fingers unfolded to measure the length of his male organ. "Lower my trousers, sweet." His hips lifted, and with only a minute hesitation, she obliged his request, bending low to slide his garments down his legs.

He wore no shoes or stockings, and the denim pants and soft, cotton drawers slid off easily. Her haste in casting them aside gave him new hope, and he held out his arms to her as she turned back to him. "Come lie down with me. Here, by my side. I want to kiss you and feel you against me."

She obliged, readily, he thought, stretching out full length next to him, her feet only reaching to his shins as they faced each other on his pillow. Against his chest, her breasts were firm, and she moved, brushing them across the width of his broad body, closing her eyes as her breath trembled in her throat. His arm was beneath her, holding her close, and he took her mouth, teasing her lips with his tongue, careful to allow her the choice of accepting him or refusing the intimacy he asked with silent pleading.

She opened to him, hesitant for a moment, and then eager as he explored her mouth and drew her tongue into a duel. With timid gestures at first, she ran her own across the roof of his mouth, then into the caverns of his cheeks, and he shivered and gasped at the sensations that flooded his body.

A chuckle erupted from her and he drew back to watch as she grinned at him. "I like that," she told him. "I didn't know kissing could make me feel so shaky inside."

"Where inside?"

"From top almost to bottom." She shook her head, as if unable to explain the wonder of her awakening. "I feel all twitchy."

"Where?" he asked again, already knowing the answer, and then slid his hand to cup her soft mound. "Here?"

She nodded, inhaling sharply as his fingers gently separated the folds of flesh and found her softness. She was slick beneath his fingertips, and he explored tenderly, brushing against her feminine flesh with delicate movements, yet with pressure firm enough to bring wonderment to her eyes.

"Do you like that, sweet?"

Augusta nodded, squirming against his fingers. "It makes me shiver, way inside. How can it do that, Jon?"

"It's the way you're made, love. We're all born with the ability to experience joy and pleasure in the marriage bed." And then he pressed within the tight opening and heard her gasp, a combination of astonishment and fearful anticipation. "Shh," he whispered. "Let me do this. It'll make it easier for you."

She was trusting, his Gussie, and her eyes closed as she relaxed beneath his caresses, allowing the presence of his hand to do as it would. He followed her lead, listening for each breath she took, aware of each movement of hip and thigh. And when her legs parted to allow him the access he needed, he kissed her deeply, and his fingers found the depths of her body, stretching and preparing her for his taking.

A moan sighed from her throat and he eased from her, then searched out the source of her pleasure and was rewarded by soft cries that encouraged his attentions. She clung to him, her hips unable to cease their movement. She bit at his mouth, and her tongue raced to imitate the rhythm he created against her flesh. Her body was damp with the straining of her flesh for the completion he offered, and then, with a gasping cry, she stiffened in his arm and arched against his touch.

"Ah, Gussie, sweetheart," he whispered, holding her against himself as she shivered and sobbed, his hand petting her, easing her, and bringing her to yet another peak of pleasure.

"Sweetheart…ah, baby." He held her close, rocking her gently, even as his body demanded satisfaction. And when he could wait no longer, he whispered against her ear, his words hopeful.

"Can you move up here and lie on top of me? I don't think I can manage to love you the way I want to, sweet. But if you'll do as I say…"

"Yes…all right," she whispered, her voice a series of breathless sounds as she followed his directions to straddle him. He eased her thigh from the site of his wound and she shifted obligingly, and then he lifted her to guide himself to the very rim of her female opening.

"You'll have to do this," he said, subduing the urge to thrust upward, ignoring the pain that burned his hip with each movement. Her fingers clasped him, and he inhaled sharply, reining in the terrible need to surge against her touch. "Ease down on me, sweetheart," he gasped. "Take me inside." And as she worked to obey him, he could only wish, for the first time in his adult life, that he'd not been so generously endowed.

She lifted her head as her body opened to him, their eyes meeting, his narrowed, hers widening as the pain of his penetration became apparent. Quivering, she bit her lip and forced herself to contain him, tears squeezing from her eyes as she closed them from his sight.

"If it hurts too much, we'll wait," he said, his words harsh as he sought to catch his breath.

She shook her head, clenching her jaw stubbornly. "No, I can do this." Her head thrust back as she lifted a bit, easing from him, and then she lowered herself quickly, crying out as the membrane of her virginity was breached by the length of his manhood. Leaning forward, she clutched his shoulders and her head lay against his throat. He held it there, aware of waves and curls cascading over his body like a soft, silken veil.

"Is that all?" she asked, her breathing shattered, her body trembling.

"No, not by a long shot," he told her, lifting her hips with his wide hands and then lowering her again to enclose himself within her depths. Again he lifted her, and by the third time, she'd caught the rhythm he needed and rose on her knees to accommodate him.

"Ah, Gussie, sweetheart." His voice rose and fell as he called her name, whispering the endearments he'd stored up for just such a time.

In this moment it mattered not that he'd been with other women through the years. Their memories were as if they had never been, erased by the magic of holding Augusta against his body, of knowing she'd chosen to give herself into his keeping.

This, *this* was what his soul had yearned for all those times when he'd taken his pleasure in the body of a stranger or someone he'd shared himself with for a short time, knowing it was only a breathing space. Knowing that he had yet to find the woman who would complete his life and be his for all the years to come.

And now, with Gussie in his arms, with her slender body containing him, gloving his manhood, giving him the very essence of her feminine strength, he was fulfilled, recognizing finally that this woman, and all she represented in his life, was what he'd been seeking. He strained upward, touching the depths of her womanhood, aware of nothing but the slender creature who held him with the force of passion unrestrained.

And when he felt the rush of heat, the overpowering sensation of losing himself in her, he cried aloud words he'd never before offered to another.

"I love you. Ah, Gussie, I love you."

During the next four days he rested, only rising to use the slop jar Augusta left in the corner for him. She changed his bandage daily, spending hours cooking for him, and then returning to the shelter for the afternoon. Their nights were spent in each other's arms, Cleary aware that he'd been fortunate not to harm himself during the events of their wedding night.

His vow to leave Augusta alone, allowing her time to heal, was partly for his own benefit, the thought of not being in control somehow going against his grain. Today he felt a renewal of strength, bending a bit, checking the wound for seepage and exercising his leg with walks through the house.

She'd barely closed the door after dinner, promising to return in time to prepare their supper, when he decided his wound had ceased paining him enough to allow his seeking out the bedroom upstairs. Augusta would have a fit, he supposed, but he was determined to try hoisting the mattress on his back.

To his relief, Nicholas stopped by, and between the two of them they hauled the heavy, awkward burden back up the stairs and onto the bed where it belonged. If Nicholas spotted the barely discernible bloodstain on the sheet Augusta had scrubbed to remove, he didn't mention it.

Cleary knew it was there, had watched her, listening to her mumbling as she worked at removing the spot that first morning. Now the memories it brought to mind gave him satisfaction in the proof of his bride's purity.

Nick broke into his thoughts, his question casual. "Are you sure you'll be ready to ride in a week or two?"

"More like two, probably," Cleary answered. "I want to get this whole mess cleared up, Nick. I need to get on with my life."

"I don't blame you." He sounded relieved. "In the meantime, I'll see that everything is going according to schedule. The men from Washington are coming in next week. Messing with government funds will put this whole gang in prison for a long time." He dropped to a chair near the window.

"Now tell me again about this brother of Augusta's. I'll see if I can pick up anything on him through my contacts in Colorado and Wyoming."

"Did you ever have a hunch, Nick?" Without waiting for more than an agreeable nod, Cleary plunged ahead. "Well, I'm willing to lay odds that he's the fella I knew as Gus in Wyoming. He was sent to prison in Colorado, while the rest of the gang was held in Laramie. He had second thoughts all along, I think, and he's not a hardened criminal."

His pause was long, and he sought understanding from the banker. "I almost wish there wasn't a chance in hell of him showing up here. I'll bet you a plug nickel, when he sees me my cover's gonna be blown to kingdom come."

Nicholas grimaced. "And how is Augusta going to feel

when she realizes you were responsible for putting him in prison to begin with?''

Cleary shrugged. ''I guess I'll have to take my chances with that, won't I?''

''She's a bright lady,'' Nick said bluntly. ''She's not going to support him and turn her back on you.''

''He's her brother. And if he sees me here, he'll fill Augusta in, and she'll be madder than hell that I haven't been honest with her.''

''Doesn't she have a clue what you're up to? Where does she think you've been going when you leave town?'' He leaned back in the chair and folded his arms across his chest. ''I can't figure out how you ever managed to persuade her to let you get this close.'' And then he looked down at the toes of his boots, and Cleary thought he hid a smile.

''On the other hand, maybe I don't want to really know the answer to that one.''

''Maybe not.'' Cleary sat on the edge of the bed, wishing Augusta would show up and make him lie down. His hip throbbed unmercifully, probably due to the workout it had gotten hauling the damn mattress up the stairs.

The bandage was seeping, not much, but it was bloody, and he couldn't reach it well enough to change the padding. He could only hope it wasn't staining his trousers. She'd have to scrub them out after she worked on his hip.

And that thought made his heart beat just a tad faster. Hell, the thought of her cool, slender hands touching him was enough to get him all in an uproar again, and he shifted uncomfortably on the mattress.

Nick was astute enough to read the signs, although he probably attributed Cleary's scooting around to discomfort. ''You need to get off that hip. I'm going to find my way out your front door, and you'd better find a comfortable spot on that mattress. It's time for me to get back to work. Dinner hour is over.''

Cleary couldn't hide the smile of satisfaction that settled on his face as he watched Nick cross the room and head out into the hallway. The sound of his boots on the stairs and then across the foyer announced his departure, and the opening and closing of the big front door was accompanied by a murmur of voices.

''Jonathan?'' Augusta's voice floated up to the second floor, and she announced her intentions. ''I'll be up in a few minutes. I came back early to bring you some hot soup Bertha made for you.''

Cleary stood and slid from his loosened trousers, tugging his stockinged feet from the pants legs, then turned his head awkwardly to peer down at his bandage. It was stained, but not badly. If he kept it from contact with the sheet, he wouldn't make another mess for Augusta to clean up.

She carried the tray up the stairs, frowning as she thought of the men hauling the mattress between them. Cleary shouldn't have been exerting himself, and she would let him know she didn't approve. In fact, before she walked through the doorway, she'd begun. ''You know, you'll never heal if you don't take care of that wound.''

He was on the bed, and aside from the bandage that circled his hips and the unbuttoned shirt he wore, the man was naked. Stark naked. And then she focused on the white sheeting she'd used to bind his wound. Stained with both fresh and dried blood, it brought fear to her heart and she made haste to deposit the tray on the bedside table.

''Let me look,'' she said, reaching into her apron pocket for the scissors she'd brought along. The pocket was deep, holding her supplies, along with another piece of soft muslin to use as a pad.

''You've made it bleed.'' Her words scolded him, and

he didn't even care, she thought, bending to cut the strips that circled his hips.

The pad was stuck and she dampened it with water from his pitcher, easing it from the wound with care. Only a bit of oozing was evident now, and Augusta breathed a sigh of relief. "It's stopped again," she murmured. "But you've got no business running around when you've been wounded."

The woman was a tyrant, he decided, but she was *his* tyrant. He grinned at her. "Yeah, I found that out." Her hands against his hip sent a message that threaded its way to his nether parts, and he grimaced as her gaze touched the swelling he could not control.

"Jonathan, how can you think about..." Exasperation was apparent in the glance she cast, and he did his level best to look sheepish.

"Some things a man can't help, sweet. And I'm afraid that's one of them."

She attempted a nonchalance her crimson cheeks belied. "Well, just keep it under control while I replace your bandage and get some carbolic salve on that wound. I've got a roll of adhesive plaster that should hold the padding in place. It'll be better than wrapping you up." She worked quickly, and he watched as her blush grew in proportion to the expansion of his male parts.

"You look about ready to run for your life," he said as she smoothed the plaster across his hipbone. "Do I still frighten you?"

"Of course not." She shook her head and sorted out her belongings, dropping them into the cavernous pocket from whence they had appeared. "I want you to eat this soup, Jonathan. It'll be good for you. Bertha said it would be especially good to help replace the blood you lost."

"All right." He was more than agreeable, so long as Gussie would stay with him. Damn, he'd eat her soup and mind his manners, and even cover up with the sheet, if she'd only sit by him and offer her company.

Propped with four pillows, he held the tray before him and spooned the soup into his mouth. "It's good," he told her between bites of savory chicken and swallows of thick broth. She looked pleased, he thought, her hands smoothing the sheet, her fingertips touching his leg through the fabric. "What are you thinking, Gussie?"

Her gaze lifted to his face. "That I'm a most fortunate woman."

"How do you figure that?" He swiped at his mustache with the napkin and replaced it in his lap. "Getting married, you mean?"

"Partly. And because I'm doing the work I came here to do. Because I met you, mostly." Her eyes were a deeper shade of blue than he'd ever before noticed.

"I never thought to marry anyone, Jon. You know that. And now I have a husband and a home. I'm thinking maybe you'll be done with your wandering around the countryside on these mysterious trips you've been taking, now that you're a family man."

The soup suddenly lost its flavor. "Well, I may have to disappoint you a bit, Gussie," he said. "I've got one more job to complete before I can settle down to being just a husband."

And I'm afraid your brother will show up and prove me right, and you'll be angry enough to walk away from me. And that was the fear he would live with until he was proved wrong or right about the identity of the man he'd known as Gus.

"You're leaving again?" Her skin grew pale, and he rued the words he'd spoken. "When, Cleary?"

Not *Jonathan,* he noted. It was a withdrawal of spirit, as though she must gird herself for the parting.

"Not for a while, maybe in a week or two."

She rose from the bed and shot him a cool look. "Well, that should give your wound a chance to heal nicely before you get shot again."

"No one said I was heading for trouble. I have a job to do, and you know it."

"No, I don't," she said, her words succinct and as chilled as the icebox in the kitchen. "All I know is that I married a man who keeps secrets."

"So do you." It was a challenge, and he knew it as such. Yet he cast it at her deliberately, waiting for her rebuttal.

"You know about me," she said, defending herself with a reserve he had to admire.

"Yeah, I know your name, and I know you come from back East. But I don't know what drives you, what made you take on the job of buying a house and filling it with women who need a future. There's more to it than you've told me, and whether you'll admit it or not, that's just as hard for me to swallow as what you expect of me."

"That doesn't make sense," she said sharply, leaning to pick up the tray from his lap. "Your job involves something clandestine, and you know it. My work is only a reflection of my upbringing. My mother taught me to be kind to others. She called it being my brother's keeper." Her eyes gleamed as she looked down at him, watched as he slid down inside the sheets and tucked his hands beneath his head.

Her lips twisted as she considered that thought and her words were quiet. "Maybe 'my sister's keeper' is more appropriate."

"You've never been a loose woman in your whole lifetime, Gussie. It doesn't apply."

"No, but I've—" She halted, her jaw tensing. "We all do what we have to. And this is my calling. Take it or leave it, Mr. Cleary."

"If I want you, I suspect I'm stuck with the shelter, and

all it entails," he said. "And trust me, Mrs. Cleary, I want you." His eyes darkened as he scanned her figure from top to bottom, noting the whitening of her knuckles as she gripped the tray with a fierce strength.

"I've got to walk to town and see if my catalogue order is in yet," she said. "I'll be back later."

"Don't be too late, or I'll come looking for you," he warned. "And, Gussie…"

Her lifted brow told him he had her attention. "Stop by the livery stable and get my buggy. Use it today in case you have a bundle waiting for you. I don't want you carrying heavy packages all the way home. And tell Sam Ferguson at the livery stable to pick up the buggy here later tonight."

"Is that all, sir?" she asked, her mouth pressing in a straight line as she awaited his reply. "Do you have any other orders for me? Perhaps a special menu for your supper?"

He stifled a chuckle. Augusta in a snit was a sight to behold. Tonight couldn't come too soon to suit him. "No, just a simple request for a kiss to tide me over till you come back." He did his best to look humble and contrite as she reflected on his words, tilting her head to one side. Looking humble wasn't going to cut it, he decided, and he'd pushed her about as far as she'd go, so his voice was softer as he gave it his best shot.

"Please, Gussie?"

The tray met the table with a clunk and she sank down onto the mattress beside him, leaning to rest her head against his shoulder. "You don't have to ask for what's due you," she mumbled. Her face turned to his throat and she kissed the skin that held a day's worth of whiskers, up his cheek and across to his mouth.

"You're all scratchy," she told him. "All but here." Her mouth met his with a warmth he hadn't expected.

He sat upright, holding her close, his arms circling her as he lifted her to his lap. She was soft and pliant and he felt a surge of emotion he couldn't name. Hovering somewhere between the need to protect and the urge to possess, his feelings for her meshed in a blend of warmth and appreciation as he clasped her to himself.

"Do you remember our wedding night? When I told you I loved you?" he asked. He felt her head nod against him, and his mouth was warmed as she lifted her face to touch his lips again with her own. She tasted sweet, and the surrender of her kiss sent triumph soaring through him.

"I've never wanted to possess a woman before, Gussie, to keep her beside me as my own, for all the days of my life. And I've never said those words about loving to another woman."

Her palms against his cheeks, and her head resting against the support of his arm, she looked up at him with a sober countenance. "I didn't think you had, Jon. I don't think you give your love lightly. I only hope the time will come when you feel you can trust me with your secrets."

"And when will you whisper your confidences into my ear?" he asked, his smile softening the words. "I'm planning on spending the rest of my life with you. There isn't anything a lady like you can tell me that will change my mind and send me packing."

"Maybe not on a permanent basis, but you're going to be packing before you know it to leave me, Jon," she reminded him.

"Ah, but I'll be back before you know it, and then we can take up our life and make plans for the future." He brushed his mouth across hers, teasing a bit as she opened her lips for his kiss. "You won't let me undress you, I suppose," he murmured.

She relaxed in his arms and her eyes softened as she

searched his face. "I don't want you to hurt your wound and start it bleeding again."

"Find a towel to put beneath me so I won't stain the sheet, just in case." He heard a gruff note in his voice and noted the hesitation in her response. "I won't ask you to do anything you—"

"Hush." The single word was quick and her retreat from his bed was even more rapid. She crossed to the washstand and found clean towels, then returned to where he sat in the middle of the bed. "If you'll roll to one side, I'll make sure you don't soil the sheets."

He did as she bade him and she bent over him, opening two towels to spread under his wounded hip. "Just like that?" he asked, his heart pounding as he recognized her surrender to his need.

Augusta stood beside him, undoing her dress, her eyes on his face, her cheeks rosy, her mouth trembling just a bit. "If you'd rather do this for me..." She slid from the dress, and snatched it from the floor to place it neatly over the nearby chair.

"No." He shook his head. "I think I'm enjoying this, sweetheart." He waved a hand, a silent signal to continue the process she'd begun.

Her vest and petticoat were next, and then she slid her drawers from her legs and, bending, removed her shoes. A pair of simple stockings, held in place with plain white garters were her only covering and he reached to touch the soft skin above them. "Leave those on," he told her, his hand sliding to the back of her leg, drawing her closer.

"Now, come here to me."

Chapter Eleven

She was late getting back to the shelter, arriving with a flurry of dust as she drew the buggy to a halt before the front gate. Honey looked up from her weeding below the front porch and waved. "Hi. We thought you got lost."

"No. I just had to go to the livery stable and get the buggy, then on to pick up my catalogue order. Everything took longer than I thought it would." She felt a flush rise to cover her cheeks as she made her excuses and climbed from the buggy seat.

"That looks like too much for you to carry," Honey said, rising quickly. "I'll give you a hand."

"I don't want you carrying anything heavy," Augusta told her. "Call out for Pearl. She's strong enough to wrestle an ox, bare-handed."

"Is that so?" From behind the screened door, Pearl questioned Augusta's statement, and received only a joyous laugh in return. "Leave it be, Honey," the woman said, sauntering onto the porch and then down the steps. "I could wrestle two fellas at a time if I had to. A couple of bundles from Sears, Roebuck shouldn't give me much trouble."

She joined Augusta at the buggy and her grin was knowing as she viewed the other woman's appearance. "I'd have sworn you had on a different dress last time I saw you, ma'am. You get the blue one wrinkled?''

Augusta felt the flush rise to cover her cheeks, and she shot a sharp glance at Pearl. "No, I just spilled something on it.''

"Make sure you spot it right quick," Pearl said blandly. "Some stains are hard to get rid of." She picked up the largest package effortlessly, and Augusta was struck by the knowledge that, indeed, this woman could probably wrestle an ox and come out the winner, hands down.

They hauled Augusta's booty into the house and Honey followed close behind, her curiosity aroused by the shipment of goods. In moments the strings were cut and the individually wrapped contents exposed. New curtains for the kitchen and two bedrooms were first, then heavy draperies for the parlor. At the bottom of the last bundle a brightly colored calico dress was folded neatly inside a brown paper sack.

"This is for you, I believe, Honey." Augusta handed the open package to the girl, and felt anticipation rise within her. The purchase of a dress designed specifically for a woman in Honey's condition had been an impulse, one which Augusta, who was far from being an impulsive creature, had kept as a secret.

Now, the look on Honey's face as she viewed the creation, was worth every penny spent on the garment. "Oh, Miss Augusta." It seemed for a moment that those words would be accompanied by tears, and then Honey held the dress up before herself and looked down, preening just a bit. "It's so pretty," she managed to whisper, and the joy filling her soft eyes was payment enough, Augusta decided.

"About time you had something that fit decent," Pearl grumbled, reaching to smooth out a wrinkle in the colorful skirt. "Go put it on, girl."

"I'm weeding." As if that were enough reason to postpone the wearing of a new dress, Honey's words were shocked, her expression dubious.

"Forget the weeds for now," Augusta told her. "We're almost ready to put supper on the table, and you need to look pretty."

So it was that when the knock came from the front of the house, just as the food was being served up, Honey sashayed from the kitchen and down the corridor to answer the summons. The women in the kitchen heard her voice, then the sound of the screened door opening. A male voice responded, and Augusta looked up quickly from the basket she was packing, preparatory to leaving for the night.

"Ma'am?" Honey's eyes were wide, her cheeks flushed as she returned to the kitchen, her gaze fastened to Augusta. "There's a gentleman who says he's come calling on you." She half covered her mouth with one hand, and her whisper was almost inaudible. "Do you suppose it's your brother?"

Footsteps as silent as the night carried Augusta past the girl and toward the front of the house. Hat in hand, a tall young man stood near the parlor door, and Augusta came to a halt a good ten feet from him. Her eyes scanned the weary features, the whiskered face and the blue eyes of her brother.

"Wilson." Tears flowed freely as she held out her arms, and the young man stepped forward, hesitantly, to be sure, but with a half smile reeking of affection on his lips. "Is it really you?" Augusta asked foolishly, her arms around his shoulders finally, her head bending to place her forehead against his shirtfront.

"I'd say so, sis," he murmured. "Not that I thought you'd recognize me under the layers of dust and whiskers."

"I'd know you anywhere." The words were fervent as she drew him with her to the kitchen. "Are you hungry? Have you eaten supper, yet?"

"Yes and no," he answered, his chuckle dry, as if his

throat held a generous portion of trail dust in its depths. "I'd take a drink of water first, and then whatever leftovers you can spare."

The women standing around the table were silent, their eyes alert, Honey still blushing and Bertha holding a wooden spoon in her hand. Wilson halted in the doorway and took their measure.

"A man in town told me there was a houseful of women here," he said. "Warned me I'd be taking my life in my hands if I came nosing around." His grin appeared again and Honey shifted to stand behind a chair, as if it might hide her. "You don't look too threatening to me," he told them.

"If you're Miss Augusta's brother, we'll welcome you," Pearl said bluntly. "If you're a stranger lookin' for a handout or a woman, we'll chase you out faster than a dog can tree a possum."

"I'm Gussie's brother," he said. "And I'll work for my supper, if that'll make you happy." His gaze touched each woman, sliding from one to another with a cheerful grin. Until he got to Honey, and then, as if he must reacquaint himself with her, he nodded and spoke.

"Ma'am? I didn't catch your name."

"She didn't throw it," Pearl said, her eyes narrowing at the young man.

"I'm Honey."

"I can see that," Wilson said quietly. "Pleased to make your acquaintance, ma'am."

With a flurry of movement and uplifted voices, the kitchen came to life, as if Wilson's words had somehow set loose a small tornado amongst them. Augusta directed him to a chair, the ladies all sat down, and Bertha finished serving the food.

"I'd like to ask a blessing," Augusta said quietly, reaching her hands to those on either side of her. Wilson grasped her fingers, offering his free hand to Janine, who sat next. Augusta's head bowed and she spoke simple words, directing her thanks to heaven for the food and the safe arrival of her brother.

"Amen," Honey said, echoing Augusta's final word, drawing Wilson's attention. He seemed unable to take his eyes from her, and her fingers trembled as she picked up her fork to stab a piece of meat from the platter.

"How did you—" Augusta began.

"I've been—" Wilson said in unison with her. And then waved a hand, urging her to continue.

"I just wondered how you found us."

"It wasn't hard. I asked where a yellow-haired gal with the prettiest eyes in Texas lived, and everyone seemed to know who I was referring to." His voice teased her, even as his words were spoken in a solemn cadence.

Augusta rolled her eyes and shook her head. "You haven't improved a bit. Still the silver-tongued rogue."

He sobered, bending to fill his fork with potatoes and gravy. "Oh, I've changed, sis. More than you can imagine." And then he smiled quickly. "But for now, I want to hear how you ladies came together here, and what I can do to earn my keep."

"I thought you weren't coming back," Cleary said, aware that his words smacked of petulance. He'd missed her, and for a moment there, just as the sun sank below the horizon, he'd wondered if his impulsive lovemaking after dinner had put her off. Maybe she wouldn't be back tonight. Perhaps he'd offended her sense of dignity by his wanton behavior in the middle of the afternoon.

"The most wonderful thing happened," Augusta said, settling herself on the edge of the mattress. "Wilson showed up just at suppertime, and I had to stay long enough to get him settled."

"Get him settled." Three simple words had never held such dire portent, Cleary decided. "What do you mean?"

Augusta waved a hand dismissively. "Oh, you know. Deciding where he'd sleep and sending his horse back to the livery stable when Sam came to collect your buggy."

"He's sleeping in your house?" He surveyed the food she was taking from the basket on the floor, and found his appetite taken by the picture of Augusta making room for a criminal in her house. No matter that the man in question was her brother, she was putting her reputation on the line.

"Yes, he is," she said quietly. "And it is *my* house, Cleary. I'll take the responsibility for sheltering him. You're off the hook."

"On the contrary," he said quietly. "You're my wife, and I'm responsible for whatever you choose to do, whether you like it or not." He looked down at the plate of food she'd somehow managed to settle on his lap and his hand gripped the fork she provided.

"Please eat," she said, lifting anguished eyes to meet his gaze. "I want you back on your feet, with your wound healed. It won't happen unless you keep your strength up." She watched as he nodded, digging into the generous helping of beans she'd provided. A sigh escaped her lips and she reached for a slice of bread, spread thickly with butter.

"Bertha sent jam along."

"That's fine, just the way it is," he told her, knowing his words were stilted yet unable to retreat from the stance he'd taken.

Augusta watched him and he found her expressive eyes to be a fount of information. At first she pleaded mutely for his understanding; then, as he remained silent, the blue appeared to darken, and her mouth tightened as anger touched her pale features.

"He's my brother. I can't turn him away. No one needs to know he's there, at least not for now."

"And when the sheriff comes to call—what then?"

"There's no need for him to visit. He never has yet, and I doubt he will now." Her chin tilted in a stubborn gesture, and Cleary felt the urge to haul her across his lap and kiss the bejabbers out of her. The foolish woman was putting herself at risk, and...

No, he admitted to himself. *He* was the one at risk. Jonathan Cleary, U.S. Marshal, a man with a badge. A hidden badge, to be sure, but a lawman, nonetheless. And once Augusta found out what he suspected she would, should her *Gus* and his be one and the same man...

He felt a chill travel the length of his spine. He could not, he would not, lose this woman. No matter the price he must pay, Augusta was his. She'd been his wife for five days, and already he was immersed in her so deeply he could not imagine his life without her presence in it.

"I'll see what I can do," he said quietly.

She looked askance at his somber features. "What are you talking about?" Her words were hesitant and he watched as her fingers formed fists in her lap.

"I have a little influence, Gussie. I'll call in a marker or two."

Bewilderment colored her features. "What sort of influence?" And then she rose, a napkin falling from her lap to the floor. Leaving it where it lay, she stepped back from him. "Who do you have influence with, Cleary?"

"The name is Jon," he reminded her quietly.

"Right now your name is Cleary," she told him. "Jon is my husband, a man I know. *Cleary* is a man with secrets, and I fear that is your identity tonight."

"You're wrong, Gussie. Tonight I'm the man you married. You can use any name you like to identify me, but the bottom line is that you're my wife, and you're my responsibility." He reached out, his hand snaking to clasp her wrist, drawing her back to the bedside.

"I suppose you want me to climb in that bed with you," she said stubbornly. "But you may be in for a grand awakening."

"No, I think you're the one with a surprise in store, sweetheart." He swung his legs over the side of the bed, retaining his hold on her with very little effort. Standing carefully, he drew her closer, his free arm circling her waist. "Whether or not we disagree about your brother, one thing will not change," he told her, aware of the weakness that gripped his legs.

He widened his stride, balancing himself, taking her weight as he held her. "You will sleep in my bed, Gussie. You don't have to fear that I'll manhandle you. I probably couldn't if I wanted to. And I'll never force myself on you, so don't be looking at me like a wounded puppy. But, you'll sleep here. With me. Not just tonight, but every night."

Her backbone felt as stiff as the broomstick in his kitchen, but her breasts were soft against his chest and he felt the reaction begin in his groin, the heat gathering as his firm arousal pressed against her. She looked up at him quickly, already aware of the needs his body could not conceal.

"Get undressed, Gussie." And then he waited for her nod of agreement, releasing her from his grip as it was reluctantly given. He accepted it as a solemn promise. Gussie would not walk out the door and leave him alone. Not tonight, anyway. And if he was very cautious, if he whispered the words that sheltered in his heart, she would sleep in his arms.

She could not deny him. She'd promised to obey, and the knowledge that Cleary would never hurt her, would not take advantage of her, allowed her to undress as he watched. He was aroused—of that she was certain. He wanted her with a passion she recognized, his eyes narrowing, glittering in the lamplight, his mouth thinned and drawn taut. And yet, he would withhold his desire, control the urge to take her to himself.

He'd promised, and Jon Cleary was an honest man.

Her nightgown fell into place and she removed her drawers from beneath its folds. If there was a trace of disappointment in his eyes at her hidden maneuvers, he concealed it well, glancing aside as she leaned to blow out the lamp, holding the sheet high for her to crawl beneath its concealing cover. And then he reached for her, his hands careful, his touch gentle.

Settling her head on his shoulder, he turned, his wounded hip uppermost, and his arms surrounded her. One broad palm pressed against her back, just beneath her waist, where her hips widened a bit, where her bottom grew taut as she felt once more the unfamiliar pressure of a man's touch. His other arm beneath her head, he folded it to surround her, and in his embrace she recognized anew the knowledge that Jon Cleary was her master in this area.

Lips that softened as they touched her skin pressed without urgency against her forehead. Words that murmured beneath his breath told her of her beauty, and she was cradled against a masculine form that left no doubt in her mind that desire ran rampant within the man she'd married. His male member twitched against her thigh, and she inhaled sharply.

"I promised. Remember?"

"I know," she whispered in return. And yet, she was not satisfied. She'd thought to remain aloof, to obey his edict and sleep beside him, ignoring his male physique and all that the awakening flesh he pressed against her represented. But it was of no use. No use, whatsoever. The memory of his loving was alive in her mind, along with the tingling sensation she recognized as his hard flesh nudged the triangle where her thighs met.

"Jon?" Her whisper was soft, questioning, and he stilled the movement of his hand against her hips, that subtle circling that edged her ever closer to his arousal. "Jon, you don't have to keep your promise. Not unless you really want to."

"Are you angry with me?" His voice seemed to come from somewhere deep within him, vibrating against her ear.

She shook her head. "No. I might not agree with you entirely, but—"

His rumble of laughter welled up and his arms tightened their hold. "Now, that's an understatement, if ever I heard one," he murmured, brushing his lips against her temple. He lifted to his elbow, and his fingers twined in the cascading length of her hair. "I don't care if you're madder 'n hell, to tell the truth, sweetheart. If you'll let me, I want to make love to you. We don't have to always agree on everything. You've found that out already."

He bent to kiss her, and she opened to him, holding her breath as his teeth touched her lower lip, biting gently, then suckling the tender flesh. "You can deny me, and I'll live through it," he said quietly. "But you'll be denying yourself, too, and you know it. I'm glad you're able to acknowledge that you want me. Maybe not as much as I want you, but I think I can make you happy and give you pleasure, if you'll let me."

Her arms lifted to circle his shoulders, her fingers sliding into his hair, pressing against his scalp. She returned his kiss, and as if it were a signal, he responded eagerly. With leisurely movements, his hands caressed her willing flesh. With softly spoken queries he discerned her needs, and his gentle touches answered the cry of her weeping flesh.

She moaned and he inhaled the sound. Her hands trembled and he placed them against his firm arousal, showing her with his broad palms and agile fingers what would please him best. Shivering against him, she submitted to his loving, her hips lifting to seek the succor he provided. And when her cries rose in the darkness, he heard them with a satisfaction he'd never known before.

She was his. *His.* And that knowledge brought him to the brink of completion before he was ready. He lifted her leg over his side, and she curled it around his waist, careful to stay clear of the bandage she'd put in place. He sought and found her warmth, and she welcomed him, curving against him, accepting his mastery over her body as he pressed home into her tender depths.

It was an easy, gentle possession, and he reveled in the silken softness of her womanhood. Her internal muscles were tense, holding him in a tight, intimate embrace, her whispers of pleasure akin to music in his ears.

He filled her with the essence of his yearning, claiming her body with a tenderness she had not expected. His fingers clutched her thigh, holding her where he would for his enhanced pleasure, and she pressed against him. She ached for a deeper touch from that invasive part of him, thankful for the care he took with her fragile flesh, yet arching against him as if she would invite him deeper yet. Invite the sweet fire of his possession into her very being.

His husky sounds of rapture were breathed into her ear, and he felt the dampness of tears against his throat and chest. "Gussie? Have I hurt you?" He lifted from her, but she would not allow him to set her apart from him, clutching at his neck with fingers that strained for purchase.

"No," she whispered. "You didn't hurt me, Jon. I just want to be a part of you and hold you closer."

His eyes closed as he felt a prickle of tears rise to invade their surfaces. It would not do for him to weep. He hadn't shed a tear since...

He couldn't remember the last time. Perhaps when his

father died, and he was left to mourn the man who had sired him. At sixteen, he was still a lad, yet had been forced to become a man.

Now, at thirty-four, a man full grown, he was burdened with a past containing both good and bad, and it seemed at times that the bad weighed far the heaviest. Thirty-four, and for the first time in his life, loving a woman beyond any expectation he'd ever had in that direction.

He was a husband, holding a beautiful woman in his arms, a woman he'd kept in ignorance. And for that he might pay a high price. Fear overwhelmed happiness for a moment, and desperation tightened his hold on the slender body he held. For he faced the possibility of being exposed as a liar, should events fall into place—as they surely would.

He bent to kiss her, deeply, fervently and with all of the love he could bestow upon her face and form, wondering if it might be the last time she would lie thus by his side. Praying in his deepest heart that the bond he'd forged between their bodies would be sufficient to bind their hearts as one.

"Where's this husband of yours?" Wilson stood before her, a belligerent thrust of his jaw making her aware of the determination he harbored. "I've been here two days already, and you haven't seen fit to introduce me to the man."

Augusta scanned his bedraggled appearance and smiled sweetly. "You don't look fit to meet a hound dog, brother dear. Where've you been?"

"Cleaning out your attic, as if you didn't know." His age showed in the youthful petulance he displayed, she thought, and her heart was touched by the fleeting glimpse of the boy he'd been.

"I thought Honey was doing that."

"I'm helping her," he said defensively. "She shouldn't be handling heavy boxes."

"There aren't any up there," Augusta said quietly. "I only asked her to sweep and open the windows to air out the place."

Wilson's hands rested on his hips, a defensive position she recalled from his youth, and then he grinned, as if he recognized his own foolishness. "Well, it happens I wanted to spend time with her," he confessed. "She's a pretty girl and I think she likes me."

"And she's pregnant." The words were nonjudgmental, but Augusta knew her gaze held a warning.

"She's had a rough time of things."

"Do you see yourself as her rescuer?" Augusta turned away from him and lifted the basket of trash she'd carried from the kitchen. The burn pile was at the furthest point from the house, and she'd taken on the task of gathering up all the bits and pieces that needed to be disposed of today.

Close on her heels, Wilson double-stepped to reach her side, taking the basket from her with a quick movement. "Let me carry that," he said gruffly. "You do too much, Gussie. Mama would roll over in her grave if she could see how hard you work. And if she knew what you've done with your inheritance."

"And what did you do with yours?" Her glance in his direction held accusation and he flinched.

"Generally made a mess of things," he admitted.

They reached the hole in which household trash was burned and he dumped the basket, then reached into his pocket for a box of matches. She watched his profile as he lit one and bent to hold its flame to a piece of paper. He squatted there, watching as the fire caught and flared, his gaze attached firmly to the blaze.

"I'll take you to my husband's home this afternoon," she said quietly.

"His name's Cleary," Wilson said. "Honey told me."

A chill touched Augusta's spine as her brother's voice hardened, spitting out Jonathan's last name as if it were a bit of garbage he'd brought to his mouth.

"Yes, it is," she murmured. "Have you heard of him?"

"Maybe. I ran into a fella by that name, up in Wyoming, last year."

She searched her memory. Had Jon mentioned being that far north? It seemed she should be able to recall if he had. His scant referrals to his past had lodged in her brain, and she'd reviewed them frequently. "His family is from hereabouts," she said. "He's a Texan, born and bred," she said, unconsciously quoting Jonathan's claim.

"That doesn't surprise me," Wilson told her, rising to stand beside her as the smoke filled the air around them.

They stepped back from the fire, waiting till it should burn down before they left it unguarded. "What do you mean?" Augusta looked up at him, shielding her eyes from the sun overhead.

"The man I knew was some sort of government fella. I wondered then if he might not have been a Texas Ranger."

"He was a lawman?"

Wilson nodded. "Working with the Wyoming Cattlemen's Association." He turned to meet her gaze and his own was shielded, as if he hid secrets he would not share.

"Did he arrest you?" Her heart beat faster, its rhythm wild as she considered the possibility of Cleary hiding such a thing from her.

"We're not talkin' about your husband, sis. We're discussing a man in Wyoming, and the likelihood of them being one and the same is pretty far-fetched, don't you think?"

"Did he arrest you?" she repeated.

"Sort of."

"Sort of? Did he send you to prison?"

He shot her a look of astonishment. "I did that to myself. You can't blame someone else for your crimes. I found that out over the past few months."

"And now you're on the run." She felt quick tears behind her eyelids, and her gaze dropped to the fire pit. "If my husband should be the man you knew, would he be obliged to turn you over to the sheriff?"

"Does he know I'm here?"

She nodded. "He read the letter you sent me." Her hands thrust deeply into her apron pockets. "He hasn't mentioned you."

"If it's the same fella, he knew me as Gus."

"Gus?" She lifted bewildered eyes, whispering the lone syllable with a hissing sound that made him smile.

"I didn't use my name, sis. Remember how I used to tease you and tell you that Mama should have named me Gus, not you? And how we used to call ourselves Gus and Gussie?"

She nodded, her mind frantic as she considered the possibilities of what this day might bring. "He's not a lawman," she stated fervently. "He has something to do with banks. But if he were a lawman, he'd have told me that."

Wilson shrugged. "Then we have nothing to worry about, have we?"

"The house needs cleaning," Augusta said as she opened the front door. "I haven't had time to turn out the corners yet. I thought maybe I'd bring the ladies over tomorrow and we could do a thorough job of it."

"You don't need to explain anything to me," Wilson said, waiting for her to step over the threshold into the entry hall. "I think you're nervous, sis, and I don't want you to be. I'll face whatever happens here."

"You're my brother," she said tightly. "Nothing is going to happen to you. I won't let it."

"You always cheered for the underdog, even when we were kids," Wilson remembered. He looked around, admiring the high ceiling, the wainscoting and the wide, curving staircase. "It's a beautiful house. You'll make a beautiful home here, sis."

"Not if I find out Cleary has lied to me," she said fiercely. "I can't tolerate a liar. Especially not a man who—"

"A man who what?" The voice came from the parlor, and with silent steps, Cleary moved from the doorway into the entry hall. "A man who married you and took you to bed, Augusta? Would that make me more than a liar?" His glance slid past Wilson to focus on the woman whose face had gone pale at his words.

And then he allowed his narrowed gaze to touch the man beside her once more. "Hello, Gus. Fancy meeting you here."

Augusta murmured a word that gripped his heart and, as she slumped to the floor, Cleary stepped forward to take her weight in his arms. He grunted at the pain he'd managed to inflict on his wound, his lips tightening as he lifted her.

"Let me have her," Wilson said quickly. "Tell me where to take her."

"I've got her," Cleary murmured, unable to inhale deeply enough to speak in a normal tone. *I've got her.* Perhaps for the last time he held his wife, given her words only moments before.

He relished the slight weight of her, unwilling to give her to the other man, clasping her against his chest with ebbing strength. He'd thought himself healed, almost ready to face the coming task. And he laughed silently as he recognized his own foolishness.

The sofa beckoned, and he bent to relinquish Augusta's form to the horsehair cushions. Her arm hung to the floor and he lifted its limp weight, placing it across her waist. Then he knelt beside her, and his hand was warm against cool, seemingly lifeless flesh. Her cheek was waxen, her eyelids closed, concealing the bright blue of her sparkling eyes.

Yet, he knew that when they opened and met his own, they would no longer be filled with warmth. The soft light of love they'd held so recently would be gone, and he would be faced with the desolate black pit of hatred. It was the other side of love. He'd heard it spoken thusly and never before understood the meaning. Now it faced him with the intensity of a pain he might never escape.

"Gussie." His whisper was soft, his voice calling her back from the escape her mind had sought. He looked up at the young man beside him. "Go into the kitchen and bring a glass of water. Dampen a towel so I can wipe her face."

He needed these moments with her, he thought, listening as Wilson left the room, aware of his footsteps in the hallway, the swinging of the kitchen door as it opened and closed.

Bending over the woman he loved, he touched her cheek with his own, seeking to infuse her with the warmth of his body. His hands held hers and he rubbed the slender fingers, then lifted them to his mouth, his lips tasting the sweetness of her skin.

"Sweetheart, wake up for me." His whisper was desperate, needing to reach her, probing the depths of unconsciousness into which she'd retreated. "I love you, Gussie." He whispered the words against her ear, words he'd spoken to no other woman. She knew already of his love; he'd made it clear. Even the first time they'd come together, he'd murmured the words in her ear. And yet, he repeated them again, as if by hearing them once more, she might forgive him his sins against her.

Her eyelids fluttered, and beside him Wilson squatted, glass of water in one hand, the damp towel in the other. Cleary took the towel and wiped her face, his touch tender as he strove to awaken her fully. She blinked, frowning, and then stared at him, her blue gaze blank for a moment, as if she tried to recall where she was.

"Have a sip of water," he said, his voice gruff with emotion. He lifted her, one hand beneath her shoulders, and she sipped at the cool water from the glass. And then, with a single turning of her head from one side to the other, she refused any more. He slid his arm to her neck, supporting her as he lowered her to the sofa cushion. "Do you feel ill?" he asked.

Her eyes swept open again and he caught a glimpse of hopeless, helpless sorrow in their depths. "I've never felt more sick at heart in my life," she murmured. "Not even when Mama and Papa were buried."

"I'm here, sis," Wilson said from beside her. "Let me help you up."

"I'll take care of her," Cleary told him harshly. "She's my wife."

"Yeah, so she is," Wilson told him, his gaze raking over the man who had become his brother-in-law so recently. "More's the pity."

"We need to talk," Cleary told him. "But not now. I need to speak to Gussie. Alone."

"And then what?"

"Go, Wilson. Leave us alone." Augusta's voice was quiet but firm, and she struggled to sit up on the couch. Pushing away the hands that would have helped her, she swung her legs to the floor and looked eye-to-eye into her brother's face. "I'll see you later," she told him. "Go back to my house and keep an eye on things. Tell Bertha I'll be by later.''

"Not today," Cleary said, denying her words. "For now you'll stay here, till we get this hashed out, anyway."

Wilson's mouth opened as if he summoned a retort, but Augusta's reproving look silenced him as he rose. "All right," he agreed reluctantly. "But I'll be back." Then he was gone, turning to leave the room and, seconds later, the house, the front door closing quietly behind him.

Chapter Twelve

"Are you planning on holding me captive?"

She stood before him, hands folded at her waist, and he was tempted to toss her over his shoulder and haul her up the stairs. Only the sure and certain knowledge that such a task was beyond his capabilities today stopped him from making a total idiot of himself. And yet, he could barely subdue the anger within him.

Augusta blamed him. Blamed him for her brother's problems, plus the ones even closer to home.

"You know better than that."

"Do I? I'm not sure just what I can trust about you."

Her words stung and his jaw firmed. "I haven't lied to you," he said.

"*Really.*"

He wasn't certain if bored or dubious described her tone of voice. No matter which, she looked down her nose as she denied his claim.

"*Really.*" His own assertion was firm. "I'm not lying now. I just didn't tell you everything. Before long I'll come clean with you, and you'll realize that I have good reason for what I've done."

Her fingers tightened their grip, her knuckles whitening

as if she took pains to contain her anger. "I can hardly wait."

He sighed, frustrated by her stubborn behavior. "I love you, Gussie. I wouldn't do anything to hurt you. When this is all over and done with, we'll start a new life here together."

"Will we?" Her voice softened, just a bit, but enough to lend hope to his apprehension. "And what will you be doing to earn a living? Take on a new assignment chasing lawbreakers?"

"I hope not. I'd like to think my days as a lawman are about at an end. I've already talked to Nicholas about another line of work."

She looked askance at his words. "I can't see you at a banker's desk."

"And you probably won't," he agreed. "When I get things worked out, you'll be the first to know my plan, Gussie. You're my wife. I won't keep you in the dark. But for now, I need you to promise me something," he said quietly. "I want you to stay here, let the ladies cope with things on their own for a couple of weeks."

"Why? Are you afraid my brother will let me in on more of your secrets?"

"No, I'd just like you to recognize that those women can cope very nicely on their own. One of these days, this will be your home, full-time, after you've decided just how to designate someone there in charge. Will you do that for me?"

She nodded dubiously. "I suppose so, if that's what you want." Her mouth pressed together and then she spoke, repeating her fears aloud. "You're sure it's not because of my brother and what he might tell me about you?"

Cleary shook his head, meeting her gaze head-on. "He doesn't know any more than he's already spilled into your ears. And if he did, it wouldn't be anything I don't want you to know anyway.''

"What sort of lawman are you, Cleary? Surely not just an ordinary sheriff or constable.''

"Your brother told you I was a lawman?'' At her nod, he drew in a deep breath. "Let's go sit down, Augusta.''

"Do I need to be seated to hear this?'' She turned obligingly toward the parlor and took a seat on the sofa.

"Maybe.'' Settling himself in a high-backed chair, he lifted his foot to rest on a tapestry footstool. "I'm a U.S. Marshal. I worked with the Cattlemen's Association in Wyoming during my last assignment, and then I was asked to come here. Kinda killing two birds with one stone, so to speak. While I healed from a gunshot wound, I was to settle in and make a place for myself here, then wait to be contacted.''

"By the sheriff?''

He shook his head. "No, the banker.''

"Nick Garvey? No wonder he asked such personal questions that day. He already knew all about you, didn't he?''

Cleary grinned, remembering. "He just likes to give me a bad time. Nick's a sharp fella. He'd have made a good agent. In fact, it won't surprise me if he heads in that direction one of these days.''

"Leave him alone in his bank. He'll be a safer bet for some unsuspecting woman right where he is.''

"Like you?'' His words sounded terse to his own ear, and he watched her with a half smile as she considered his query. "Don't be looking at Garvey, sweetheart,'' he said, admonishing her softly. "You're already taken.''

He watched as a rosy flush climbed her cheeks. "I didn't mean *me*,'' she said sharply. "I'm very well married, in case you've forgotten.''

Cleary shifted in the chair as he considered the import of those words. "Not a chance, honey. I won't be forgetting our wedding night." He lowered his foot to the floor and rose. "Or the afternoon I invited you into bed. Or that night either, now that I think about it." His gaze took a lingering inventory of her, his reaction to her instinctive as he mentally drew her clothing aside to reveal the woman beneath the crisp percale dress she wore.

She cast him a glance, apprehension painting her features. And with good reason, he decided. If Augusta thought for one minute she could put him off with her fit of temper, she had another think coming. He reached for her, drawing her unwilling body from the sofa to stand in the circle of his embrace. Brute force wasn't his style, especially when it came to women. Most especially when it came to Gussie.

But he was determined to keep her aware of his presence in her life. And if constant reminders served that purpose, he was not averse to using them to forge new links in their relationship. His arms held her close, and he bent to her, his mouth covering hers readily. She was acquiescent, only a faint trembling of her hands against his chest divulging her uncertainty.

The kiss was soft, undemanding but most satisfactory, he decided. Taking her to bed would have been a bonus, but he was dead certain she'd put up a fuss should he instigate such a thing right now. His mouth touched her eyelids, closing them gently, and then he whispered soft words of praise for her beauty, for the elegance of her bearing and the pleasure he found as he held her in his arms.

She sighed, leaning closer, her hands clutching at his shirt, her head tilting to afford him access as he brushed numerous kisses across her throat. One hand lifted to her head, and experienced fingers slid pins from the twisted locks she'd arranged high on her crown. The silken length fell from its moorings, and his fingers clenched in the glory of golden curls. Pins fell silently to the carpet, and she pressed against his groin. Cleary felt his arousal answering the call of soft female flesh against its turgid length.

"I'm trying to behave here, sweetheart, and you're not helping matters." His whisper was husky, his words bordering on a plea for her permission to take his loving a step closer to full-blown seduction. Her murmur was barely discernible, and he bent, the better to catch the broken words she spoke.

"It's full daylight," she whispered.

"I know."

"Someone may come to the door."

"Do we care?" His arousal was becoming a serious problem, and he shifted his stance. "Will you go upstairs with me, sweet?"

She sighed and levered herself from him, meeting his gaze with stubborn blue eyes. "If I'm not allowed to leave here, I may as well make myself useful, Cleary. This room is a shambles," she said primly, looking over his shoulder to where he knew cobwebs continued to hang in the far corner of the parlor. "And besides, you're still healing from a bullet wound."

"And you well know that in a couple of days I'll be leaving the bandage off, Gussie. I'm a fast healer." He released her, reluctantly but with good grace, and then grinned as a knock sounded from the front of the house.

"You were right, Gussie. We have company."

She backed from him and blinked, as if her own state of disarray had only just come to her notice. Her hands lifted to her hair, and a look of astonishment colored her features. "How did you manage that?" she asked, her fingers busy as she twisted and coiled the heavy length atop her head. "Where are my pins?" She bent her head, one hand holding the arrangement in place, the other searching the surface of the end table.

"On the floor, I'm afraid," Cleary said, bending to pick

them up and place them in her outstretched palm. "I'll get the door," he said, grinning widely as she grumbled beneath her breath.

"I came to help Miss Augusta." Standing on the other side of the screen, Pearl was a formidable opponent, he decided. The door opened beneath her touch and he stepped back as she crossed the threshold into his house. "Where is she?"

With a great show of deference, he ushered her into the parlor and took note of Gussie's flushed cheeks as she tucked the last pin in place. "There she is, safe and sound," he told Pearl, smug in his success. Another few minutes and he'd have had her up the stairs and beyond the reach of any intruder. He'd give Pearl a few hours to make certain that her chick was unharmed. And then she'd be gone, and he'd have Gussie to himself again. At that thought, his smile widened into a grin.

He could wait.

Within thirty minutes Glory showed up, bucket and rags in hand. "Bertha said you probably had soap aplenty, but she wasn't sure Cleary owned more than one bucket to tote water in. Where do you want me to start?"

"The kitchen floor is a mess," Augusta told her. "And so are the windows. Maybe we could just work on the kitchen and parlor today. I'd be happy to have two clean rooms. And if we have time for the front entryway, that'd be a bonus."

Glory went off cheerfully to the kitchen, and Augusta saw Pearl's backside tilted upward behind the sofa as she wiped down the woodwork with gusto. On hands and knees, she was making her way around the room. "No sense in starting in on the carpet till the mop boards are clean," she muttered, wringing out her rag in soapy water.

She'd settle for the corners, Augusta decided, wrapping

a rag on the end of a broom handle. Reminded of the night she'd salvaged cobwebs for Cleary's wound, she was industrious with her weapon, as if she would erase that memory from her mind.

She'd been so worried, so afraid she wouldn't be able to halt the bleeding. Lying beside him throughout the long, dark hours had been an awakening for her, a night during which she'd found herself responding to the call of masculine flesh and his need for her.

She'd known then, recognized in her secret heart that Cleary possessed her. Not in the physical sense, but with an invisible chain he'd forged over the past weeks, tying her with unbreakable bonds. Her body aching for his presence, her mind aware of him during each waking moment, she'd become a slave to her own emotions.

And once their marriage had been consummated, once she'd known the touch of his hands and mouth and body against her own, her whole life had changed.

Now she recognized the attachment as permanent. No matter his lifestyle, she was committed to the man. Lawman or not, secrets notwithstanding, she was his wife. Even the love she bore her brother lessened significantly when compared to the overwhelming magnificence of Cleary's impact on her life.

She was saddened by the thought of losing Wilson; yet, his flight from prison haunted his every step. Surely Cleary would find it necessary to report his appearance in Collins Creek. As a lawman, he was obligated to do such a thing.

She lowered her broomstick, noting with satisfaction the gray gathering of dirt she'd accumulated on her journey around the parlor walls. Enough of this woolgathering, she decided, scolding herself silently. Tonight would find this house in decent condition, given the efforts of the two women who were working with her. She would concentrate on that for now.

* * *

"Your brother was downright upset when he got back to the house," Pearl muttered as they put together a slap-dash meal. "Me and Glory decided we'd come on over and keep an eye on things."

"I was fine," Augusta told her, her brow lifting in surprise.

"Yeah?" Pearl grinned. "Looked to me like he was about to haul you up those stairs and take you to bed."

Augusta bent her head, unwilling to meet the other woman's gaze. And that, in itself, she realized, was a dead giveaway. "He wouldn't hurt me," she said finally.

"No, I suspect you're right," Pearl agreed. "Wilson thought old Cleary was pretty hot under the collar, though. He doesn't know the man as well as we do."

"He knew him in Wyoming," Augusta told her. "Cleary's a lawman."

Pearl was silent, her spoon moving slowly as she stirred the beans lest they stick. "Somehow, that doesn't surprise me," she said finally. "How'd your brother happen to meet up with him?"

Augusta told her briefly, not making excuses for Wilson, busy slicing the cold roast beef Bertha had sent along for their dinner as she spoke. She watched as Pearl nodded her head in understanding.

"No wonder he got sent off to prison. Rustling's about the worst crime a man can commit. It rates right up there with stealin' a man's horse, I reckon. And Cleary was the one to catch him?"

"There were some extenuating circumstances, I think."

"Yeah, you could say that," Cleary said from the kitchen doorway. He sauntered closer, one hand in his pocket, peering over Augusta's shoulder to see what his dinner would consist of. "Your brother probably saved my life, Gussie."

She turned her head quickly, her voice sharp as she uttered a reply. "How? What happened?"

"I was sent in to rescue a woman rancher and found that your brother had been watching out for her, trying to keep her safe from the rest of the gang. When we headed out of the canyon, he cut her loose and covered us while she rode hell-bent for election, with me stickin' like a burr behind her. She rode that stallion like a circus rider. Between them, they kept me from being trampled under the herd, or bleeding to death from a gunshot wound."

"Who is she?" A surge of jealousy struck Augusta like a rushing wind, and she felt the blood drain from her face as she wondered how Cleary could so easily leave such a woman behind.

"The wife of a rancher. Chloe was..." His pause was long. "I thought she was my ideal woman for a while."

"And now?" The question left her lips before she thought to hold it to herself.

He took the knife from her hand, placing it on the table. Then with firm fingers on her shoulders, he turned her to face him.

"I believe I'll go get Glory and tell her dinner's about ready," Pearl said, sliding quietly through the doorway into the hall.

"Now, sweetheart," he began. "Now, there's you. And once I saw you there on my porch that day, once I lost my heart to blue eyes and golden curls and the innocence that shone from your face, I forgot that Chloe ever existed. I've never been one to poach on another man's woman to begin with, so she was out of bounds from the beginning.

"And after I caught sight of you, with the sunshine makin' you look like an angel from heaven, all fresh and new, and as pretty as a picture...well, there wasn't any other woman on the face of the earth that could have held a candle to you."

"You liked me right away?" she asked, unaware that her voice and eyes begged for assurance.

"You betcha," he said softly, bending to kiss her with a heated blending of lips. "I knew you were the woman I wanted."

"You wanted to marry me so soon?" She cocked her head, doubting his word.

"I knew by the second time we met that it would have to be marriage," he told her. "There wasn't any way I was gonna get past Bertha and Pearl with anything less than a wedding ring on your finger."

The days passed in a flurry of activity. Augusta cleaned and cooked, her efforts aided by the presence of Glory and Pearl on several occasions. When her ladies were in residence, Cleary retreated to a room he'd designated as his office, scanning reams of paper as if his life depended on the plans he formed. As indeed it might.

Breaking the concentration he shed on his work, he lifted his head as Nicholas Garvey peered past the doorway. With a wave of his hand, Cleary invited him in and nodded toward the open door. "Close it please," he said quietly. "Find a chair, Nicholas. I have a favor to ask of you." His words were succinct as he shared the problem he'd been stewing over, and Nicholas's reaction was about what he'd expected.

"You want me to *what?*" the banker roared, and then at Cleary's pained expression and dour glance at the closed door, he lowered his voice. "You're going to put your reputation on the line for an escapee from prison?"

"He's Augusta's brother." And as if that were reason enough, Cleary leaned back in his chair and folded his hands across his flat stomach. "The man saved my neck in Wyoming last year," he explained. "I owe him."

"The man is a rustler." Nicholas held his tone to a gruff

murmur, probably in deference to Augusta's presence in the house.

"He *was* a rustler. But I have the feeling...hell, I had the feeling a year ago that he was in over his head and was doin' his best to get out of the mess he was in."

"And you're ready to go to bat for him." Nicholas sat down and propped his hat atop his knee.

"If Augusta was your wife and that young scamp was your new brother-in-law, what would you do?" A grin tugged at the corner of Cleary's mouth as Nicholas digested the query.

"Hell, probably the same thing you're wantin' me to do." He grinned suddenly. "Doesn't pay to argue with you, Cleary. And if you've got the clout to pull this off, you might as well do it. If Augusta was mine, I'd no doubt move heaven and earth to make her happy."

"You bet you would," Cleary agreed. "She's one in a million, and I won't have her worrying about the only family she has left."

"Are you going to put her mind at ease?"

Cleary shook his head. "No, not yet. Not till we know for sure that we can swing this thing. I want him to have a full pardon, Nick."

"You may have to do some finagling to pull this off," the banker warned him.

"I'll do whatever it takes."

An occasional rumble from the office reached Gussie's ear. And once she distinctly heard the sound of Nicholas Garvey's voice raised in a shout. Yet, try as she might, she was unable to make heads or tails of their conversation. It was troubling to her, but she set it aside, aware that she must trust Cleary in all things.

Doggedly she concealed her aggravation from the women who pitched in a few hours each day to help her, scrubbing and cleaning in her wake throughout the large house. She was naturally an impatient woman, and Cleary's silence regarding his involvement with the undercover work he'd taken on loomed over her head like a dark cloud. She'd come to recognize that he and Nicholas Garvey were two of a kind, both of them open and aboveboard in their conversations with others, but secretive beneath the bland surface they offered.

Yet, she loved the man she'd married, without reservation, and Cleary made no bones about his need for her. Each night, she was ushered with haste to the big bedroom upstairs, his impatience with her attention to after-supper chores not allowing her to linger in the kitchen. He wiped dishes with a will, locked the doors and blew out the lamps, moving at a steady pace throughout the house, ever vigilant that his home be secure for the night, especially now that Augusta dwelled within its walls.

And then he found her, whether she be in the pantry searching out items for their breakfast, or standing at the parlor windows taking a long, last look at the quiet street and the flickering lights of town. On occasion, he found she'd preceded him up the curving staircase to their room, and on those nights he hastened his steps, aware that she waited for him in their room.

Now he stood with his back against the closed bedroom door, watching her as she brushed her hair in the glow of two candles. They reflected in her mirror, and as she looked up to find him behind her, she was framed by the tall, shimmering tapers. She was breathtaking, he decided, her beauty having increased with her self-assurance. That she was wanted, that his need for her grew daily, would have been apparent to a blind man, he thought ruefully.

And she was thriving on the attention he gave her. Her skin glowed, her eyes sparkled as they met his in the mirror and her cheeks took on a soft flush that only magnified the fragile grace of the woman. Her brush dropped from her fingers as she caught his gaze upon her, clattering against the top of her dressing table. Around her face, her hair flew in wispy disarray, and with supple grace, she lifted her arms to contain its length in her hands.

He shook his head. "Please," he said quietly, and she dropped her fingers to rest in her lap, aware of the request he would make.

"All right." Tonight, it seemed she was especially acquiescent to his needs, and he gloried in her submission. And she did submit to him, each time he came to her, as if it were a joy to give over to him the access to her body he demanded. And yet she did not only receive his loving, but, little by little, her confidence grew apace with the pleasure he brought to her. Her hands were wont to seek his flesh without urging, her lips tasted his skin and found it pleasing, and she grew bolder as the nights turned into the weeks he'd demanded, and then became a month.

A month he'd salvaged for himself, pleased that events allowed him to remain here with Gussie. Satisfied with the marriage they'd begun to forge, with bonds of flesh and nights of passion.

But now, it seemed this would be a time of reckoning, if the look on his wife's face had any bearing on the matter. "Tomorrow," Augusta began, hesitating as if she would judge her words well before allowing them utterance. "Tomorrow, I'm going to the house to catch up with things. I've left Pearl and Bertha too long in charge."

Her chin tilted, a bit of defiance adding an edge to her words. "Besides, I miss my brother, and Pearl fears that he and Honey are becoming more than friends."

"Is that bad?" Cleary asked quietly. "I thought you approved of him living there."

"I do." She inhaled deeply and turned from him, her

fingers working at the buttons at her spine. Her eyes were wary as she awaited his response.

"You'll go over there in the morning?"

She nodded, intent on reaching the middle of her back. "Is there a problem with that?" Releasing the dress from her grip, she mumbled words beneath her breath.

"No, it's fine. I should get my horse from the livery stable and ride him for a while. He'll be stale from standing in a stall so long."

"Are you healed well enough?" she asked.

"As good as new," he said, aware that he'd been malingering. His healing process had been complete well over a week ago. His grin was lazy, as if he had all the time in the world at his fingertips. "I had a most competent nurse." And then he smiled widely as he viewed her flushed face, and the dishevelment of her gown.

"I'll do that for you," he offered, and moved quickly to pull down the window shade before he stripped her from her clothing. It was a ritual he enjoyed, this deliberate removal of dress and petticoats. Of drawers and vest, and lastly, the peeling of her stockings from slender, well-formed legs.

She stood before him, as naked as the day she was born, and he sensed a residual of that modesty she wore that proclaimed her a lady. Even here, in their privacy, she was unable to be bold or blatant with her body. Yet, within the layers of darkness, after he'd blown out the lamp and pinched the candles, she offered herself to him without restraint, unlike the faint shyness she still wore when he viewed her in the light of day.

But he could not complain. His Augusta was exactly what he wanted, the very essence of feminine beauty and strength. If Nicholas Garvey sometimes eyed him with a bit of envy apparent, it only served to enhance Cleary's enjoyment of her, secure in the knowledge that she looked no further than her husband for the satisfying of her needs.

Her hair was long, covering her breasts as he drew it over her shoulders, and his fingers were lost in the curls and waves. He sought her flesh beneath it, the soft curves of her breasts, the hardening crests that puckered at his touch, and bent his head to suckle with a desperate need.

She murmured softly, her hands at his nape, holding his head against herself, and he lifted her, his movements hasty, his hands rough against her waist, as he carried her to the bed.

She was on her back, beneath him, wiggling against his clothed body and muttering darkly about his abundance of apparel. Her hands worked swiftly, unfastening buttons, loosening his belt, and her urgency brought laughter to his lips.

"You in a hurry, Gussie?" he asked, nuzzling her neck and biting carefully at her ear. She'd managed to tug the fabric down his arms and he was captured by the shirt-sleeves gathering at his wrists. With a jerk that came near to tearing the seams, he escaped their hold and tossed the garment aside. His arousal pressed for release against his drawers, and he cast them impatiently to the floor.

Hampered by his weight, Gussie wiggled beneath him, then lifted her feet, nudging at his trousers, reaching to ease the heavy denim down his legs. He delighted in her haste, reveled in the muttered imprecations she flung in his direction, and finally shed the last of his clothing by the side of the bed.

And then he came to her, finding the fork of her thighs, recognizing the damp, slick folds as an invitation to his entry.

It was hasty and headlong and she trembled, crying out. Halting his forward movement, he hesitated, fearful of stretching her beyond her ability to contain him so quickly.

But she would not allow it. Her arms circled him, her legs found purchase and surrounded his hips, and she lifted to meet his thrust. Shivering, she moaned anew and clung to him with a fierce strength that only served to bring him to a shattering climax.

"Sweetheart." He dropped his head to her shoulder and groaned the word with a sense of disgust at his own lack of control. "I'm sorry, Gussie. I took advantage of you. I didn't take care with you, and then I left you far behind." His words were uttered between breaths that rose from his depths. He was stunned by the force of his desire, the graceless, greedy fashion in which he'd used her body. Appalled by his harsh, hasty treatment of her, he lifted himself, peering down at her in the dark.

She was a shadow beneath him, her hair pale against the pillows, her breath sweet as he bent to touch her lips. "Forgive me, love." It was all he could say, knowing he'd failed to bring her the pleasure she deserved.

"You were magnificent," she whispered, her hands finding their way to his head, burying her fingers in his hair, tunneling through its length. "I've never felt so much like a woman in my life."

He turned them to their sides, and heard her words with a sense of puzzlement. "How so?" he asked.

"You wanted me…maybe 'needed me' is a better description," she said haltingly. "You couldn't have been held off by a herd of wild horses."

"I looked at you too long in the mirror," he said glumly. "I get so riled up watching you when you do your woman thing at night, I can hardly keep my hands to myself."

"I don't want you to," she said airily. "I like it when you act starved for me."

"You do?" He breathed deeply, satisfied that he'd not harmed her or placed a strain on the budding relationship. "I'm still hungry," he whispered, leaning closer to touch her mouth with his, suckling at her lip and nipping it lightly.

"So am I."

She'd never been so forward with him, and delight sang in his veins. "I can fix that," he promised, his hands searching out the curves and hollows of her flesh.

"I'll just bet you can," she sighed. "I'll just bet you can."

Chapter Thirteen

"I'd begun to think you were in jail," Wilson said, his eyes scanning Augusta, as if he searched for injury of some sort. "Does he always keep you at his beck and call this way? Or am I the reason you've been out of touch?"

"You know better than that," she said. "I've just been busy."

Wilson's gaze was skeptical. "Too busy to see your brother after all this time apart? I think your husband doesn't want you hanging around me, sis."

Augusta bristled and glared in his direction. "I thought it was time to give my ladies a chance to operate without supervision." She glanced around the parlor and then stalked toward the hallway. "It looks to me like they've done just fine without my guiding hand."

"Don't be mad at me, sis," Wilson said quickly, following in her wake. "We were all wondering where you were and what was keeping you from home."

"I *was* home," she said quietly, halting in her tracks to straighten a picture on the wall. And then she slanted a look in his direction. "You don't seem to understand. I'm married to Cleary. I owe him my loyalty, and my time is his to direct as he pleases."

"And that's what this is all about? Letting Cleary boss you around?" Wilson lifted a brow, sliding his hands into his trouser pockets. "This is my sister? This paragon of housewifely virtue?" He walked toward her and she moved from his path. It was no use. He only circled her slowly, his gaze on her as if he peeked beneath the layers of clothing to find the sister he'd once known.

"I'm married," she repeated. "That may not mean anything to you, but it does to me. One of these days I'll be giving over the leadership in this place to someone else, and I need to know that when that time comes, I have in place a woman capable of the job." That she was repeating Cleary's words to her didn't occur to her until she'd finished giving chapter and verse to the young man standing there.

"Which woman are you talking about? Not Honey, I hope."

She shook her head. "No, probably not Honey. She's in need of a husband and a home of her own, not the job of tending to ladies who would probably run roughshod over her."

"She may already have someone in mind for that position. That of a husband, I mean," Wilson said quietly.

Augusta's brow lifted in inquiry. "Really?" Her heart beat just a mite faster as she saw his jaw tense and his mouth tighten at her tone of voice.

"Yeah, really," he said, his words just a shade threatening.

"You have enough on your plate already, my brother. You don't need to be looking at Honey and worrying about her future. It's more important that you find a safe place to land and begin making plans to get there."

"Why? Is the lawman ready to turn me in?" His cheeks colored as he asked the quiet question, his trace of arrogance gone, as if worry had sent it flying.

"He hasn't mentioned it, but surely you know he's obligated to do that very thing." As much as it hurt her to think about it, facts were facts, and she could not be disloyal to Cleary in this matter.

"Maybe I'd better get my gear together then. I sure wouldn't want to bring the law down on your head, sis." She sensed a note of worry as he faced her head-on. "You've got your hands full running this place. Half the folks hereabouts are unhappy about having a houseful of shady ladies on the edge of town as it is."

"Where'd you hear that?" she asked, although she was aware that it was true. More and more, her original sponsors had withdrawn their physical support, even though occasional bits of help came by way of cash and baskets of clothing and garden produce left on the back porch. She was still in the black, but unless she found some financial help she would be in trouble.

"I hear things in town. I was in the saloon the other night, and a gal was waiting tables, making up to me and in general trying to invite me upstairs with her. She had some bruises on her arms and a purple lump under her eye." He shifted his stance and his cheeks reddened again.

"I told her to come here if she needed help, and she said you probably didn't have room for another woman in the house, that this place was likely gonna fold soon anyway, since the ladies in town were reneging on helping out here." His discomfort increased as Augusta eyed him sternly. "She told me she didn't dare come here, that the saloon owner would kill her."

"They all get that song and dance when the people who earn money from their activities get worried about them running off," she told him. "Most of the women who work in brothels and saloons are afraid for their lives. I'd just like to know what you were doing to contribute to their misery."

"Don't look at me that way, sis. I was only having a drink. I didn't plan on abusing any of the women there." He looked past her at the kitchen doorway and his eyes widened.

"Hey there, Honey," he said, sidestepping Augusta to approach the young woman watching him, her eyes misty. "I only stopped by the saloon for a few minutes, Honey," he said in a low, cajoling tone.

"I'm sure what you do is your own business," Honey told him, as her voice quavered, a dead giveaway to the tears she was about to shed.

"Where is everyone?" Augusta asked quickly, calling attention to herself as she caught Honey's eye. Unless she missed her guess, the girl was already besotted with Wilson. He probably looked like the proverbial knight in shining armor to her weary eyes. And at this point the girl was open to hurt, too fragile of spirit to be exposed to a man who might not stick around for the long haul. Given Wilson's past record, she could expect little from him when it came to being a stick-to-it sort of fella.

"Bertha's fixing dinner and Pearl's cleaning corn on the back porch." Shoving her hands into the deep pockets of her printed percale wrapper, Honey smiled, a shy gesture aimed at Augusta. "Janine is at work and Glory's hoeing out the chicken coop."

"I hope you haven't been overdoing it," Wilson said, his voice aggressive, as if he dared anyone to place more on Honey's slender shoulders than she could bear. "I told you I'd do the gardening this afternoon."

"I have to earn my keep," Honey told him, her chin jutting forward. "I can't let everyone else pitch in and not do my share."

Augusta sent her brother a measuring look. "I think we're taking good care of Honey," she said bluntly. "She managed before you arrived, and I'm sure she'll be just fine when you leave.''

"You kickin' me out?'' he asked, his gaze swerving in her direction. His jaw was clenched, his mouth grim, and Augusta found herself wishing she'd stayed home with Cleary where she belonged this morning. Arguing with her brother was the last thing she wanted to do today. Not when her heart yearned to hug him and assure him of her love and concern.

"No, I'm not sending you on your way,'' she said, firming her voice with an effort. "I'm just telling you not to give Honey any false hopes.''

"If she's got any hopes where I'm concerned, they're not false,'' he said quietly, stepping closer to the vulnerable young woman who seemed on the verge of shedding a bucket of tears. His arm across her back earned him a tremulous smile as Honey nestled close to his side.

"I'm planning on marrying her, sis,'' Wilson said firmly. "No one has to know I'm here, except for the preacher. And if you don't believe I'm ready to stand behind my promise to her, you can go fetch him right now.''

"And when you run from here, will you take her with you?'' Augusta heard her own words with disbelief. That she would speak to her brother in such a way was beyond her comprehension. And yet, he'd turned her world awry during the past weeks, and somewhere she'd found her loyalties shifting in another direction.

"I'll do whatever I have to, in order to spend the rest of my life with Honey.''

From the entryway, where the front door stood open wide, a voice spoke, its rough, harsh tones causing Augusta to spin in a half circle, her hand covering her mouth. "Seems to me you'd better start listening to your sister, *Gus.*''

"Don't call me that,'' Wilson said, his eyes narrowing.

"I've been sorry for the past year for using Gussie's name in such a way. I had no right."

"Are you ready to straighten up and be a law-abiding citizen? Ready to get a job and earn your keep honestly?" Cleary threw his queries at the young man relentlessly, hands on his hips, his gun bound to his thigh with a leather thong, his clothing dark, his visage sinister.

Augusta shrank from the knowledge that the image he presented at this moment was no doubt the real person behind the facade of caring he'd offered her when she'd pledged him her loyalty and obedience. This was Cleary, the lawman, the U.S. Marshal, the seeker of vengeance on the behalf of those he'd worked for back in Wyoming.

"I said I'd do anything to have Honey in my life," Wilson told him. "I can rope a steer or ride a bronc. I'm a good cowhand."

"What else are you fit for?" Cleary's words were sharp, his gaze assessing as he faced the young man. "What do you know about business?"

"If you're asking me whether or not I've been to college, the answer is no. If you want to know if I'm smart and capable of learning, then I'll be glad to work at anything you've got in mind to prove myself."

"All right, son." His reply was quick, as if he'd only waited for Wilson to offer his compliance. "I want you to take the chore of keeping records for this house off Augusta's shoulders," Cleary said. "I want you to figure out a way for the ladies here to earn enough money to support themselves. They're already making progress, but a man can help them more than the most competent woman in the world. And Gussie is backing off from her responsibility, a little bit at a time."

"I can do my job," Augusta said staunchly. "What if the law comes after Wilson?"

"There's not going to be anyone on his doorstep this

week. I'll almost guarantee that," Cleary drawled. "This may be the only chance he's ever going to get, as far as I'm concerned, Augusta. I'd like to see just how well he can handle responsibility. This seems like a good place to start, wouldn't you say?" His eyes were dark, holding old secrets in their depths as he turned them in her direction. The firm tone he offered gave her no choice but to agree, at least for now. She would not argue in front of an audience, and well he knew it.

"What are you doing here?" she asked sharply, suddenly aware that his appearance at the front door was not a part of his plan for today. "I thought you were going to ride your horse this morning."

"I was...I am," he said. "Just as soon as I have a talk with your brother." He motioned toward the back of the house. "Join me in the yard, son." He glanced back at Augusta. "Don't go far. I want to talk to you, too."

She watched as he steered Wilson across the kitchen and out the back door. Something was going on, something beneath the surface. Cleary was not acting himself.

"He's pretty upset, ma'am," Honey said quietly. "I hope he doesn't send Wilson away, Miss Augusta." Her eyes filled with a renewal of tears. "I sure do love your brother. And finding someone willing to take me on—" Honey broke off, wringing her hands as if all hope had fled.

"Cleary isn't mean," Augusta said quickly, hoping to reassure the girl. "He'll do whatever's best for all of us. And if that includes bringing Wilson up to snuff, then that's exactly what will happen." And if that didn't work, then Wilson might as well wave goodbye, she thought sadly.

"I hope you're not mad at me, Miss Augusta." Honey's hankie mopped at her tears and she blew her nose with a lusty sound. "I wasn't trying to go behind your back when I took up with your brother. He was kind to me, and he hasn't taken advantage of me." She halted as if she considered those words. "Not that he probably wouldn't like to," she said quietly, as if she must be painfully honest.

"He'll treat you like a lady, Honey," Augusta said firmly. "And you'll expect that sort of treatment from him. I hope I've taught you that much." She held the girl's shoulders in her hands and then sighed, stepping closer to hug her tightly.

"Wilson is a good person, deep down. He's made some mistakes in his life, but if Cleary can get him on the right track, and if the law doesn't catch up with him first, he'll be a fine husband for you."

The words began as a soothing panacea to Honey's turmoil, but to Augusta's amazement, she recognized them as the truth, and her heart felt lighter. Through the back door, she caught a glimpse of Cleary and Wilson, heads together as they stood near the doghouse, Henry begging attention at their feet.

Something was going on this morning. Her instincts were raging. His wound nicely healed, she'd lay odds that Cleary was about to head for parts unknown once more. And her heart sank as she considered what that might mean.

It was late in the day when a knock sounded at Cleary's front door, and Augusta hastened to answer the summons. Cleary stood before her on the porch, and Augusta thought sadly that this was where it had all begun, on the day she'd come to solicit donations for the shelter. This time she faced him from the front hallway, Cleary on the threshold, awaiting entry. If he gave recognition to their meeting in a way reminiscent of that day, his demeanor showed little sign of it.

"Can I come in?" he asked, as if unwilling to remove her from his path. "I didn't think I'd need to knock on my own front door, Gussie."

"I had it locked for safekeeping while I was in the house alone," she explained, though even to her own ears the reasoning was flawed. No one in Collins Creek locked their doors during the day. Indeed, most of them didn't bother at nighttime, either.

But she'd known that Cleary would show up before the day was over, known he would be looking for her after her sneaky departure from the shelter earlier today. And she didn't want to be caught unaware by his arrival.

"You were hiding from me." He looked at her, his gaze noting her stance, her hands folded at her waist, her chin held high. "Do I frighten you?"

For a moment she thought to answer with a nod, then honesty prevailed, and she shook her head, a brief, single movement. "Only the man you become on occasion frightens me, Cleary."

He nodded in understanding. "Ah…the difference between *Cleary* and *Jonathan,* I assume." His smile was crooked, its warmth questionable. "Will we never get past this, Gussie?" His own arms were folded now over his broad chest, and she thought the gesture was only a symbol of the gap between them today.

Her shrug was diffident and her gaze dropped from his face to touch those wide shoulders, the long, muscular arms and well-formed hands. *The hands that touched with gentle care and a tenderness past imagining.*

Somehow the image of Jonathan and Cleary could not be joined in her mind today. Today he was Cleary, the lawman, and she must hold herself apart from him, lest she be hurt beyond repair should something happen to take him from her life. Already her heart ached as she waited for his words of farewell. They were not long in coming.

"I ran into Nicholas on my way to the livery stable to get my horse," he said quietly. "I'm afraid I'll need to leave for a few days."

"You knew that when you came to the shelter earlier, didn't you?"

He nodded. "I didn't want to talk about it in front of the rest of them."

She was silent, her stomach churning with despair. So easily he bade her goodbye, without care or concern for her well-being or whereabouts during his absence. And then he shattered that concept with a short, succinct reminder.

"I'll expect you here when I return, Gussie. I've put Wilson in charge at your shelter, and Pearl knows what to do in an emergency, though I doubt one will arise. You have everything in good order there. It only needs supervision."

"You expect me to remain in this house for an unknown amount of time, while you trot around the countryside, doing whatever it is you do? And I'm not supposed to ask questions, or wonder where you are or what's happening to you?" She was amazed at her reasonable tone, her firm words and her ability to remain dry-eyed in front of the man.

Her gaze sought his face, noting the thinning of his lips, the narrowing of his eyes and the faintly ruddy hue of his cheekbones as he considered her queries. "Yeah," he said finally. "I guess that's exactly what I expect of you. Is it too much to ask?"

With those words he hung her high on the fence of indecision, and she grasped for a handhold, seeking a reply, sensing a deep, gaping hole on either side of her. If she was biddable, as a good wife should be, she would forever give up what small shred of independence she'd managed to retain in this marriage. If she defied his edict, she might forevermore wonder what her marriage could have been, for surely her blatant disobedience would cast her into the role of a woman who had dishonored her marriage vows.

And so she sought the middle ground. "I don't know, Cleary. Maybe I'll have to think about it."

"You promised to obey," he reminded her, his eyes glittering with intent. He stepped closer and she was forced to retreat, backing into the hallway. He followed her, one foot lifting to close the big door behind himself. His arms circled her and she was drawn against his body, its hard lines ungiving against her tender flesh. Her breasts were mashed against his chest, her thighs enclosed by his as he widened his stance and lowered his hand to her hips.

Wide lips enclosed hers, seeking to dominate, and she was acquiescent, aware that she could not win such a battle of wills. He was stronger, and his anger rose like a red tide between them. His hands measured her waist, and as she shifted to remain clear of the pulsing arousal he'd managed to wedge between her thighs, he slid those broad palms down to clutch at her bottom.

Passion rose to claim her, and for a moment her lips gave way to his demand, opening to accept the movement of tongue and teeth. Then she shivered and turned her head aside, gasping for a breath. She could not allow this.

Bending his head, his voice was raw against her throat. "Gussie. Don't turn me away."

She closed her eyes to his appeal, her heart to his plea, and her answer was chilled by the ice that settled to encase her heart. "You promised to cherish me, Cleary. Is that what you call this?"

"This?" he asked, rubbing the thick ridge of his manhood against her. "I'll do more than cherish you, sweetheart, and well you know it. I'll give you a memory to hold while I'm gone."

"Don't be obtuse," she said sharply, pushing him away, catching him off guard. "I love you, but I won't be treated like a village idiot. I'm a woman, not a creature you can cajole into bed whenever it pleases you. Keeping me a prisoner inside this house may have worked during the last several weeks, while you were in residence, but short of tying me to the bedpost, you'll not keep me here while you're gone this time.''

''I didn't consider you a prisoner. I thought of you as my wife, the woman I love. And if you choose not to do as I ask, there is little I can do about it.'' he said quietly, his hands hanging by his sides, fingers held tightly inside fists that could inflict dire bodily harm, should he so choose.

She eyed them a moment and lifted her gaze to his. ''You look frustrated.''

''With good cause, don't you think?''

''I think you'd like to take a swing at me, Cleary.'' Her chin tilted upward as if offering a target for his consideration.

He felt a pang at this evidence of her mistrust. ''Have I ever hurt you, Augusta?''

She considered her aching heart, wondering if that qualified according to his criteria. And then she shook her head. ''No, of course not. I'm sorry. I know better.''

''I can only tell you that I'd rather you stayed here at night, so I'll know where to find you, or so Nicholas can reach you, should he need to. He won't want to call on you at the shelter if there should be news that would distress you.''

And then he grinned with just a trace of his old arrogance. ''Not that it would bother you overmuch should I not return. In fact, it would probably solve a couple of problems for you.''

''Don't say that,'' she whispered, seeking in those dark eyes a trace of the love he'd pledged to her. ''You know better.''

''Do I?'' His grin was crooked now, and she caught a glimpse of sadness, a tightening of his jaw and a flexing of those long fingers. "I want to tell you something. I've done what I could for your brother. I can only hope my actions will bear fruit on his behalf. And as for you, I've tried to treat you fairly, Gussie. I've given you more than I ever thought I could."

"I—"

"Hush," he said, placing his hand over her lips to halt her words. "Not in monetary things, I know that, but by putting you first in my life, almost neglecting my work in order to put our marriage on a firm basis." He looked down at her and his hand slid from her mouth.

"I can't do that today. I told you before that there's a cleanup operation to be handled, and I'm the only one who can tend to it. Nick may be out of town next week, and you'll be on your own when that happens. I just thought you ought to know." His smile was tinged with a remnant of desire as his hand touched her face, a gesture she knew was meant as a farewell of sorts.

She felt a pang of regret that she'd turned him away, and yet, she could not allow her heart to forever dictate her responses. There must be a compromise, a middle ground she could hold. Her hands lifted to his chest. "Will you kiss me goodbye?" she asked, her fingers clenching in the fabric of his shirt.

"Hell, yes." He bent his head and she offered the warmth of her mouth to him, opening to the thrust of his tongue, the biting edges of his teeth that touched her lips and then moved to her throat. His big hand moved her bodice to the side, sliding two buttons undone in order to attain his goal. He murmured words against the tender flesh of her neck, opening his lips to suckle the skin, then moving up to nuzzle beneath her ear.

She inhaled deeply, holding his scent as a memory against the coming days. The dark, forbidden aroma of Cleary, the masculine, seductive smell of Jonathan, and the sharp, acrid wisp of gun oil that rose from his holstered pistol.

His fingers closed the buttons at her throat and his hands cradled her face as he bent to bestow a last, almost chaste, touch of his mouth on her lips. "I'll be back."

And then he was gone, the door opening and closing soundlessly behind him. Augusta's hands rose to her face and she dropped to the floor, bending her head to touch her knees, her fingers already damp with the tears she shed.

His horse broke into a sharp trot as Cleary headed for the edge of town. His bedroll tied behind the saddle and his rifle secure in its sheath, he was as ready as he'd ever be to face the culmination of this operation. The last, he hoped, as an undercover man for the government. The men involved would be in one place, readying themselves for this, the largest shipment of gold yet.

That those who had plotted and planned their downfall were aware of his movements would hopefully not occur to the gang. Cleary was certain he'd infiltrated the group with sufficient skill that they would not suspect him of being anyone but who he pretended to be. He was a renegade, a former lawman, a money-hungry gunslinger, all of which were not so far from the truth that he couldn't substantiate his claim. Even Wilson's appearance in Collins Creek had not done damage to this operation, and for that Cleary was most thankful.

No matter what happened, Nicholas was sworn to pull the necessary strings to get the boy a full pardon, and Cleary had instructed the banker to call in all the markers he had available to accomplish the deed. At least, should he not return, Augusta would be left with one fond memory of him.

His lips tightened at that thought. It would not do to allow her image to intrude over the next few days. It would take every bit of his concentration to accomplish this task, and for now Gussie was safe, secure in his home and his bed.

The hotel room he found was a long way from a bedroll beneath a tree, and even the sounds of revelry from outside his window could not keep Cleary awake as he drew the sheet up to his waist. The thought of Gussie alone in his bed in Collins Creek entered his mind and he doggedly erased it, his long training allowing him to concentrate solely on the work that was ahead.

The streetlights in Dallas lit the interior of his room, and he watched the flickering glow on the ceiling as he considered the days ahead. First, he had to notify the men of his arrival, then follow the designated member to the hideout, a place he'd not been privy to until now.

He'd be in danger, but the plan Nicholas was setting into motion would cover that angle, once the men gathered and heard their instructions. He'd given the nod when Nicholas told him that the Pinkerton Agency was involved. The knowledge that those men were unrivaled in their skill, and that the results of their work were without blemish gave him an edge that would allow him to concentrate fully on the task at hand, knowing that his backup was secure.

The banks were paying a high price for the Pinkerton promise, but unless this group of outlaws was caught and sent to prison, they would lose much more than the cost of hiring the detectives. The net was closing, and the Pinkertons were arriving in town one by one, their disguises as close to perfection as his own.

He closed his eyes, counting sheep, secure in the knowledge that not only was his room locked, but any touch on his doorknob or the heavy wooden structure itself would rouse him from slumber.

He'd been here before. Not in this place, perhaps, but in

many other such situations. He touched the butt of his revolver, moved it closer to the edge of his pillow and closed his eyes.

Augusta rose behind his eyelids and he allowed himself a long look at the beauty of the woman he'd married. And then he forced himself to play through the schedule for the next few days.

Chapter Fourteen

The days passed more rapidly than she'd expected. But the nights were long, her bed chilled with the cool night air and the absence of Cleary beside her. Whether it was because she was a dutiful wife, or because he might think of her and picture her waiting in his bed, Augusta went home at night.

The image of a dutiful wife made her smile, knowing she was far from that state of perfection. Cleary had married an independent woman. What she gave him, she gave gladly and from her heart, not because of a vow she'd spoken the day she'd accepted his ring. And yet, he'd given more—a spoken promise of his love—on more occasions than she could count. And her own avowal had come sandwiched in the midst of a quarrel, barely significant enough to take his attention.

She walked the distance from one house to another, smiling as she thought of her loyalty to both of her homes. That Cleary's white, comfortable house on the better side of town would be her home in the years to come was a given. She would live there gladly. But her own place, the shelter in which she'd invested more than a good share of her nest egg, would always have a place in her life. She owed that to her mother.

The mother she still had not acknowledged in Cleary's hearing. And for that, she knew regret. It would be first on the agenda, once he came home and they took up their lives again. She owed him much, the least of which was her trust in this matter.

Once he came home. Those words were a litany she spoke daily, planning the small things that would please him, her memory of their last, ambiguous moments together becoming a tender parting between two lovers in her mind.

She could not afford to dwell on what might happen, on the danger he might even now be in, wherever he might be.

A knock on the door halted her hands in their task as she sorted through a box of belongings she'd carried home last evening. The last of her boxes, found in the dark corner of a closet, not taken when she'd moved into Cleary's house.

Wiping her fingers on the rag she'd used to dust the small collection of colored glass ornaments gathered through the years, she walked quickly toward the front door. The shadow apparent through the leaded glass panes was large, broad through the shoulders and too tall to be a woman. Perhaps Nicholas had come to call.

"I'll bet you're surprised to see me, Miss Augusta." Roger Hampton stood on the porch, his thumbs tucked nonchalantly into his front trouser pockets, his grin tainted by a hint of sadistic pleasure. "I come bearing good news for you."

"I somehow doubt that." Her heart beat heavily in her chest as she announced her skepticism. "The only thing you've ever given me has been trouble, Mr. Hampton."

"Tut-tut," he said, his smile denying her claim. "I distinctly recall offering you a proposal of marriage, and the promise of a diamond ring to grace your lily-white hand.''

She glanced down at the delicate band she wore, and her eyes blurred as she recalled the day Cleary had settled it into place on her finger. ''My hands are not lily-white,'' she said quietly. ''And as I recall, I turned down your proposal—several times, in fact.''

She looked up to meet his gaze and surprised a look of avid desire on those harsh features. Mr. Hampton's eyes roved her body and a dark flush covered his cheeks.

''Perhaps you won't be so hasty the next time,'' he told her. His voice had taken on a rough texture, and as he stepped forward, her natural instinct for protection caused her to reach for the door. His brow lifted in surprise. ''Do you think to keep me on the porch while I tell you the news?'' he asked. ''I think not, ma'am. You'll want privacy to hear the sad tidings I carry.''

''You told me you had good news to report, sir,'' she said. ''And you can tell me right here, without coming into my home.''

''Well, the news can be considered either good or bad, depending on which viewpoint you assume.'' He opened the screened door, and with a swift movement, captured her waist in his hands, lifting her and setting her aside to insure his entry. The heavy interior door closed behind him and he leaned back against it, releasing her from his hold.

''Now, isn't this better?'' His chest rose and fell, but to Augusta's eyes it was not because of the effort of moving her from his path. He inhaled again, deeply, as if he drew in a scent from her clothing and the body beneath that caused his lungs to expand in a deliberate effort. ''You must have used rosewater on your hair, ma'am. I declare I can catch a hint of flowers when I stand this close to you.''

''Then by all means, step away, sir,'' Augusta said stiffly. ''I did not invite you in.''

"Your husband told me you wouldn't be eager to see me." His voice was musing as he uttered the words, and his eyes narrowed, taking in her lush figure. She wore a formfitting dress today, and it emphasized a problem she'd noted over the past weeks. This simple cotton shirtwaist seemed to be the only one in her wardrobe that buttoned easily at her waist. And beneath its smooth, ironed surface, her breasts felt stifled by the bodice that clung to her like a well-fitted glove.

"You are looking lovely this morning, Miss Augusta," he said politely. He lifted one hand and touched her cheek with his index finger. "Hmm...no tears visible. I'd thought you might be pining for your husband, him being gone for a week already, and you waiting here like a good wife, all by yourself."

She flinched beneath the subtle brush of his fingertip against her skin and turned her head. Never in her life had she felt so vulnerable, so unable to cope with a situation.

Roger looked around the foyer and through the wide doorway into the parlor. His gaze roamed up the curving staircase to the second floor and then returned to her. "It seems you are alone."

"Yes," she said shortly. "I'm alone. Does that suit your purpose?"

"Well, it seems I'm to be designated to comfort you in your loss. I won't deny that I'm planning on obtaining a certain amount of satisfaction at that thought."

She felt the color drain from her face, and her legs trembled beneath her. "What loss are you talking about?"

"Why, the missing gentleman who can't quite seem to decide which role he should play in the general scheme of things, ma'am. He's dabbled in banking, owns a silver star that proclaims him a U.S. Marshal, and now, as of last week, I do believe his name and face are on Wanted posters." His smile was feral, his teeth glittering as his lips drew back to expose them. "Although they'll be able to tear those down very soon."

Augusta lifted her chin, determined not to allow this man access to her fear. "I haven't the least idea what you're talking about."

"He's been deeply involved in a series of train and bank robberies, ma'am. I warned you about him, but you chose not to listen to me. And now, he's been shot. They tell me he probably won't live long enough to hang with the rest of the gang."

Her back met the wall, and Augusta's hand dropped to clutch the curved arm of a small bench that graced the foyer. "What are you talking about?"

"Exactly what I said, Augusta." His facade of elegance disappeared as easily as did the polite edge his voice had worn. "I think you'd better sit down, before you fall down," he told her coolly.

"Cleary is wounded?"

His nod confirmed the image in her mind, of Cleary bloody and unconscious. She had prior knowledge of such a thing, recalling the night when he had lain on the kitchen floor as she'd cleaned and bandaged his wound. And now, he was... She lifted a hand to her temple, feeling the blood rush from her head.

"Where is he?" Her eyes closed as her mind sought frantically for a plan that would take her to him.

"Almost fifty miles from here," Roger said, and his words were fuzzy in her ears.

As if in a dream, she felt his hands on her, moving her to sit on the bench beside her, and then his palm pressed against the back of her neck as he pushed her head to her knees. Her mouth filled with bile, as her breakfast threatened to erupt from her stomach, and she gagged, causing him to step back hurriedly.

"If you're going to vomit, please turn aside," he said roughly. "I don't care to have my boots soiled."

And wasn't that typical of the man? She swallowed with effort and lifted her head. "I have no intention of losing my breakfast in the foyer," she told him, encouraged by the clarity of her vision and the warmth that returned to her body.

"I'll be happy to take you to see him," Roger said politely, and she thought he resembled the snake in the Garden of Eden. The apple he held before her was tempting, but the messenger was Satan personified, and she was not going to allow him to involve her in a wild-goose chase.

"Is he dying?" she asked, amazed at the cool tones of her query.

He pursed his lips and thought about it. "Most likely," he said finally. "Train robbers don't get the best of care, ma'am. The Pinkerton men likely feel they'll be saving the price of a length of rope if he gives up the ghost on his own."

"I doubt he's a bank robber." She felt her optimism waver as she thought about the last bullet wound Cleary'd received.

Roger shrugged. "You'll have to believe what you please. I'm just trying to make his last hours happy, bringing his wife to his side. As to the rest of it, ask the sheriff if you want the truth." He drew his pocket watch from his vest pocket. "I'll be back in an hour if you want to come back to Dallas with me. The sheriff's in his office, if you'd like to talk to him. I'm sure he can give you the details."

With a last piercing look that brought her to her feet, he opened the door and stepped onto the porch, then turned and tipped his hat in a gesture of ironic gentility.

Augusta watched as he departed, stood in the doorway as he mounted his horse and turned the animal in a tight half circle before he headed back toward the center of Collins Creek. And then she climbed the stairs, hastening to her bedroom, approaching her mirror and peering within its depths. Her hair was a bit disheveled, her cheeks pale, and with a quick swipe of her brush and a splash of cool water, she was ready to visit the local lawman.

It took ten minutes to walk the distance to his office, and she stood before the closed door for another full minute before she knocked on the solid, wooden panel.

"Come on in." It was a gruff, bold invitation and she turned the handle with the tips of her fingers, as if it held the dirt from a hundred filthy outlaw hands.

"Roger Hampton told me you had news of Cleary," she said, and was given a look of satisfaction from the broad, lined face of the man behind the desk.

"Cleary? That rascal you married, ma'am? I thought Mr. Hampton would have already given you the news about your husband."

"He told me Cleary was wounded."

"And did he tell you that he took a bullet while he was robbing a train, along with a whole slew of fellas?"

"He's not a criminal," Augusta said firmly.

"Well, I beg to differ with you, ma'am. He was right smack in the midst of the whole thing, they tell me. I sent Mr. Hampton down to tell you the news. He thought you might want to tell your husband farewell, but it doesn't look like you're gonna do that now, does it?"

"No, I'm not." Her chin held high, Augusta vowed not to give this cretin the pleasure of seeing her wilt before him. "In fact, I'm going to wait until I hear from him before I do anything."

"You'll wait a long time, ma'am," he said slyly. "Maybe you'd best go to the general store or that there ladies' furnishings place across the street and buy yourself a black dress to wear to his funeral."

She turned from him and walked back out into the sunlight, aware that the interior of the sheriff's office held a bad odor and she was in dire need of a breath of fresh air. She turned to walk down the sidewalk and felt the presence of hot tears against her eyelids. What if Cleary was, indeed, wounded? And she had refused to go to him. What if he died, without her being there to kiss him and whisper a farewell?

She stiffened her spine, willing the tears to vanish. Before her eyes the sunlight was shredded by a sparkling mist, and through that mist strode the figure of a woman. *Pearl.* Augusta reached out a hand beseechingly and spoke the single syllable of her name, as if it were a plea for help.

"Pearl?" An aura enveloped the strong, voluptuous form, a golden haze that blurred into darkness as Augusta felt her knees collapse beneath her.

"I declare, I never saw such a thing in my life. I knew you was strong, Pearl, but carrying Miss Augusta all the way home must of about wore you down to a frazzle." Honey's words were both respectful and disbelieving as she uttered her admiration aloud.

Rough hands clutched at Augusta's fingers, and Wilson's voice was thready as he called her name. "Augusta. Look at me. Open your eyes, sis."

Blue eyes, the exact color of her own, met her view as Augusta's eyelids lifted a bit. "Where's Pearl?" she asked, amazed at the wispy sound of her own voice.

"I'm right here," the woman answered, and Augusta turned her head to see Pearl seated in a chair, a damp cloth in her hand. With a quick swipe she brushed back a stray lock of hair and then ran the cloth over her face. "You 'bout wore me out, girl, totin' you all the way home."

"Miss Augusta told me once you were strong enough to wrestle an ox, bare-handed, but I guess I didn't believe it before now," Honey said, her voice subdued. "I never saw anything like it, you carrying her up the street and through the gate the way you did."

"Well, I never want to see anything like it again," Wilson stated firmly. He bent closer to Augusta. "Are you sure you're all right, sis? I can't imagine what made you lose consciousness that way. Do you think we should get hold of the doctor?"

"She'll be fine if y'all just clear out and let her breathe," Bertha said from the doorway. Her eyes were shrewd as Augusta sat up, lifting her eyes to meet the older woman's gaze. "I'm thinking there's nothing wrong with her that a little more than seven months' time won't cure."

Augusta pressed her lips together firmly, aware of the intake of breath beside her as Wilson plopped down on the sofa where her feet had been only moments before. "Is that true, sis?"

"I've only just begun to figure it out myself," she admitted. "How did you know, Bertha?" She caught a glimpse of good humor in the woman's dour countenance before a frown replaced it.

"Been there a couple of times in my life, and seen enough in my years to spot a woman in the family way, right off."

Pearl waved a hand, as if dismissing that particular problem in order to search out the answer to another. "What happened to you in town?" she asked, her words not allowing any dithering on Augusta's part. "Something musta upset you in a mighty way to cause you to faint."

With a rush of agony that struck hard at her heart, Augusta recalled the reason for her walk to town. "Roger Hampton told me that Cleary was wounded during a train robbery and the sheriff confirmed it," she said bluntly.

"And you believed that Hampton fella?" Pearl asked skeptically. "He's been after you since the first day I met you. Probably before then, if the truth be known."

"You're right, he has," Augusta said tonelessly. "But I don't have any reason not to believe him, I suppose, not with the sheriff backing up his story."

"I'd doubt anything that came out of that man's mouth," Pearl decreed. "Seems to me that our honorable sheriff ain't much of a fountain of truth anyway. He's a scalawag if ever I saw one. He gets his women for free, both at the saloon and the Pink Palace, too, lest he give them any trouble. And he's left behind more than one bruise, let me tell you. He's about the most slipshod lawman I ever heard tell of."

"Well, I don't know what to do. If Cleary's really wounded…" Augusta halted, her hands clenching in her lap. She looked up at the concerned faces surrounding her. "Roger said that Cleary was one of the gang, and he was shot by the Pinkerton men."

"And you believe that tale, too?" Bertha asked.

Augusta shook her head. "No, of course not. He's never told me a whole lot about what he does. But I can't imagine that he's a crook of any kind. And I don't trust Roger any further than I can throw him." She looked around, her gaze fastening on the mantel clock. "He said he'd be back in an hour to take me to Cleary."

"Here?" Pearl asked disbelievingly. "He's coming here?"

Augusta shook her head. "No, he'll go to Cleary's house."

"Well, you're not going to be there," Wilson said firmly. "You'll not go anywhere with a strange man. As a matter of fact, you're not going anywhere with anybody. You'll be staying here where we can keep an eye on you."

Pearl laughed aloud. "And your sister thought you'd never get a backbone and grow up, youngun." She looked fully at Augusta then. "Do you think Cleary's been shot?

Or do you think that fella's just tryin' to get you away from here for his own reasons?''

"I don't know." Her voice sounded weak and uncertain, and Augusta shook her head. "I really don't know what to think." She looked around her at the circle of faces, Glory and Janine having joined the group in the parlor. "If Cleary's been hurt, I should be there, I suppose. But I told the sheriff I was going to wait till I heard for sure before I did anything."

"Well, that oughta deliver a killing blow to old Roger Hampton's plans for you, I suspect," Pearl said sharply. "I'll warrant that man thought he had you right where he wants you, and if I know anything, I'll bet he's gonna plot to be sure Cleary is deader than a doornail, one way or another."

Her heart ached with the uncertainty of it all, and Augusta felt a great weakness overtake her. For the first time in years, she was hesitant about the direction she would take next. Somehow she couldn't sense that Cleary was near death, for certainly she would know, would feel the impending doom hanging over her like a dark cloud. And if he was on the side of the law, as he claimed, he'd return to her either with or without another wound for her to tend.

Struck with the vision of the ambiguous future before her, she leaned her head against the couch. "I'm tired," she said flatly. "I've just nicely discovered that I'm going to have the child of a man who's traveling on the edge of the law. He's never made it a point to be totally honest with me from the beginning. And I think I'm tired of see-sawing back and forth."

Her eyes opened wide and she fastened her gaze on Glory. "Go on upstairs and find me a place to sleep, Glory. I'm staying here until I know which end is up."

"I've never taken testimony from a dead man before," the judge said, settling himself into a chair beside the bed.

"But if this is the way the Pinkerton Agency wants to handle things, I'm willing to go along with it."

Cleary focused on the man beside him, willing the urgency of his pain to recede. The wound was not nearly so bad as others he'd suffered through the years, and head shots always bled like the very dickens. He'd been living with a banger of a headache for three days. Three days during which life had gone on outside this building.

He'd known, from secret visits with Judge Horace Hodges, that the Pinkerton man in charge of this operation had loaded a rough wooden coffin with a couple hundred pounds of rocks. With less ceremony than tossing a dead woodchuck over the fence, it had been buried in a pauper's grave, purporting to be that of J. Cleary, gunman and bank robber.

Cleary ached for Augusta, fearful that news of his death might have reached her already. There was no way to reassure her, and the success of this mission depended on secrecy, anyway. His testimony was essential to the outcome of the hearing and trial of the defendants who now sat in solitary confinement.

Lest anything happen to him, the judge had decided to take his testimony today, at his bedside. That he would also appear in the courtroom, three days hence, was a given. But this was a precaution, one Cleary could well understand.

"All right," Judge Hodges began, "I've got my clerk here ready to write down your statement. Let's get to it."

Cleary's head pounded with a vicious rhythm, but his thoughts remained clear as he spoke. The medication was gone from his body, and he'd spent a miserable night with no relief from the pain, but the doctor promised a dose of painkiller as soon as this ordeal was done. To that end, Cleary set out to describe the plan he'd formed and put into motion, beginning almost a full year ago when he'd settled in Collins Creek. He told of being notified by Nicholas Garvey that events were underway, putting Cleary at the forefront of the action. Then he continued with a detailed description of his activities since that time.

The clerk's hand flew across page after page of lined paper, and though some of Cleary's testimony was already known to Judge Hodges, he listened intently. "How many bankers were in on this?" he asked finally.

"Three in all," Cleary told him. "Nicholas Garvey set things up and called me in. I asked for the Pinkerton men to back us up, and then spent six months involving myself with the gang, searching out their leaders."

"More than one?" the judge asked.

"Yeah. That was the problem. We needed to get to the man at the top, and in order to do that, the banks took losses. Now, with almost the entire kit and caboodle of them in custody, we stand to retrieve some of the gold and cash they took. Some of it's gone, but with this mess cleaned up, it should be safe for the banks and the government to transport whatever they need to. There's one more man to nail, and I suspect he'll be here at the trial to gloat."

He grinned and his voice hardened with promise. "We'll grab him then." Sobering as he considered the future, he spoke a prophecy he feared was all too true. "At least things will be safe until someone else comes along and decides to take up where this gang left off."

He looked at the judge and felt a pang of regret as he spoke his mind. "I fear we'll have the criminal element with us so long as there are banks to steal from and trains to rob."

Judge Hodges nodded, his mouth twisting with a wry grin. "I'm afraid you're right, son. But we can only catch one at a time, and this bunch is gonna get sent up for more years than they can count."

He rose and flexed his shoulders. "I've got to get back to the courtroom. There's another case on my docket this afternoon." He looked at Cleary with a measuring eye. "I'll expect to see you in court on Friday. Till then, you lay low and keep yourself safe. I don't want to take any chances with someone sneaking in here and getting rid of our star witness."

"I go along with that," Cleary told him, aching for the promised dose of oblivion the doctor had promised, once this interview was a thing of the past.

From the doorway, the medical man met his gaze and, seeming to recognize Cleary's thoughts, he entered the room. "I think my patient needs to sleep, Judge. I'll have him on his feet by Friday, one way or another. You just leave us a deputy here to keep an eye on this room."

"Already seen to it," Judge Hodges told him, offering a hand to Cleary.

His head banged in rhythm to the firm handshake the judge offered, and Cleary winced, then closed his eyes.

"He's here," Pearl said sharply from the door of the parlor. "I figured he'd show up. The man's not about to turn you loose, Augusta."

Rising from the sofa, Augusta cast a long look at her friend. "I might as well see him for a minute. He needs to know he's not welcome anywhere near me. If Cleary was here, he'd nail his hide to the wall."

"If Cleary was here, a lot of things would be different," Pearl said tartly. "And you don't need to be getting upset again. We just nicely got you calmed down."

"I'm fine." Augusta waved aside her concern and walked across the parlor toward the screened door.

"I'd think you'd have given up," Augusta told the man waiting there. "I don't know why you followed me here. I'm not going anywhere with you, Mr. Hampton."

Roger shrugged, and shook his head. "Sorry to hear that, ma'am. I've got to take my leave. I'm heading back to Dallas now. I can't miss the hearing and the trial, and if your husband lives long enough, I'll see him there. I'll be sure to give him the message that you didn't want to see him one last time."

"You do that," Augusta said sharply. "And don't bother to come back here again."

She watched him leave, thankful that she'd met Roger this time surrounded by friends. He'd struck a note of fear in her that hovered yet in her mind. She'd had a close call with him, had not been smart enough to discourage him right off that day in Dallas when he'd approached her as she left the bank. He'd offered a five-dollar gold piece, asking if it were hers. Had she dropped it?

Stunned that a man so honest could be found in the city, Augusta had dithered over his query, then felt a blush cover her cheeks as she sensed his regard for her person. Before many days had passed, she'd begun to recognize him as a fortune seeker, and her flight to Collins Creek had been a twofold retreat.

Her shelter would, she'd decided, be more effective in a small town, where her soiled doves might find work or perhaps even a husband, once they were trained for a new venture. And leaving Roger behind had sealed her decision. She did not trust the man, and became aware that her money held an appeal he could not resist.

In fact, looking back now, she wondered if he might not be somehow involved himself, in the whole fabric of Cleary's problems in Dallas.

"You sent him packing, I see," Pearl said from behind her, joining her to watch Roger ride down the road.

"Yes. I don't trust the man. Never have and never will."

"He's a looker," Pearl observed. "But I've seen his kind before. I'd call him a four-flusher, rotten to the core."

"Well, he almost fooled me right off, when I met him in Dallas. He had me nailed as a woman with means, and he was determined to get his hands on my money. It didn't sit well when I came to Collins Creek, so he came after me. I suspect now he's just determined to get his pound of flesh one way or another. And Cleary seems to be his target."

"He's no match for Cleary," Pearl said stoutly. "You'll see."

"Well, I'm not sure I am, either." Augusta stepped back from the doorway. "My husband has a lot to clear up before I'm willing to go back to his house. I don't propose to be left in the dark any longer, Pearl. I wanted a husband who could be honest with me, and I won't have a man who's determined to trot off and get himself in a peck of trouble every time I turn around."

Pearl grinned. "Anytime you want to call it quits with him, I'll bet there's six or eight other females more than willing to take your place, ma'am." She laughed aloud. "In the meantime, just settle in here and let us tend you for a while."

"That's exactly what I plan on doing." Augusta headed for the stairs and began the climb to the second floor. "I'm going to ask Janine to help me let my dresses out tonight. I need some breathing space, in more ways than one."

Chapter Fifteen

"Miss Augusta? May I come in?" Nicholas stood on the porch the next morning, his hat in hand. Augusta touched the latch and the door swung open, the spring protesting as it stretched.

"Certainly, you may," she said politely. "How did you find me here?"

His grin was quick. "Everyone in town knows you've left Cleary's house to move back into the shelter," he said cheerfully. "You're quite the topic of discussion."

"Well, I certainly never meant to be," she said sharply. "I don't appreciate folks following my every move."

"Then you shouldn't be so much in the public eye," he told her, strolling behind as she walked into the parlor. He took a seat, looked around and leaned back in the chair he'd chosen. His boots were polished, his trousers sharply creased, and his hair gleamed like a crow's wing in the sunlight. An altogether attractive man, Augusta decided.

But he couldn't hold a candle to Cleary, she thought glumly, as she sat upright in a straight chair. And why that should be was not a puzzle as far as she was concerned. Cleary, though not handsome in the conventional sense, had a quality, an appeal that no other man possessed, to her way of thinking.

He'd made her love him. With very little effort, he'd claimed her, heart and soul, and even the flashing good looks of Nicholas Garvey held little appeal to her senses.

"What can I do for you this morning?" she asked, hoping in her heart of hearts that he carried news of Cleary's whereabouts and well-being.

"I thought I'd drop by to see if you were handling things well," he said quietly. His smile was gone, his eyes serious as he held her gaze. "I know you're worried, Augusta. I don't blame you. The news from Dallas is not good."

She stiffened. "What have you heard? The same claptrap Mr. Hampton tried to pass off as the truth?"

Nicholas looked down at his boots, as if a weighty matter merited his consideration. "I think you came close to disaster with that man, Augusta. There may have been plans in the works for you to be taken to Dallas, in order to convince Cleary not to testify against the gang."

"Then why didn't it happen?" She felt a sick fear grip her heart, adding to the concern for Cleary that occupied her thoughts.

"I don't know for certain," Nicholas said. "He may have had second thoughts, or maybe he cares about you more than we realize. Whatever his reasons, he left alone on the early train to Dallas. I consider it good riddance, and I have a notion he's going to come to disaster once he reaches there. However, the story he used to lure you to accompany him might not have been a total fabrication, my dear."

"He said Cleary was wounded, and probably would die in jail." She made the blunt statement without embellishing it in any way, and held her tears in abeyance while speaking the words. Her pillow was still damp from the abundance she'd shed during the night hours. She felt drained, her eyes dry and burning, her heart sore within her breast.

"Well, Cleary's not in jail. That much I know for certain. I got a wire from a Judge Hodges in Dallas this morning. He tells me that a coffin was buried two days ago in a pauper's grave on the outskirts of Dallas. The wooden marker bears Cleary's name."

Augusta felt a rushing wind fill her body, clouding her thoughts and causing her hands to tremble as she lifted them to her face. "Is he sure?" she asked, holding her voice steady with an amazing effort.

"He's sure there was a coffin buried, yes. But I thought it was odd that he didn't tell me there was a body in it."

She lowered her hands slowly to her lap and lifted her gaze to his. "I don't think I understand."

"I read it three or four times before it sank in that he was telling me something beyond the words themselves, Augusta. No doubt there was a chance that the wrong element would be privy to the wire, no matter how secret such things are supposed to be. I think, and God above knows I hope I'm right…I think Cleary's alive, and they're holding him, probably hiding him somewhere, until the trial."

She stood and paced to the window, forcing her legs to be strong, her knees to hold her body erect. Outside, the trees still held the green hues of summer, but the corner of the garden visible to her eyes contained only tangled tomato vines, with a few green specimens still clinging tenaciously. A few feet over, dried plants aboveground hid the hills of potatoes beneath, waiting to be dug. She thought of using the three-tined spade to bring them forth. A good job for her this afternoon, she decided.

"Augusta? Are you all right?" Behind her, Nicholas's voice was concerned and quiet, filled with dark whispers of doubt. She heard him approach across the carpet, felt his

warmth behind her, and with a wrenching cry, she turned
to him.

His arms circled her with gentle care, one hand touching
her shoulder, the other patting at her back. "He's alive,
Augusta. I feel it, deep inside, where such things as trust
and a belief in God's justice abide." He looked down at
her, one palm moving to cup and lift her chin, until her
gaze met his. "I want you to have faith in the man."

Tears flowed silently, and agony seemed to grip her with
iron claws. Yet, in the face of Nicholas Garvey, she saw
an optimism that penetrated her despair. "I hope you're
right," she whispered. "I've lost my parents and my home,
then found a new family here in Collins Creek. My brother
has returned to me, but in exchange I've lost Jonathan."

"Jonathan? So that's his name." A grin enveloped the
dark features as she watched. "He signed his account with
just his last name," Nicholas explained. "Wouldn't say
what his Christian name was, and I didn't press him. He's
not the only man I've met who doesn't tell all he knows."

He reached into his pocket and drew forth a clean white
handkerchief. Unfolding it, he offered it for her use, and
Augusta took it thankfully. Her eyes wiped free of tears on
its pristine surface, she held it in her hand.

"Thank you for giving me a shoulder to cry on," she
said, attempting to smile. "I'm taking back the statement I
just made. I don't know for sure that I've lost Jonathan, do
I? And I'm not willing to admit defeat." She sniffed once
and drew a deep breath. "Besides, I'm quite angry at him,
and if I believe he's truly alive, I can work up to being
really furious and enraged by the time he shows up on my
doorstep."

"And what are you so *furious* about?" Nicholas asked,
his lips curving in a tender smile. "You're too nice a lady
to hold a grudge."

"Well, I've been working on this one for a while," she

admitted. "He's never been honest with me, and the longer I think about it, the angrier I get."

"Did you ever think that maybe there were things he couldn't tell you?" he asked.

She shot a look of disgust in his direction. "You make a good pair. Are you certain you're not related?"

He backed away, picking up his hat from the sofa and holding it at his side. "No, not by blood, but we probably have some similarities, deep down." Eyes that took note of her tearstained cheeks and then settled on the clenched fists at her waist were dark with mystery.

"I can't tell you anything else, Augusta, only that I'll keep my ear to the ground. We probably won't know much more until things are settled in Dallas. In the meantime, I may be reading between the lines, but the honorable judge didn't tell me to come post haste to Dallas to claim Cleary's coffin, and that gives me reason to think that we just need to sit tight."

"Then you'll be here, after all?" she asked, following him to the doorway. "Cleary told me when he left that you might be going to Dallas yourself."

"He was right. The judge did tell me I need to appear there for the trial, so I'll be leaving soon, perhaps tomorrow. By the time I've been there a day, I should know more about Cleary's whereabouts. In fact," he said, turning to face her, "if I have to turn into a grave digger myself, I'll find out for sure exactly what was in that coffin they buried."

"Thank you," she whispered, then lifted a hand to press it against his forearm. "Do you think I should go along?"

He shook his head. "No. You're safe here. Don't go home. Let Wilson and the ladies take care of you." With long strides, he was out the door and down the steps.

"I was listening, sis." From behind her, Wilson's words

were quiet. "I'll be willing to lay odds that Cleary's alive. And I suspect the banker thinks so, too."

"That's about what he said," she murmured, watching as Nicholas stepped into his saddle. She lifted a hand as he looked back at the house, and he touched the wide brim of his hat in silent salute.

"What do you think?" Wilson's arm curled around her shoulders and he bent to press a silent kiss against her temple. Before she could reply, he laughed quietly. "My bet is on Cleary. The man's too ornery to die, sis. Don't forget, I watched him get shot, and then a week later saw him in a courtroom. He bled like a stuck pig, and I wouldn't have given him a chance to live through the night." He smiled, remembering. "A few days in bed had him on his feet, as good as new. They'd have to do more than put a bullet in Cleary to keep him away from you."

"I'm trying to be hopeful," she said. "Nicholas seemed positive, didn't he?"

"I'd say so." Wilson's hands turned her from the door and back toward the parlor. "Now, come on in here and talk to me, sis. I think we've got some catching up to do."

"I need to know how the books look," she told him, "and what ideas you have for moneymaking projects for my ladies."

Wilson winced. "Here I thought we'd be having old-home week, and instead you're wanting a detailed account of my work for the past weeks."

"We can do both," Augusta told him. "We've got time."

The courtroom was filled to overflowing, with guards standing at alert around the perimeter as more than twenty men were led into the suddenly cramped area. The judge peered over the top of his spectacles at the motley crew and tapped his gavel as the observers' voices rose in a low rumble of sound.

"We'll have order in my courtroom," he said sharply. His keen eyes scanned the extent of his jurisdiction this morning, nodding several times as his gaze met that of various men he apparently recognized. From the hallway just beyond the courtroom door, Cleary watched, disgusted by the doctor's orders prescribing more salve covered by a white bandage that circled his head beneath the hat he wore.

And yet, he knew himself fortunate to be here at all. His patience was at an end, both with the medical man who had kept him close to a bed for several days, and to the circumstances keeping him from Collins Creek and Augusta's presence. Once this thing was over and done with, nothing would be able to halt his departure. The next train out of Dallas in the general direction of home would find him occupying a seat in the coach, while his horse traveled in a livestock accommodation.

Beside him, as tall and broad shouldered as himself, Nicholas stood guard, his revolver holstered, but his eyes vigilant for trouble. On his other side a well-dressed gentleman kept equal watch. A Pinkerton man, if Cleary's guess was right. He'd be willing to warrant that more than one other guard was behind him, but his head did not lend itself to sharp movement yet, and he decided to leave that observation to chance.

The gang stood before the bench, with both hands and feet bearing heavy chains. The men were attached to one another by the chains on their feet. A veritable train of crooks, Cleary thought, headed for the gallows, if things went as predicted. With one piece of the puzzle missing, he felt restless, prone to rush through these proceedings in order to locate the final man he wanted brought before a judge.

"Let's go in," Nicholas said quietly. "The judge has called the court to order."

Cleary murmured assent, his mind on the trial, one he knew would be short and to the point. The hearing had been quick, and the men accused of a federal offense. Now they awaited trial and the appearance of the key witness. Their only prayer was in the purported death of that man, and Cleary was here to put paid to those hopes.

He settled in the back row, where three seats had been reserved for him and his escorts. The man on his left nudged him, nodding at the hat still settled firmly on his head, and with a dark look, Cleary lifted it gently and rested it on his knee. Eyes turned to view him, whispers rose as his bandage was noted, and the judge slammed his gavel on the desk once more.

"There will be order in my court," he said loudly.

The preliminaries were quick, the men on trial seeming to understand that they were at the end of the road. In the midst of the prosecutor's speech, another man entered the courtroom, standing just inside the double doors.

Nicholas nudged with one elbow and Cleary glanced to his right, beyond where Nick sat, noting the late arrival. As he did, one of the nondescript-appearing men standing guard stepped to the latecomer's side and grasped his elbow, glancing at Cleary, as if for confirmation.

"I didn't think he'd be fool enough to show up here," Nicholas said in an undertone, reaching one hand to put pressure on Cleary's arm. "You stay put," he said harshly beneath his breath. "Let the law take care of him."

Cleary exhaled and nodded at the guard as the new arrival turned to catch his eye. Roger Hampton's face blanched, the color leaving his ruddy cheeks in a rush, and then there was turmoil as he attempted to jerk free from the hand that held him fast. Another agent joined the effort, and Roger was escorted to the front of the courtroom, where the judge eyed him with scorn.

"I beg your pardon," he said to the prosecutor, interrupting him mid-sentence, "but I think we've just gotten our hands on the final defendant in this case."

"I'm no such thing," Roger said, blustering as he stood between two stalwart lawmen. "I'm here as an observer."

"Well, you've observed yourself right into a trial," the judge said sternly. He rapped his gavel again. "We'll take a ten-minute break while we add this man to our list of defendants."

"It didn't take long, did it?" Nicholas looked up at the blue sky, as if he welcomed the sun's warmth after an hour of observing the scum of society getting their just dues.

"No," Cleary agreed, standing on the courthouse steps, inhaling deeply of the fresh air. "I feel clean for the first time in a year. I was getting so deeply involved in that mess, I had to wonder some days if I'd ever be my own man again."

"I think someone else has a claim on you, my friend," Nicholas said wryly. "You stopped being your own person a couple of months ago."

One corner of his mouth turned up, and Cleary allowed the grin full sway. "I've lost some weight. The doctor's wife was no great shakes as a cook. Suppose Augusta will recognize me?"

"I think she'll know who you are," Nicholas said with a grin. "But don't expect a hero's welcome, my friend. She's madder than a wet hen."

Cleary sighed, gloom settling over him rapidly, even spoiling his pleasure in the beautiful day. "I figured she would be."

"She still doesn't know for certain that you're alive. Want to send a wire?"

Cleary shook his head. "No, I want to go home. I think I need to deal with this myself." He looked down the length of the wide avenue before them. "How far is the train station?" If it was a considerable distance, he wasn't certain he could make it on foot, but admitting it, even to Nicholas, was not to be considered.

Nicholas gave him a measuring glance. "Not far. We'll whistle down a hansom cab and head there now. I've sent our belongings ahead, along with the horses."

"Thanks," Cleary said, more than willing to go along for the ride, storing his strength for the ordeal he was certain to face once he turned up at Augusta's front door.

"She's staying at the shelter," Nicholas said. "At least that's where I saw her last."

"I thought she would be. Once she heard they'd buried me, I didn't think she'd want to be alone. And I feared that Hampton had something in the works that involved her. I shouldn't have asked her to stay at the house in the first place."

"She has her doubts that you're really six feet under, my friend. In fact, I told her I was dead certain you were in hiding. I thought they'd be secreting you in a closet somewhere, waiting for the trial, lest some of those men had friends out looking for you."

"Hampton was the only one left. I can't believe he was foolish enough to get caught up in the net," Cleary said glumly. "I was really hoping to get a few minutes alone with him myself, after the way he hounded Gussie in Dallas. And then he gave her a hassle after she got to Collins Creek. It wasn't bad enough that he was a go-between for the gang. The man's a criminal of the worst kind, preying on helpless women."

A hoot of laughter met his words, and Cleary looked up in surprise. Nicholas's grin was wide, his teeth flashing as he tossed his head back in a gesture that invited smiles from onlookers.

"Augusta is about the least helpless woman I've ever met," the banker said. "She'd give any man a run for his money, you included."

"I know," Cleary told him dryly. "That's what I'm worried about. I think I'll be eating humble pie for the next six months, trying to get back on her good side. I didn't leave her with much to remember me by the last time I saw her."

"Well, at least she loves you," Nicholas told him. "If ever a woman was besotted with a man, it's your wife. You're a lucky so-and-so, in my book. And whatever you have to do to get back in her good graces will be worth it, to my way of thinking."

Cleary perked up a bit at that, stepping off the sidewalk as a cabbie stopped his vehicle before them. "The train station," he told the man, climbing into the interior of the enclosed cab. He settled back in the seat, breathing deeply. "I don't care what I have to do to please her—damn, I'll eat crow if I have to, Nick," he said quietly. "No matter what it takes, I want Augusta in my life for all the years I have left on this earth."

The kitchen table was stretched to its full length, the leaf in place. Bertha smoothed the oilcloth with a damp rag and wiped it dry with the dish towel she'd slung over her shoulder. "Honey, come set out the plates," she called. "Supper's about ready."

From the backyard, Honey's voice answered, and then her laughter rang out, bringing an answering smile to the women in the kitchen. "She sure sounds different than she used to, don't she?" It was a question requiring no answer, and Augusta only nodded, aware of Honey's reason for happiness.

Wilson was courting her with dogged determination, this

afternoon digging the potatoes Augusta had planned on tending to several days ago. Honey was ensconced in a chair, watching from the edge of the ragtag garden as Wilson dripped sweat in her behalf. Piles of potatoes sat here and there, awaiting a final rinsing in a bucket before they were stored for the winter months.

A fruit cellar beneath the house was cool, winter and summer alike, and carrots were already piled atop boards in its depths, keeping them off the ground. Sacks of onions hung from hooks overhead, and jars of canned fruit and vegetables lined the shelves in the cool cavern. Now the potatoes would be added to the bounty stored there.

Augusta felt a sense of well-being as she considered the progress made during these months of summer. If she never accomplished anything else of value in her life, she would look back at this place and these women and recognize the worth of this project.

Honey entered the door and washed her hands quickly, speaking of Wilson and the gardening in a rapid recitation that sailed completely over Augusta's head. "Don't you think so, Miss Augusta?"

The words caught her ear and she turned quickly, aware that her expression was blank. "I'm sorry, Honey. I missed what you said."

The girl's face took on a sorrowful look. "I sure wish we'd hear some news pretty soon, ma'am. You look like a lost duck in a thunderstorm these days. That Cleary has a lot to answer for, not getting hold of you."

"The man might not be in any shape to send messages," Bertha said glumly. "Last we heard, he might well be—"

Augusta put her hands over her ears. "I don't want to hear such a thing," she said sharply. "Let's get this table set for supper."

In less than ten minutes the family had gathered, and the food was brought to the table. Bowls of vegetables and a platter of leftover ham from dinner were passed from one hand to the next, and Glory began a story about the dress she was sewing.

Janine offered words of encouragement, and then Wilson proposed an idea he'd apparently been mulling over. Suggestions for setting up a shop in the front parlor sailed over Augusta's head, only a word here and there penetrating her thoughts. Pearl chimed in and Augusta recognized the air of amusement as she spoke, finally recognizing that she was missing something that could be important.

"Cleary told me to be thinking of moneymaking ideas," Wilson said stoutly. "I think a bakery or dressmaker's shop of our own would be a good idea."

"Whoa," Augusta said quickly. "I think we need to back up a bit here."

"I gave the man a job to do. Don't discourage him." From the hallway beyond the kitchen door, the statement held them in stunned surprise.

Then Augusta rose to her feet, her chair falling on the floor behind her. Glory whispered a soft prayer of thanksgiving, and Honey burst into tears. Pearl looked up and grinned with apparent delight.

A bandage circled his head, and his muscular frame appeared to have lost some of its bulk, but there was no doubt that the man walking in the kitchen door was Cleary.

"Got room for one more around the table?" he asked, his eyes never leaving the woman who faced him from across the room.

Wilson moved quickly from his seat between his sister and Honey. "Here, sit in my chair. I'll get another from the dining room," he offered. His eyes darted to Augusta as if he hesitated to leave her side, but Honey nudged him into action.

"Thank you. I believe I will," Cleary said, circling the table and holding his wife's chair for her to reseat herself.

She looked at him blankly, her face ashen, her eyes wide, and he bent to her, his lips brushing hers in a quick kiss.

"Miss me?" he asked. He touched her chair to the back of her legs and she sat down, abruptly to be sure, but perhaps just in time, as she seemed unable to take in the sudden turn of events.

"Pass the man some spuds," Bertha said, aiming the platter of ham in Cleary's direction as she spoke. "I'll get more gravy." Her eyes shone with an unfamiliar gleam as she turned to the stove, and Augusta was unbelieving. Surely Bertha would not be teary eyed. Not this no-nonsense woman who ran the kitchen with an iron hand.

And yet, looking around the table, there was more evidence of emotion on the faces of those who had waited with her for some solution to the problem that was Cleary. Glory fished a hankie from her pocket and wiped her eyes, while Janine sniffled once as she held out a bowl of green beans in Cleary's direction.

"I haven't had a decent meal since I left home," he said, piling the food high on his plate. "I've been looking forward to this. I can't resist your cooking, Bertha." His left hand fell to his lap and in seconds had made its way to Augusta's right thigh, where it opened wide against her dress, his fingers spreading to capture the warmth of her skin.

He bent his head in her direction and his lips barely opened as he whispered words audible only to her ear. "I missed you, sweetheart. I'm sorry I didn't send a wire before we left Dallas, but I only wanted to get home as quickly as I could."

She could not speak. The mixture of joy and aggravation bubbling within her breast held her speechless. Joy for his safe return, aggravation that he walked in like the cock of the walk and acted as though he'd been on a short jaunt to the hardware store for a bag of nails.

She had wept and wailed, crying until there were no more tears to be shed. Now he sat here beside her with a bandage wrapped around his head, not one word being said to let her know what lay beneath the white strip of fabric. Anger joined the aggravation, and joy went flying as she rose and deposited her half-eaten meal on the drain board.

"All done?" Cleary asked, his eyes narrowing as he took in her stance.

"You bet I am." She turned away and sailed across the kitchen. Behind her, the sound of another chair hitting the floor barely caught her attention, and when his hands spun her in a half circle to face him, she looked at him with blue eyes blazing with fury.

"Welcome home," he said mockingly. "Go on. Say the words, Augusta. Even if you don't mean them, at least make the effort." He caught her elbow and hauled her behind him as he marched out of the kitchen.

"Hold on, Cleary." Wilson's voice was harsh. "Don't get her upset. She doesn't need any more on her plate than what you left her with."

Cleary looked back into the kitchen. "And what is that supposed to mean?"

Bertha stood, a formidable figure, and pointed an index finger in Cleary's direction. "You hurt that child, or that baby she's toting under her apron, and you're a dead man, mister."

"What baby?" His words were choked, caught in his throat and barely audible. He turned Augusta toward him, his eyes wide as they fed hungrily on her face. *"What baby?"* He repeated the words, this time for her benefit alone, and she felt relief as twin streaks of crimson touched his cheeks.

"Yours," she answered quietly.

"Mine?"

"Do you doubt it's yours?" She looked into his eyes,

the dark orbs that had promised more passion in her life than she'd ever thought possible. Now they blazed with hope, if she was any judge of it.

"Hell, no, I don't doubt it. Of course, it's mine," he stated equivocally. "You're mine, too. And don't you forget it."

"I thought you might be dead," she said, unwilling to state as fact the fear she'd lived with over the past days.

"I thought I might be dead, too," he said agreeably, his lips twisting in a cruel suggestion of a smile. "Matter of fact, I wasn't sure I wanted to live for a day or so there."

She looked at the bandage he wore. "Gunshot wound?"

"Just nicked my scalp." He grinned at her doubtful look. "Well, a bit more than that, but I survived."

"I thought I might not," she told him quietly.

"You will," he told her. "Let's head for home, Gussie. You'll have to ride on the back of my horse."

"I'm staying here for now," she told him. "I'm still mad at you."

"Because I almost died? Or because I didn't?"

"Neither. Both, maybe. Mostly because you find it so easy to walk away from me. I can't do this any more, Cleary. I'm tired of wondering where you are and what's happening to you. This isn't the way I want to live my life."

"I understand that. But that isn't the way it's gonna be from now on."

"Really."

His nostrils flared as he inhaled sharply. "Yeah, really."

Bertha approached the doorway, arms akimbo, eyes narrowed as she spoke his name with stubborn intent. "Cleary. She doesn't have to leave if she doesn't want to."

He spared her a sharp glance. "She doesn't have a choice. She's my wife, and she's going home with me. You can send someone over with whatever stuff she brought here with her.''

He bent to scoop her into his arms and Augusta clutched at his neck, lest she fall to the floor. Over his shoulder, the occupants of the kitchen watched, frozen in place as they beheld the Texan stomp his way down the hallway to the front of the house. His hip nudged the screened door open and he stepped onto the porch, Augusta grasped firmly in his arms, her skirts in disarray.

At the front gate stood a buggy, Nicholas holding the reins of the brown mare standing before it. ''Thought you might need some transport,'' he called out to Cleary, and then tipped his hat to Augusta. ''Good evening, Mrs. Cleary. I told you I'd be back.''

He watched as Cleary approached, bearing his burden, then stood aside as Augusta was bundled summarily onto the seat. Nicholas's smile was brilliant as he shot her a look of triumph. ''I found out there were rocks in the coffin.''

Chapter Sixteen

"Upstairs with you," Cleary said gruffly as he escorted Augusta through the door.

"What about the buggy?" She stopped in the middle of the foyer and set her jaw. "You can't leave that animal out in front of the house all night."

"You're more concerned about that damn horse than you are your husband," he told her. And then he relented. "Nick will take care of returning it to the livery stable. Sam knows to wait for it to arrive before he closes up for the day."

"I have things to do," she said, wary of climbing the stairs with him hot on her trail. The sun had settled against the western horizon as they drove across town, and now twilight settled around the house like a shroud. Maybe a light would help.

The hall table held a shaded kerosene lamp and she took three steps to where it sat, near the curving staircase. A box of matches sat beside it, and, as she picked it up Cleary moved swiftly, snatching it from her hand. She looked up into his face, biting her lip as tension hovered between them. "I wanted some light."

"You don't need a lamp to climb those stairs."

"I thought we might go into the parlor and discuss things."

"We can say anything that needs to be said after we get into bed." His jaw was set, his eyes in shadow, and she heard a forbidding note in his voice. If the man was trying to intimidate her, he was doing a credible job of it. He dropped the matchbox onto the hall table and grasped her waist, turning her in a half circle, then up the stairs.

It seemed Cleary was not in a mood for small talk.

She entered the bedroom before him, almost tripping over a throw rug that lay rumpled near the doorway. He tightened his grip and she heard a quick breath escape his mouth. "Are you all right?"

"Yes, I'm fine. Just clumsy."

"Stop where you are," he said quietly, his hand tightening its hold, fingers pressing with firm strength against her hip. He turned her until her back was presented to him and she offered no resistance. Swiftly his deft fingers made short work of her buttons, and she relaxed her stomach muscles, aware that this dress was not one Janine had worked on for her.

Bertha said that some women carried extra weight right off when they got in the family way, and it seemed that Augusta was fated to be one of them. She felt waterlogged, her breasts sensitive, the swollen crests darkening more every day. And the puffiness extended to her once narrow waistline, her one small vanity sacrificed on the altar of motherhood.

"Your dress looks like it shrank," Cleary said.

"No, I just grew." She might as well be straightforward with him. He had another seven months of this to live through. "I'm sleepy a good share of the time. I've been throwing up for the past several mornings for no good reason, and I tend to cry a lot."

"I'd say you had a mighty good reason to lose your breakfast. Don't they call it morning sickness?"

She huffed harshly. "A lot you know. Breakfast has nothing to do with it. I've barely made it out of bed the last few days, before I'm gagging and retching in the slop jar. Bertha tells me I probably have that to look forward to for a month or so."

"Well, if that's gonna be a regular occurrence we'll have to put the thing a little closer to the bed." He slid her dress down her arms and pushed it past her waist to fall on the floor. The strings of her petticoat were loosened and it followed her dress. Standing before him, she was garbed in drawers and a lace-edged vest, with dainty garters holding her stockings securely just below her knees.

"Let's get these off," he murmured, lowering her drawers to join the petticoat and dress, and then lifting the vest over her head. "Now step out of there," he told her, grasping her hand as she moved away from the clothing. He tilted his head to one side, as if he were examining her figure, bit by bit.

"What are you looking at?" she asked, aware that her anger was fading in the light of his obvious desire. Even in the dusky light from the bedroom windows, she could not miss the evidence. His eyes glittered with a passion she'd become familiar with over the past months, and an obvious bulge in his trousers gave away his interest in her.

"I haven't seen you in well over a week, sweetheart," he said, his words slow, his voice rasping. "But I don't know how I missed the signs before I left."

She looked down at herself, noting the response of her breasts to his survey of her figure. As she watched, the crests tightened and she caught her breath, looking up quickly to meet his enigmatic gaze. His lips thinned, and then his eyes took in the fullness that had caused her dress to pull at the seams.

"Damn, you're pretty." The husky tone was familiar. A gauge of his desire, his voice deepened in increments as he allowed his passion full sway. And it seemed tonight was to be no different, no matter that she'd protested his dragging her home. The man was incorrigible, a veritable roughneck with only one thing on his mind at this moment.

And with sudden clarity, Augusta recognized that all of her womanly instincts savored that very quality about Jonathan Cleary. He wanted her. *Desired her* might be more to the point, she decided, and if he was to be believed, he loved her. There was a certain satisfaction to be gained from being the object of a man's desire. And she was too honest not to admit her own fascination with his body and the pleasure it was capable of bestowing upon her.

He lifted one hand to touch one dark, pebbled peak, his fingers closing over the sensitive tip with a gentleness she had become familiar with. A shiver ran the length of her spine and he smiled, a dark, knowing expression lighting his face. "I think I'd like a lamp lit now," he murmured.

"No." Her reply was quick as she shot a glance at the windows, their shades at half-mast.

"I'll pull the shades first," he said quietly, and then looked into her eyes. "But I want a lamp lit." And then at her indrawn breath, he grinned. "I'll settle for a candle."

Her voice wobbled. "There are several in my dressing table drawer." Standing before a fully clothed man, being clad only in white stockings, held up by pink garters, gave her a feeling of vulnerability. And Augusta was not accustomed to that state of mind. And yet, there was a joyous anticipation flooding her female parts that would not bow to her normal inhibitions.

She was upset with the man. There was no getting around the anger she'd allowed to build whilst he was gallivanting around the countryside, putting himself in danger and getting himself shot. Yet now that she had him before her, and the opportunity was presenting itself to vent her wrath, she found herself melting into a willing woman.

He'd pulled the shades, then found the candles, a series of events that made her laugh as he pawed through the dressing table. "Why didn't you find the candles first?" she asked.

"I can't think straight," he said gloomily, striking a match and holding his hand behind the wick as the flame caught and flared. He looked up into the mirror over her dressing table and she saw the candle glow reflected in his eyes, herself a pale shadow in the background.

The small crystal holder on her lamp table held the candle nicely and he stood in the flickering light, his hands working slowly to strip his clothing, tossing it aside with careless gestures. "I should have taken a bath," he said. "But I can't wait that long."

She trembled in the warmth of his appraisal, his eyelids heavy, his hair rumpled. The picture of a man set on seduction. He flipped the quilt and top sheet, tossing them to the foot of the bed. Rescuing the pillows, he replaced them and nodded at her.

"Get in." As invitations went, it rated pretty low on the scale, she decided, but it didn't seem she would receive another. As she hesitated, he stalked around the foot of the bed, and in less time than it took her to catch a hurried breath, he was beside her, lifting her and placing her with care upon the clean sheet.

"Now, let's talk about this baby." He was beside her, parting her legs with gentle hands, then taking his place over her, the length of his manhood pressing insistently against her flesh. He lifted to his forearms, taking his weight from her body, and only the twitching of that male member gave notice of his urgency.

"What do you want me to say?" she asked.

"How long have you known?" His hand curved to cup her cheek and his fingers nestled in her hair.

"Not long. A few days. I'd just about figured it out the day before I went to the sheriff and then fainted dead away on the sidewalk."

He frowned. "You fainted? How'd you get home?"

"Pearl was going into the general store and she carried me home."

"Damn! I knew she was a tough one, but that takes the cake."

"About wore her out. When I roused enough to know where I was, everyone was standing around in the parlor and Bertha let the cat out of the bag. She told them there wasn't anything wrong with me that a little more than seven months' time wouldn't fix."

He grinned. "How about that. Must have done the deed on our wedding night." And then he sobered. "What did the sheriff say to you?"

"Not much. He isn't a very nice man."

"He's a flunky for some of the powers that be in the city. They gave him the job because they figured he couldn't get in a whole lot of trouble in Collins Creek. He's not a bad man. He just isn't a very good sheriff. And I'm thinking he's not going to be around for long."

She glared up at him. "Well, don't get any ideas about taking on the job yourself. You're going to find some sort of occupation that doesn't involve guns and lawbreakers."

He bent to drop a kiss on her open mouth. "You still mad at me, sweetheart?"

"Yes. But I love you, anyway." She felt tears come to the surface, filling her eyes and overflowing against her will. "I was so worried, and frightened that you wouldn't come back. Promise me you'll never do that to me again, Jon."

He beamed. "I'm back to being Jon. How about that?

For that alone I'll make any promise you like, sweetheart.'' He bent his head and took her mouth in a long, intimate melding of lips and teeth and tongue. She was the object of his desire, the fulfillment of this long day of weary travel, and the hope for his future. His every instinct told him that by the time this night was over, he'd have peeled back the layers of his wife, to find the hidden secrets of her past.

She sighed into his mouth, a soft whisper of words he cherished, confessing her love, words not easily spoken by this proud woman, and all the more precious because of her reticence when it came to declaring her emotion. ''I can't seem to stay angry with you, face-to-face. It was easier when you weren't here.''

''Good. Because what I have in mind doesn't allow for you being in a snit.''

She wiggled beneath him and he stayed her with the firm pressure of his body. ''None of that. I want to talk to you first.''

''Talk?'' Her brows lifted in surprise.

''Tell me something, sweetheart. I've thought of it for days, when the ceiling in that room was the only thing to hold my attention, and you and your secrets occupied my mind.''

She bit at her lip, as if she knew what he would ask. He brushed a kiss across her mouth. ''Don't chew on your mouth that way. I don't want it all red and sore.'' Another kiss brought a reluctant smile to her lips.

''Now,'' he said firmly. ''I want to know what you've been keeping to yourself for so long. There's some sort of cover-up tucked away inside you, and it's enough to make me feel like you're hiding from me.''

She closed her eyes as if to escape his scrutiny, but he wouldn't have it. ''Gussie.'' He whispered her name, pleading for this last bit of secrecy she'd harbored, aware that so long as she held it sacrosanct, he would never know the fullness of the woman he'd married. "What makes you tick, sweetheart? What brought you here to Collins Creek, and made you so adamant about sheltering those women you've gathered together?"

She opened her eyes, and he saw fear reflected in their depths. "I've deceived you from the beginning," she said, her voice trembling as if some great, shuddering beast dwelled within her and she must conceal its presence. Then the tears flowed, and with them the confession he'd urged from her.

"When my mother died, I found her journal, and I was excited, because I really didn't know a lot about her or my grandparents, and I thought this was my chance to get all my questions answered." She swallowed, and then began anew, her voice growing stronger, fueled perhaps by the release of secrets she'd harbored too long.

"I found that my father had met my mother in a bordello, where she was known as Little Dove. He fell in love with her, and bought her freedom from the woman who ran the place. And then married her and took her away."

Cleary schooled his features into a mask, unwilling to reveal his shock at her revelation. Augusta coming from the body of a whore was not to be believed. Not this woman, pure and innocent and possessed of all the fine qualities he'd only known in women of the highest stature. Yet, if Gussie said it was so, he had to recognize it as the truth and accept it, whether or not it left a bad taste in his mouth.

"They had a wonderful marriage, and she was the best mother I've ever seen or heard of," Augusta said quietly. "I was the envy of my friends, with a beautiful, youthful mother and a father who adored her." Her mouth twisted in a grimace, as if the memory was too painful to recall.

"And then they died, suddenly, with no chance for Wilson and me to tell them goodbye. They were gone, leaving us a legacy of a beautiful home, money in the bank, and a journal whose pages were filled with the secrets of the life of Little Dove.''

''Were you angry with her?'' Cleary asked quietly, lifting his hand to smooth her hair from her forehead.

''Yes, I suppose I was.'' She looked surprised. ''I think I still am, now that I consider the idea. Isn't that foolish? She did the best she could, and certainly was a good wife and mother. Yet there's a part of me that hates where she came from, and another part that needs to help other women who live that life and need someone to care about them.''

''I guess I can understand that, sweetheart. It answers a lot of questions for me.'' Another thought struck him and he asked a delicate question. ''Does Wilson know all this? Or have you kept him in the dark?''

She shook her head. ''He doesn't need to know. I fear he'd lose his respect for her and I couldn't bear that his memories be tinged that way.''

Cleary nodded. ''All right. I can understand that. We'll be sure he never finds out.'' Another thought occurred to him. ''Do you still have the journal?''

''Yes. It's in the false bottom of my old valise, beneath a piece of cardboard so it can't be easily discovered.''

''Do you know what we need to do?'' he asked, and then answered his question before she could pose one of her own. ''We need to burn the journal in the stove tomorrow morning. At least the parts that have caused you such pain.''

Her eyes lit with surprise and her lips curved in a smile he hadn't thought to see. ''Can we do it now?''

Reluctantly he nodded. ''If you'll come back to bed with me and take up right where we left off.''

The stove held only ashes and Cleary patiently lit a small stack of kindling within its depths, then fed the journal pages into the flames. One by one, he placed them atop the flickering fire, then watched as they caught and blazed brightly. Augusta tore them slowly and carefully, removing a whole section from the book, offering them into his hand, as if it were some sort of ritual that must be performed and observed in a precise manner.

"Is that it?" he asked finally, watching as she closed the black, slender volume and held it to her breast.

She nodded, concentrating fully on the glowing embers, and then she lifted her gaze to meet his. "Thank you, Jon. I wouldn't have thought of this. It's put a seal on the memories of the past for me. Maybe now I can read the rest of the words she wrote and just remember the good times we had, and recognize her as the wonderful woman she was."

"Our children can know her through that book," he said, meaning the prediction from the depths of his heart. "Every family has secrets, Gussie. Yours just fit into a different category than most."

She laughed, a vibrant sound that touched a chord within him. And then her hand crept into his palm, twining with the length of his longer, stronger fingers. "Let's go back to bed," she said quietly, her eyes dark in the faint glow coming from the stove. She watched as he settled the stove lid into place and then allowed him to lead her toward the foyer and up the stairs to their room.

They shed their clothing, Augusta having snatched his shirt from the floor to cover herself, Cleary garbed only in his trousers for the trek to the kitchen. The bedsprings squeaked a bit as they settled into the center of the mattress, and for a moment, he felt as though it was his wedding night once more. A different situation to be sure, and definitely a different location, but containing that same sense of newness. A fresh beginning that might very well accompany their coming together again and again in the years to come.

They were starting over again, the air cleared of nebulous memories that might cloud their future. He sought and found his place atop her once more. As if this too were a part of the rituals of this night, he moved her where he would, aligning her soft places to fit snugly against the firm structure of his muscular form, his masculine body eager for the yielding of her woman's flesh.

He begged entrance, his mouth and hands pleading silently as he readied her for his taking. Soft words were but sighs against his throat, her tongue tasting the skin there, her purrs of contentment bringing him to a peak of arousal that gave no respite but drove him to a completion that left them breathless and limp, sated by the ecstasy of their coming together.

"Did I tell you how much I love you?" he asked.

"Um...I think so." Her fingers threaded through the length of his dark hair, holding him closely to herself, as though she could not bear to have him lift his weight from her.

"I don't want to hurt the baby," he said, rising over her, her fingers reluctant as they slid from his head to his shoulders and then rested against his chest. "I didn't even get a chance to get acquainted with him."

She laughed aloud, sputtering as her fingers covered her mouth. "I'd say you were on speaking terms a few minutes ago," she gasped, catching her breath. "You couldn't have gotten much closer to him if you'd really set your mind to it."

He rolled with her, tugging her close, sorting out their tangled limbs as she settled her head on his shoulder. "We'll be happy, won't we, Jon?"

"If you mind your manners and do what I tell you, everything will be fine," he said, tongue-in-cheek, waiting for the explosion that was sure to follow.

It was not long in coming. She lifted to her elbow and

peered down at him. "I never should have said I'd obey you. I knew it at the time, but things were so confused that day that I just let it slide, and now I suppose I'll be expected to be biddable and obedient for the rest of my life."

"Ah, Gussie, that's too much to hope for," he said smugly. "I'll probably settle for you being agreeable most of the time."

"You need to know that I don't intend to abandon my shelter, Jonathan."

"I didn't think you would. I just want you to let someone else do the everyday management. I think your brother is having a good time there. You need to give him a chance to see what he can accomplish."

She settled down beside him again. "All right. That makes sense." Her fingers traced small circles against his flesh, outlining the nubs on his chest that were almost buried beneath dark curls. "What are you going to do, Jon?"

"Right now?" He grinned, knowing the direction she took.

"No, I mean in the future. Where will you work?"

"Nicholas is coming tomorrow. Things should be fitting together nicely, he says, and he'll be bringing news. Can you wait until then for an answer?"

"All right. But what will we do in the meantime?" she asked politely. "I need something to take my mind off all the things that are racing around in my head."

He lifted her, turning to his back and fitting her against himself. "Why don't you just see what you can come up with?" he asked, his knees bent, his thighs spread so that her slender form dovetailed to his broader, firmer body.

She tilted her head, watching him by the light of the guttering candle. "I think you've already come up with something," she said in a solemn whisper. "And I think I know just what to do with it."

* * *

"I knew I should have moved that slop jar closer before we went to sleep, sweetheart," he said softly, holding her against himself as she bent over to spew bile into its depths. She shuddered and he lifted his shirt from the floor, wiping her mouth with the inside of one sleeve. "Come on, crawl back in bed and I'll go get you a damp cloth and a piece of bread to chew on."

"Thank you," she whispered, feeling as if she had lost every bit of dignity she'd ever possessed. "I'm sorry," she told him. "This won't last long."

He pulled the sheet over her and then bent to find his trousers. Buttoning them as he watched her, he managed a smile. "Do you think you'll feel this way every time we start a new baby?"

Augusta shuddered again. "Don't even talk about it. Just let me get through this one first, before you start making threats." She dozed for a while, aware of his hands turning her, a warm cloth washing her face and his mouth pressing soft kisses against hers.

"Nicholas will be here soon," he said quietly. "Do you want to rest, and I'll talk to him?"

She roused, took a deep breath and recognized the loss of her early morning nausea. "No, I'm feeling all right. I'll get dressed and be right down. Start a fire in the kitchen stove and I'll fix breakfast."

Nicholas joined them, tucking into the scrambled eggs and bacon with a will. He leaned back in his chair as Augusta poured him a second cup of coffee. "We've got news," he said, waiting until Augusta regained her seat to begin his recitation. "Got a wire this morning from the banker's organization in Dallas. They've offered you what you asked for. It's the very job we described to them."

Augusta pressed her lips together, determined not to interrupt in this discussion yet aching to know what Nicholas was talking about.

"Did they agree to my salary?" Cleary asked, and at Nicholas's nod, he picked up his cup and sipped the hot brew. "Do they need my plan in writing first?"

"Didn't seem to want anything but your agreement to upgrade their security and check out their systems on a regular basis."

Cleary turned to Augusta. "This will mean going on a business trip once a month, for three or four days. Will that be all right with you?"

If Nicholas thought it odd that a man should ask his wife such a question, one pertaining to his plans for a career change, he didn't allow his thoughts to show, only sat back as Augusta considered Cleary's query. Then, as she nodded thoughtfully, she saw a smile light the banker's face.

"It will give me a chance to spend time at the shelter on a regular basis," she said. "In fact, it might work out very well."

"There's one more thing," Nicholas said, his tone offering a warning.

"The sheriff?" Cleary asked.

"Yeah. The town council wants you to take over until they can find someone else to fill his shoes. I figured it would give you something to do in your odd hours."

"I don't like the idea of you wearing a gun to work," Augusta said bluntly. "We talked about that last night."

"There's not enough crime in Collins Creek to warrant him wearing a gun every day," Nicholas told her. "To tell you the truth, it's a prime job. Not much to do but keep the floor swept and the hinges oiled on the cell doors. He'll be home for dinner every day at noon, and gets to wear a silver star pinned to his shirt."

Cleary looked at her, his face drawn into lines of concern. "I know you're worried about my being a lawman,

Gussie, but this isn't anything like what I've been doing as a marshal.''

He turned to Nicholas and opened his mouth to speak, then shot a look at Augusta. ''Can I tell him?'' he asked. ''You know, about—''

She nodded. There wouldn't be any keeping it a secret once the ladies got out and about anyway. Janine was sure to carry the news to the dressmaker. Pearl would tell the next-door neighbor, Harriet, probably the next time she carried eggs over, and once those two women heard about a coming baby, the whole town would be in on the story.

''We're gonna have a baby,'' Cleary announced, doing his best to sound casual about the whole thing, as if it were an everyday occurrence.

It was no such happenstance as far as Nicholas was concerned. He rose from his chair, drew Augusta from hers and hugged her, then extended his hand to Cleary, still holding her around the middle with his other arm. ''How about that!'' He bent a bit to peer into her face. ''Is that why you fainted a while back? Are you all right now?''

''I'm fine,'' she assured him readily.

His delight was genuine, Augusta decided as he released her and picked up his coffee cup. ''Here's to the next generation,'' he said, offering a toast. ''And while we're at it, I've got more news to brighten your day.''

Cleary rose, his hands sliding negligently into his trouser pockets. ''Did it come through?'' Though his stance was casual, Augusta sensed his excitement, and as she watched, she noted his sigh, as if a load had been removed from his shoulders. ''Gussie,'' he said, turning to her and grasping her hand. ''We need to go over to the shelter. I want to talk to your brother.''

''A pardon?'' Wilson was stunned, his eyes unblinking, his mouth twitching, as if he sought more words to speak, and was coming up dry. "You actually got me a pardon, Cleary?" And then he looked at Nicholas. "Or were you behind it, Mr. Garvey?"

"Kind of a joint effort," Cleary said, hugging Augusta to his side. "It just came through this morning. Nicholas got a wire from the governor."

"How did it happen? They don't do those things out of the goodness of their hearts," Wilson said firmly. "Someone must have pulled some strings."

Cleary shifted uncomfortably, and Nicholas grinned. "Your brother-in-law knows more strings to pull than you could ever imagine, son."

"You did it for Gussie, didn't you?" Wilson asked, facing Cleary head-on. "And don't get me wrong. I'm glad you wanted to make her happy, but at the same time, I don't like being beholden to anybody. You know that."

"Well, let's just say it erases my debt to you," Cleary told him. "Remember the day you cut Chloe loose and watched my back till she got me out of danger? That debt's been canceled. And if that doesn't suit your fancy, let's just say I couldn't stand the idea of my brother sitting in prison."

"Your brother." The stunned look returned to the younger man's face and he turned aside, clearing his throat.

Honey rose from her seat near the parlor door and took her place beside him. "Sometimes it's better just to say thank you," she told him quietly. "Accept the gift in the spirit in which it was given. No strings attached. Am I right, Mr. Cleary?"

"You're right," he answered, extending his hand to Wilson, who looked at it dumbly, then snatched it between his palms, as if the offer might be rescinded should he delay in accepting the gesture.

"I thought this might be a good day to have a wedding," Cleary said, looking Wilson squarely in the eye. "How about taking a hike to the parsonage and see if the preacher wants to come by later this afternoon.''

"Well, if I'm planning on attending, I'd better be on my way. I've got a bank to tend to," Nicholas said, breaking the awkward silence that ensued at Cleary's suggestion. He drew his watch from his pocket, checking the time as his words set off a flurry of activity. Then with a wave of his hand, he was gone.

The rest of the gathering fled the parlor, leaving Augusta and Cleary standing in the center of the room. He slipped his arm around her and glanced about the warm, welcoming parlor. "You've made a difference here, Gussie. You've given all these folks a place to call home.''

"I had a lot of help," she said, unwilling to take the credit for what others had contributed. "They've given me a family, Jon. If it weren't for them I'd never have been out looking for funds the day we met. I'd not have run across you in my everyday doings.'' She felt a pang of sorrow at the thought.

"And now you've given Wilson a second chance at life, and given him your blessing. You've made changes right and left.'' She felt tears gathering and forced their retreat, unwilling to cry when there was so much joy to be found. "I don't know how I'd face the days ahead without you,'' she confessed. "These people are my family...but you're my life.''

"Another seven months, huh?" he asked, swinging her fully into his arms. "We'll have our family circle complete before you know it.''

"I thought you said—"

"Hush," he whispered. "I did. This is only the first, but each one that comes along will only add to the circle, and each time it will be complete until another baby is on the way. It's like a set of stepping stones, one leading to the next.''

"Don't get all carried away," she told him, leaning back against his forearms and looking sternly into his twinkling eyes. "I'm not planning on more than four or five."

"That sounds like a good number to me," he said agreeably. "We've got that many bedrooms to fill. After that, we'll just have to put an addition on the back."

In the kitchen, Bertha gathered the ingredients for a cake, and Pearl watched from the back door as Wilson and Honey walked around the side of the house, on their way to visit the preacher. Glory sat on the stoop, Henry asleep on her lap, his huge, puppy paws bearing mute testimony to the size he would become. With a slam of the screened door, Janine strolled in the front door and made her way to the kitchen.

"What's for dinner?" she asked. "I've got to be back at work in an hour."

"We're celebrating today," Bertha said. "When you hear the news you may want to take the afternoon off to help plan the party."

"What party?"

"Sit down there while I mix this cake, and we'll tell you," Bertha said. "You won't believe what's in the works."

Epilogue

"I'll bet he's the only baby ever born with eight godmothers ready and waiting to welcome him," Augusta said, holding the tiny bundle swaddled in a flannel square in the crook of her arm.

Cleary looked stricken. "Tell me they're not all going to parade up to the front of the church for the ceremony."

She looked at him disbelievingly. "Of course not. Just Wilson and Honey will stand up for him. But the rest are planning on having some say in his upbringing."

There were three more women settled into the bedrooms upstairs in Augusta's shelter, Janine having found a small house of her own. Although self-sufficient, she still managed to be a regular visitor at the big house where she'd been given a second chance at life. Pearl was spending a lot of evenings with Sam Ferguson, the giant who owned and ran the livery stable, and Augusta wouldn't be a bit surprised should that twosome instigate a wedding some day soon.

Wilson and Honey were head over heels in love with the baby girl they'd welcomed several months ago, and Glory was hard at work at the business of attaining skills that would allow her to take over the books and perhaps find employment in the back room at the bank one day.

This morning Nicholas Wilson Cleary had joined the family, leading Cleary to predict that Nick Garvey would be turning up on their doorstep on a regular basis.

Having never had a child named in his honor, and stalwart in his denial of planning on marrying anytime soon, he'd been waiting anxiously for the arrival of this baby, determined it should be a boy.

"You need to walk over to the bank," Augusta told Cleary. "Bertha will spread the news at the shelter. She ought to be getting there right about now."

The stalwart woman had directed at the delivery, eschewing the presence of a doctor, claiming a long history of escorting babies into the world. Augusta was prone to believe her claim, baby Nick having arrived with only four hours labor spent in the effort of his birth. Somehow she doubted that Cleary could have withstood much more than that, his tolerance for her pain being short-lived.

Now he sat on the edge of the bed beside her, his index finger brushing at a wisp of hair. His son had arrived with a full head of golden curls, and dark eyes that, this morning, matched those of his father. Though Bertha said they might change over the next weeks. It didn't matter, Cleary had said stoutly. Whatever color eyes and hair the baby was born with, the important thing was that he was healthy, and his mother had survived the ordeal with flying colors.

"Do you want to hold him?" Augusta asked, and then with easy movements, she transferred the tiny bundle to his father's arms. He looked small, fragile and uncommonly beautiful, she decided. His eyes opened and he frowned, one small fist clinging to Cleary's index finger with a reflex action.

"Look at that. I think he knows who I am." The man who struck fear in the hearts of the few lawbreakers who'd crossed his path over the past months had become, during that same period of time, a man totally devoted to his wife and the baby they awaited. Now he looked absolutely dotty over the tiny bit of humanity he held, a baby whose miniature features reflected his own, Augusta decided happily.

She smiled wearily, ready for sleep. "Go on now," she told him. "Bertha's going to send Glory over for the afternoon. You can take care of business and be back for supper."

He looked down at the baby in his arms. "Where do you want him? Shall I put him in the cradle?"

Augusta shook her head. "No, just put him beside me. I want to look at him." She scooted carefully down in the bed and held out her arms. "I'll take him."

He seemed reluctant to relinquish possession, but, with a sigh, he tucked the infant next to Augusta's bosom. He bent lower, his mouth seeking hers, and his kiss was long and lingering. "I love you," he said, repeating the words he'd spoken a multitude of times earlier today while he'd ached for her pain as she brought forth his son.

"I love you, too, Jon." She felt her eyelids closing and made a valiant effort to smile in his direction. "Thank you for staying with me." And then as he rose and left the room, she called him back, her voice soft, her words anxious.

"You weren't put off by everything, were you? I mean, it didn't make you think twice about having another baby, did it?"

He turned to her, his face blanching as if her questions brought back the concern he'd felt for her well-being. "We can talk about it another time, sweetheart," he said. "I may have decided that two is enough."

"Two? I think not, Jonathan," she said crisply, lifting on one elbow to meet his gaze.

"You promised, Gussie," he blustered. "Remember?

You promised to obey.'' And then he was gone, and she settled down on her pillow, content for now to admire the beautiful infant beside her.

"Obey? Did you hear what your father said?'' she murmured, crooning the words as sleep overtook her. "We'll just see about that, won't we, Nickie.''

* * * * *

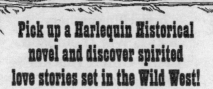

**C'mon back home to Crystal Creek with
a BRAND-NEW anthology from**

bestselling authors

Vicki Lewis Thompson
Cathy Gillen Thacker
Bethany Campbell

Return to Crystal Creek

**Nothing much
has changed in
Crystal Creek...
till now!**

The mysterious Nick Belyle has shown up in town,
and what he's up to is anyone's guess. But one
thing is certain. Something big is going down in
Crystal Creek, and folks aren't going to rest till
they find out what the future holds.

*Look for this exciting anthology,
on-sale in July 2002.*

HARLEQUIN®
Makes any time special ®

Visit us at www.eHarlequin.com

PHRTCC

Princes...Princesses...
London Castles...New York Mansions...
To live the life of a royal!

In 2002, Harlequin Books lets you escape to a
world of royalty with these royally themed titles:

Temptation:
January 2002—*A Prince of a Guy* (#861)
February 2002—*A Noble Pursuit* (#865)

American Romance:
The Carradignes: American Royalty (Editorially linked series)
March 2002—*The Improperly Pregnant Princess* (#913)
April 2002—*The Unlawfully Wedded Princess* (#917)
May 2002—*The Simply Scandalous Princess* (#921)
November 2002—*The Inconveniently Engaged Prince* (#945)

Intrigue:
The Carradignes: A Royal Mystery (Editorially linked series)
June 2002—*The Duke's Covert Mission* (#666)

Chicago Confidential
September 2002—*Prince Under Cover* (#678)

The Crown Affair
October 2002—*Royal Target* (#682)
November 2002—*Royal Ransom* (#686)
December 2002—*Royal Pursuit* (#690)

Harlequin Romance:
June 2002—*His Majesty's Marriage* (#3703)
July 2002—*The Prince's Proposal* (#3709)

Harlequin Presents:
August 2002—*Society Weddings* (#2268)
September 2002—*The Prince's Pleasure* (#2274)

Duets:
September 2002—*Once Upon a Tiara/Henry Ever After* (#83)
October 2002—*Natalia's Story/Andrea's Story* (#85)

**Celebrate a year of royalty with
Harlequin Books!**

Available at your favorite retail outlet.

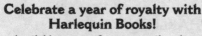

HARLEQUIN®
Makes any time special ®

Visit us at www.eHarlequin.com

HSROY02

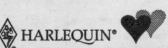

New York Times **Bestselling Author**

Stephanie Laurens

Four in Hand

The Ton's most hardened
rogues could not resist
the remarkable Twinning
sisters. And the
Duke of Twyford was
no exception! For when
it came to his eldest
ward, the exquisite
Caroline Twinning,
London's most
notorious rake was
falling victim to love!

On sale July 2002

Escape to a land long ago and
far away when you read these thrilling
love stories from Harlequin Historicals

On Sale September 2002

A WARRIOR'S LADY
by Margaret Moore
(England, 1200s)
*A forced marriage between a brave knight and
beautiful heiress blossoms into true love!*

A ROGUE'S HEART
by Debra Lee Brown
(Scotland, 1213)
*Will a carefree rogue sweep a headstrong young lady
off her feet with his tempting business offer?*

On Sale October 2002

MY LADY'S HONOR
by Julia Justiss
(Regency England)
*In the game of disguise a resourceful young
woman falls in love with a dashing aristocrat!*

THE BLANCHLAND SECRET
by Nicola Cornick
(England, 1800s)
*Will a lady's companion risk her reputation by
accepting the help of a well-known rake?*

 Harlequin Historicals®
Historical Romantic Adventure!